I Hear a Melody

In *I Hear a Melody*, Anna evokes the personal history of a character – Sarah – whose life journey, though fictional, reflects the authentic lived experience of those who fit uneasily into a society that struggles to accept or accommodate them. Themes of race and identity are explored in rural and urban environments, and found to be problematic in both. Growing up and becoming aware of these issues, coupled with oppressive gender attitudes she encounters, Sarah's innocence seems to be gradually eroded.

And yet, despite Sarah's life struggles, there is a sense of joy, and a positivity that flows throughout her life's narrative. Grounded and anchored by family and friends, our protagonist finds delight and comfort in the 'simple' things – shared meals, music and companionship.

This marks Anna's drama out from others that might deal with such crucial subjects in a less optimistic way. Above all, there is hope.

David Brett, The Word Bookshop, London

Melodies run throughout as a background to a major part of this story. It includes music which engenders a strong desire for foot-tapping, smiling or sad reflections of pain and classical pieces which include the elated yet melancholy beauty of a choir of human voices soaring up to the rafters.

I was totally engaged from each chapter to the next, being curious as to how and where it would lead. The characters are cleverly painted as to demonstrate those whom Sarah meets along the way. She comes across cultures and communities different from her own experience as she searches for her place in society, her family and loving friends always being there to support her.

I enjoyed Anna Corbett's descriptive style and imagery of people and places from the beautiful county of Cornwall to the capital city fondly known back in the 60s as 'swinging London'.

Joyce Fraser OBE: Playwright. Founder and Chair of The Black Heroes Foundation.

This poignant and captivating book kept me engrossed with relatable characters from start to finish. It gives an authentic and heartbreakingly honest insight into growing up as a Black girl in 1950s' Cornwall and life beyond in London. Anna Corbett explores this journey of identity and belonging with compassion, warmth, and understanding. The desire to fit in, in an environment where you are seen as 'other', can be extremely challenging. This is captured brilliantly in the way that Sarah's hair becomes a focal point not only for her but for everyone around her. It is viewed as embarrassing, problematic and something to be dealt with.

Being born into one culture and living in another simultaneously is tough. It is hard to find belonging, identity and home. Anna Corbett captures this journey throughout this book in unique, memorable, and brilliant storytelling. This is absolutely worth a read.

Lorna Wells: playwright, writer and lyricist:
It Tastes Like Home, the Musical, Illusions of Liberty
and *Before Birdsong*

In 1950s' England, mixed-race child Sarah is aware of her difference to others in her rural community. Music plays a large part in her family life, bringing fun and happiness. She explores her cultural identity as she grows up and leaves home to begin a new chapter in cosmopolitan 1960s' London.

Anna Corbett's novel gives a gentle and poignant narrative into the life of a Cornish coastal family as they deal with social and political societal changes. Sarah is reminded over the years of the importance of family and friends and knows she will always be special.

I Hear a Melody gives an insightful and rich perspective into how it feels to be a child growing up within two cultures as she navigates her own identity in Britain.

*Oluwatoyin Odunsi, Creative Producer & Head of Learning and
Participation, Brixton House, London*

Dedication

This book is dedicated to the memory of my eldest brother. Dear Victor taught me everything I know and love about jazz music.

I Hear a Melody

Anna Corbett

Eulipion

Copyright © Anna Corbett 2023
First published in 2023 by Eulipion
#14 London SE13 6PA
http://www.eulipionpublishing.com

Distributed by Gardners Books, 1 Whittle Drive, Eastbourne,
East Sussex, BN23 6QH
Tel: +44(0)1323 521555 | Fax: +44(0)1323 521666

British Library Cataloguing in Publication Data
A catalogue record for this book is available from the British Library.

ISBN 978-1-9162862-1-4

Typeset by Amolibros, Milverton, Somerset
www.amolibros.co.uk
This book production has been managed by Amolibros
Printed and bound by T J Books Limited, Padstow, Cornwall, UK

Acknowledgements

Thank you so much to those who kindly gave up their time to talk to me about their musical careers. I am delighted to have had the privilege to interview three of my long-time jazz musician friends. All of them have made and continue to make a huge impact on British jazz. Please check out more details about them on the Reference Pages and various chapters in the story. Many thanks to: Roland Perrin, jazz pianist and music teacher, Michael Bami Rose, jazz multi-instrumentalist and Norma Winstone OBE a highly respected jazz singer and lyricist.

★

My sister and I enjoyed a lovely day out thanks to Kingsley Rickard visiting The Great Flat Lode, one of the busiest Cornish mines in times past. Mr Rickard is a Cornish Bard and Historian for The Trevithic Society. His knowledge and expertise regarding Cornwall's industrial history is much sought after and he has spent several years giving lectures throughout the county.

About the Author

Anna Corbett was born and brought up in Cornwall. She was brought up to learn about their family histories as well as being cognisant and understanding of the society in which they lived. After they married her parents settled in Truro, Cornwall and had a family of six children. As the only Black family in the community at the time, they were very noticeable. Jazz has always played a big part of Anna's life; it was often the music they played at home and was a valued part of their racial identity. Some of their family members play instruments and family parties are always an occasion to enjoy making music, particularly jazz.

When she left school she came to London to study and enjoyed a fulfilling teaching career. Afterwards she embarked on further study: a degree in English and American Literature, followed by an MA in Creative and Life Writing at Goldsmiths University prior to embarking on writing *Masquerade*. She takes every opportunity to listen to live jazz in New York and London when she's not spending time with her family or being captivated by a wealth of other cultural activities. She recently lived in Cardiff for two years, where she was able to do further research on her first novel as well as having an exciting time co-presenting a weekly jazz show on Radio Cardiff.

Prelude

George Hodges was sitting on the train.

WWII was over.

He was reflecting on all he had witnessed along the way.

He had been demobbed a few months earlier from the US Allied Forces.

He knew what it meant to lose close friends, to watch them writhe in pain as he tried to stifle the fear for his own life.

He experienced how it was to discover a world apart from his Harlem home, and witnessed cultures which deviated so much from all that he was familiar with.

He was different from everyone else around him and knew how it felt to be an outsider.

He knew how it felt to be in love.

★

He was returning from visiting his mother back in Harlem, to spend a couple of months with her and tell her all about the new life awaiting him four thousand miles away. He and Mom had been exchanging letters throughout his military service, each of them trying to reassure the other as they scribbled away about the minutiae of their days, hiding the stark reality of their daily lives as the world toiled on the edge of disaster.

Mom's most recent letter indicated that she had something important to convey. She suggested that instead of going straight to her apartment when he arrived, they should meet the following afternoon at the foot of St Nicholas Park where she would be waiting.

He checked into a shabby looking brownstone, the sign outside declaring itself as 'Harlem's Most Welcoming Hotel'. Their proud boast was far from the truth, but he was exhausted after many hours in spent in economy seating on the 'plane, his long legs stiff and aching. In his hotel room, the hard mattress offered some comfort for a couple of hours and he spent the rest of the night lying in the dark, too excited to sleep.

★

He stepped out of the 135th street subway the next day, striding confidently along, absorbing the familiar surroundings where he had grown up. It felt good to take in the recognisable smells, hear the noise of traffic and watch people going about their business. People who looked like him.

St Nicholas Park was in view. His mom used to take him there for walks on her days off from work when he was a kid. Sometimes Aunt Flo would come along; she would pick him up and swing him around, declaring that he would always be 'her favourite man'. The two women would chat and giggle together as the three of them struggled to climb every step and reach the very top of the park to Hamilton Heights, or wander along to wonder at the grand houses on Sugar Hill.

Sometimes, they decided to stop halfway up to take a rest and look out on the busy streets below. He thought about it how it would feel to hug his mom again, to imbibe her comforting smell and look down as she gazed up into his eyes.

Her big smile greeted him as he approached. He paused for a moment as he saw that she was not alone. She stood in front of a man in a wheelchair. She stepped aside as George got closer and patted the man's shoulder, who slowly lifted his head and looked at him with a sideways smile.

★

By the end of the afternoon George's head was a mix of joy and confusion, other puzzling thoughts kept hidden. He loved his mother dearly, this brave and wonderful woman whose life journey had been compounded with struggle, pain and poverty. She had worked hard to bring him up with everything she could give. And she had done it alone.

It was heart-warming to see her looking so happy, but it was hard to throw off the inner rage that crept around in his head. He had finally witnessed the truth. It was a day he would never forget.

Chapter One

He was on his journey back to Elsie. Back to the beauty of the South West countryside of England. They had been apart for several weeks but he knew she would still be waiting for him. He took her tattered photo from his wallet, the image that had kept him going during hard times. He loved Elsie and couldn't wait to settle down and build a life with her, but there had been many occasions when he was severely reminded that he was 'a stranger in a strange land'. He smiled as he remembered the quote she had read aloud from one of her Shakespeare books: 'My love is as boundless as the sea' How lucky they were to have met one another. Nothing else really mattered.

The train seemed to take forever, the engine slowing as it groaned to a halt at every small countryside station, their place names echoing signs and symbols of a dying Celtic language. There were hardly any passengers getting off at each stop. He watched through the window, as they strolled along the platform before disappearing into the afternoon sun, their relaxed pace in tandem with the quiet beauty around them.

Chapter Two

It was January 1954; Sarah was seven years old. Her mum had gone to see a film with her best friend Maureen. They went once a week no matter what was showing. Although if her dad asked about what they had seen, she would sometimes just grunt, saying, 'British film' and that would be the end of the discussion. As far as Elsie was concerned, America ruled the magic screen.

Sarah was allowed to stay up late because it was the weekend. She and her dad had just finished the washing the dishes; they were in the sitting room. She sat on his lap, gazing up at his face, the colour and shine of a hazelnut shell. He raised his eyebrows and smiled, tilted his head back to scratch the shaving stubble on his neck as she began to flip his bottom lip up and down, while saying their names over and over: Elsie, George and Sarah, Elsie, George and Sarah. He tried to sing in time to her wiggling fingers, one of their favourite tunes about a place far away in America, called Dewey Square. She watched the little lump on his throat go up and down as he laughed.

She slid off his lap, took off her slippers and threw them across the room.

'I love that tune. Let's dance Dad!'

She stood quite still at the edge of the rug, scrunching her toes together as her father went to switch on the record player. Their favourite record was right on top of the pile, with the picture on the front of Charlie Parker wearing a slight smile, holding his saxophone of gold.

'OK, Miss Sarah, at your service.'

The music started with a piano introduction as he walked towards her, and the ritual began. She made a slight curtsey and waited; he put one hand across his front and the other at his back as he gave a slow bow. He glanced up sideways and winked at her before rising again. She stood on his big shoes and they held hands as he bopped from side to side, before releasing one hand to spin her around with the other. Then one of them would always shout out: 'free time!' That meant they would jump apart, spin and sway, singing nonsense words along with the tune.

Her parents had named her Sarah after one of their favourite singers of their favourite–music: jazz. It was their daughter's favourite too. It's what they listened to indoors when it was just the three of them. It was theirs. Her dad said it was a special gift he had brought from America.

When the tune was over, he went back to the records. 'OK, it's my turn to choose now.'

The needle scratched loudly on the first notes.

'I know what it's going to be: "Scrapple from the Apple".'

He gave a pretend groan, slapping one hand to his head, 'Oh no, you guessed it right.'

'I always do, don't I, Dad?'

And they danced some more.

★

Christmas was over and things had more or less settled down. But it was not like other Christmases. Something had changed.

They were almost ready to sit down for dinner. Mum was rescuing the parsnips and potatoes from the oven – they'd been in for too long, the pointed parsnip ends black and burnt as they were every time. Dad had drained the green vegetables over the sink and a large golden chicken, covered in strips of bacon, graced

7

the table like a king: a well-roasted master of festivities, festooned with a red ribbon tied around its legs.

Their neighbour, Mrs Spargo knocked on the back door, in the way that people do when it's something important. She was large and loud with chubby pink arms which shook for a few moments after the rest of her body stopped moving. She had a wide selection of wrap-around pinafores and a laugh that set the cutlery rattling.

Her culinary skills were extensive, and in true Cornish tradition she did her baking every Friday, enough to last for the week. Her repertoire included Victoria sponges, scones, heavy fruit loaf, and her saffron cake was as moist and yellow as it should be. On Saturday mornings she would visit with what she called 'a sweet surprise for tea'. Wrapped up in a clean tea-towel, the gift was regally presented on a dinner plate, followed by the pretence of finding a threepenny bit in one of her deep pockets. She would graciously place the coin in Sarah's open hand, close her fist around it, before tugging her plaits and sweeping out again. And so the weekend began.

★

'Oops, sorry to interrupt, I've left Doug in charge of operations, so I thought I'd quickly pop in.' Mrs Spargo held a parcel under her arm as she accepted a glass of rum and took a large sip.

'I'll be good for nothing after this George. You naughty boy.'

He grinned, 'Why not? After all Dot, it is Christmas.'

'Too right, to 'ell with it.' She drained the rest of her glass. 'Can't stay, I'd better check on Doug. God only knows how dinner would turn out like if I left 'im to it. And we got his brother Stan coming over. He's a misery at the best of times. And deep as Dolcoath.'

She sighed loudly and rolled her eyes.

She began to open the door before pausing, 'Crikey, nearly forgot why I came. 'Ere you are, me 'ansum. I made it just for you. A special present for a special girl.'

She handed Sarah the parcel and kissed her cheek. It was a wet kiss; Sarah could smell the rum on her breath and tried to wipe it off without anyone noticing. The parcel felt like a shoe box, so she couldn't guess what was inside. George poured Elsie another rum as they clinked glasses and raised eyebrows at one another.

The paper chains they had made the night before were draped over the top of the dresser and around the walls. The kitchen was full of steam and spice. The choir on the radio began: 'While Shepherds Watched', and they all stood up to sing the Cornish tune over it, trying to drown them out. When they reached the line, '*and glory shone around*', they broke into two parts and went into the 'call and response' style similar to gospel music, George singing one part, Sarah and Elsie singing the other. They reached the last line; George held his fork up high like a conductor's baton indicating a pause before they all slowed down to end on a theatrical flourish.

Years later Sarah read that the standard version of that carol is called *Winchester Old* but the one sung in Cornwall is entitled the *Lyngham* version, which is much more rousing. It is also popular in Southern Australia and could apparently be related to the fact that on the decline of the tin mining industry in Cornwall, many Cornishmen emigrated to Australia to mine for copper.

George had learned the *Lyngham* version when he joined a group who called themselves the Cornish Choristers a couple of years before. When he arrived in the church hall for his first rehearsal, the conductor Ted Rowe didn't bother to audition him, but put him straight into the bass section. Suppose that was hardly surprising. The choir put on three performances a year; the proceeds always being donated to a charity for Newlyn fishermen.

Elsie said the choir on the wireless were all boys who sang regularly in a famous cathedral in Cambridge, their young voices weaving and dipping into rich harmonies brought a tingle to the spine. Sarah thought they sounded like girls, but her mum knew about so many things. George often said that she knew about everything, and that even if she didn't know she would make something up.

They eventually sat back down to eat. Sarah had Mrs Spargo's present balanced on her lap under the table.

Her mum smiled: 'Go on then, you can open it now if you like. But you'll have to wait for your other presents until after dinner.'

Elsie and George laughed as she tore at the wrapping paper and threw it to the floor before wrenching the lid off the box. That dropped to the floor as well. There was a soft squishy thing inside wrapped in layers of tissue.

★

Sarah held the knitted golliwog above her head and waved it about; slowly lowering it again as she noticed the look that flashed between her parents. A sharp breeze had crept under the door and wrapped itself around their legs.

'Gosh, almost forgot the gravy.' Elsie's chair screeched on the floor as she got up and busied herself at the stove.

George put his hand out and squeezed the gollywog, his smile tight as he pinched his daughter's cheek.

'Mrs Spargo worked very hard to make that for you. Why don't you put it somewhere safe, sweetie? We don't want him to get splashed with your mum's lumpy gravy, do we?'

The child stared as he pretended to make a silly face.

'My gravy's lumpy is it? Better than how you make it, big boy.' Elsie's voice several notes higher than usual.

'Uh, oh, you think I've put my foot in it, Sarah?' He drooped and puckered his lips.

'What, in the gravy? What do you mean?' Her voice small and tight.

With a piercing laugh, Elsie came back to the table.

★

Sarah spent the afternoon fiddling with her presents while her parents drank the rest of the rum and George made up silly jokes. Elsie wouldn't join in; she was quieter than usual and went off to wash the dishes even though it wasn't her turn. In the end George suggested they go for a walk up to Trevasgis Lane.

They set out, all dressed up warm. The road was quiet apart from the barking of a couple of frustrated dogs stuck indoors with their families. A few brave paper decorations blew about in the tree branches of those who had tried to spread some festive joy beyond their front rooms. When they reached the start of the lane, the mud was frozen into stiff peaks and cows huddled together in the nearest field, probably awaiting the comfort of the barn and some winter fodder.

Their breath blew out in wisps; George suggested they walk as far as the milk churn, which was about halfway down. The milk churn was very big and heavy, made of metal with a lid on top and a handle either side. The farmer, Mr Trevasgis kept it placed on a big stone slab. George pretended to try and pick it up to shake it.

'Put your ear close to it, Sarah. Can you hear any milk sloshing about?'

She did so and shook her head. He rubbed his chin and nodded a few times, 'Ah, that means the cows must have the day off too because it's Christmas.'

Elsie groaned and blew out a long breathy sigh.

'Ten out of ten for trying, Georgie, but can we go home now?'

They trudged back down the road. There were usually a few children racing up and down on their bikes or playing outside but everywhere was quiet. No cars, no planes overhead, not even any birds. All the windows had their curtains drawn, including Veronica's house. Sarah usually knocked for her in the mornings on their way to school. Veronica Pearce was the kind of child who always noticed if someone was hanging around by themselves at playtime. She was probably finishing her dinner or opening her presents with her two older brothers.

Going along the road through the oncoming dusk, they were the only people in the world. Sarah was beginning to feel cold too and put her hand in her mum's pocket.

'What does deep as Dolcoath mean Mum? Why did Mrs Spargo say that Stan was deep?'

'Deep as Dolcoath is an old Cornish saying. You remember when we walked along the cliffs at Porthtowan with Auntie Maureen and saw those old buildings with tall chimneys? Well, that's one of the places where men used to dig big holes in the ground, called mineshafts, looking for precious metals which lay under the earth. The deepest mineshaft in Cornwall is called Dolcoath. It was very, very deep, very, very dark and very, very scary,' speaking more and more slowly and quietly with every word.

'The miners dug long tunnels which ran a long way beneath the surface. Miles and miles of tunnels. Dolcoath had twelve miles of tunnels. Now they are all covered in grass and heather. We probably walk over some of them when we go exploring along the cliffs.'

All went quiet for a moment.

'Does that mean that Stan is scary? He sometimes has a cigarette out in the garden with Mr Spargo. I don't think he's frightening. He doesn't talk much but he's got a kind face.'

'No. Being deep means he doesn't say much because he's too busy thinking about lots of things.' She paused, looking at her hard with big eyes and her bottom lip turned down at the sides.

'Deep and quiet. Like the tunnels of Dolcoath.' That voice again.

★

Much later, after dreaming of being chased through narrow darkness by Stan, Sarah woke up whimpering. She lay still for a moment before getting out of bed to use the toilet, hesitating on the landing as she listened to the voices outside. Mr Spargo was calling out goodnight to his brother Stan as he was leaving. The rest of the family joined in: Mrs Spargo and the two boys, Andrew and Derek, their voices replaced by laughter as the front door was closing. Stan gave a loud cough, followed by a gurgling noise as he spat on the path. His noisy boots gradually faded away as he went off down the windy road, between the trembling trees. The branches of the bay tree in the garden brushed against the window, just above where she sat huddled in the corner. Then – a conversation from downstairs, quiet at first and getting louder.

'... and you wanna know why I get fed up sometimes?' Elsie's strident voice, her words running together.

'I know sweetheart, but we do the best we can. We can't protect her for ever. I'll talk to her tomorrow.' George's soft American drawl sounding more pronounced than usual.

'Talk to who? Dear old Dot? Dot with her florid, fat face and her patronising attitude.'

'No. No point honey. Her intentions are good, and she means no harm. I'll talk to Sarah. Maybe it's time ...' his voice tapering off.

'Yeah, yeah, OK, Mr Oh-So-Grateful-and-Nice. You might have the Negro problem where you come from, but believe me, some people here really get my goat.'

'Yes, you're damn right we have problems.' His voiced was raised now, 'And do you know what, in the States we wouldn't even be together,' his words bouncing off the walls.

'What do you mean by that?'

'What the hell do you think I mean?'

The door slammed shut and Sarah couldn't hear any more. Why wouldn't they be together? What did he need to talk about? Her feet stiff with cold, she crept back to bed and lay in the dark.

Chapter Three

Looks like someone ate too much yesterday. Don't you want the rest of your porridge?' Her mum had made a big pot and even added extra treacle, but Sarah's throat was full of stones.

She looked out of the window and saw her dad leaning on the fence, smoking, and gazing about. He wandered about between the shrubs before stamping out his cigarette and disappearing into the shed. He came out with the clippers and started randomly hacking away at them.

Elsie noticed him too and opened the door. 'George, it's a bit late in the year to start pruning … do you want your porridge or not?'

'Yeah, yeah, won't be long.'

She made a clicking noise with her tongue and went upstairs. He came back indoors within a few minutes.

'And how's my favourite girl this morning?' He was washing his hands at the kitchen sink with his back to her.

'Alright, thank you,' her words squeezing out like toothpaste.

He got the towel, started drying his hands and put his head to one side when he saw her face.

'What's wrong, sweetie? You not feeling well?'

She shook her head and looked over his shoulder. As long as she didn't catch his eye, maybe the nasty thing would go away. It might have done if he hadn't sat beside her, putting his arm around her shoulders. That was it: tears, snot, wailing … the whole works.

Elsie came running downstairs, 'Bloody hell, what's going on? Sarah, you OK my love?'

★

The child calmed down eventually and was even persuaded to eat a piece of toast, the porridge by that time looking like dried up lava. Her voice quiet, as she tried to tell them what she'd heard the night before.

Elsie tugged her plaits. 'You know me and your dad both love you very much, don't you?'

They were in the sitting room, and she sat huddled up on the floor with two cushions, wearing one of Mum's big cardigans with the familiar smell of Pond's Cold Cream overlaid faintly with sweat. She could only nod and listen. She couldn't take the chance of talking in case the waterfall behind her eyes started up again.

'What you heard us talking about was not what you thought. We love each other very much too and we want to take good care of you. It's just that sometimes, even kind people say and do things without thinking about it first.' Mum was using her sensible voice.

'You mean like when I told Tony C that he was stinky?'

They both laughed. She added quickly, 'Yes, but afterwards I said he was only a little bit stinky … not too much.'

'What did he say?' Dad was grinning.

'He said I had nits in my hair and wouldn't sit next to me in assembly. He must know that he smells. And it was difficult when I had to walk in front of him in the Christmas play. He kept trying to tip my hat over my face with the box of frankincense.'

For the third Christmas in a row Sarah was one of the wise men in the school nativity pageant, because of her brown skin and frizzy hair. Her tight plaits were squashed under the same tea-cosy for three years in a row. She was supposed to be the man from the 'dark continent', wherever that was. The other two were Tony C and Christopher, who wore cardboard crowns, painted gold. She knew she would never be Mary or one of the angels, because they always had long, smooth hair, usually blonde. Although, on reflection, she thought that having to play the part of a boy was probably worse than not being Mary.

★

The day passed in slow motion. Elsie and George were still quieter than usual at tea-time. Afterwards George sat Sarah on his lap and they looked at one of her books for a while. Then he closed the book and put his hands either side of her face.

'Now you're a big girl Sarah, I'll tell you about someone in our family. Your American granddaddy. I think you're old enough now.'

'American? Like you?'

'That's right. His name was George too, because he was my Dad, and I was named after him. George Hodges.'

'No, you're wrong. Grandad James was your daddy. That's what you said before.'

'Yes, I know but – well - it's like this. My mom married Grandad James when I was seven years old.'

He paused, waiting for her reaction.

'Same age as me?'

'Yep.'

'That's silly, I thought people had babies after they got married, not before.'

'I know honey. Look, I'll explain. Sometimes things are a little more complicated.'

Elsie reached for her knitting and slumped on the sofa. She listened without interruption as George went on to explain that when two people fall in love, really in love, they have ways of showing each other how much they care. And that sometimes a baby comes along afterwards which is a sign of the love they have both shared.

He looked across at his wife as he said that. She grinned as her needles clacked away. Sarah watched her fingers trying to think of what she said when she was teaching her how to knit: '*in, over under, off, in, over, under, off* ...' until she got the rhythm going, only for it all to fall apart when she dropped a stitch. Then Mum would gently take the knitting and slip it back on the needle.

' ... so, when Grandma Alice met Grandad George, they fell in love, really in love. And ... erm, they showed each other. Then I was born a while afterwards.'

'Showed each other what?'

Nobody said anything. She stayed very still and thought about what Jackie Penrose had told her on the way home from school one day. Jackie was three years older than her and knew a lot of grown-up things. She remembered feeling uncomfortable when Jackie told her something about her own mum and dad; something Jackie saw one night on her way to the bathroom. Sarah thought about it later and decided that it couldn't possibly be anything to do with her own mum and dad, and dismissed it. Anyway, their family was different from everyone else.

'Why did Grandma Alice marry Grandad James if she loved somebody else?'

'Because George Hodges just disappeared. She was lonely for a long time. She wanted me to have a real daddy.'

She paused for a moment. 'You're my real daddy though, aren't you?'

'Of course I am, sweetheart. Come on, give me a big hug.'

She hugged her real dad for a long time. 'So, you never ever saw him?'

'Well, yes, I did, but not until I was grown up. I came back from the war and after a while, I married your lovely mom.'

'Yes, and when you saw her after such a long time you ran to each other like people do in Mum's magazine stories. I love it when you tell me that bit.'

Back on safe ground.

'That's right, we did. My sweet Elsie waited for me all the time I was working, and even after I had to go home for a while.'

He was looking straight across at Elsie. 'She could have done anything, instead of marrying me. She's a very clever and ambitious woman.'

'And you loved each other ...'

'Yep, too right we did.'

'But why did she have to wait for so long?'

He looked across at Elsie. 'We wanted to marry each other sooner, but we weren't allowed to.'

'Why not?

'We weren't allowed to because of my colour and because I was American. And the Commanding Officer said that ...' before he could finish, Elsie rolled her eyes and started mumbling about bedtime.

'Not yet, Mum, I'm not even tired.'

He nodded, 'It's OK, you go on upstairs, I'll tell you more tomorrow. Goodnight honey.'

Within minutes, she was falling asleep, trying to process all she had been told.

★

'You OK honey? Can't you sleep?' George squeezed up close, pulling the blankets over his wife's shoulders.

'Yes, I'm OK. I was just thinking about – oh, just things. I want to get it right for Sarah.'

'What do you mean, get it right?'

'As a parent.'

He sat up, looking straight at her. Elsie turned away and began arranging the pillows behind them.

'You're a great mom, Elsie, just remember that. We both do our best and I think we're doing pretty damn good.'

'I know, but when I think about my own mother, I realise how difficult it must have been for her. There was so much she wanted from life. When she ran off with that sculptor, I realised what was more important to her. And it most certainly wasn't me.'

'I know, it must have felt like that, but not everyone's cut out to be a parent.'

'Mmm, suppose not. I always knew that when I had a child, she or he would have everything they deserved from life, no matter what it took.'

He paused for a moment, 'Your dad's a great guy and your parents both welcomed me into their home, when you took me to meet them. Not wanting to be disrespectful, but I did think your mom was – well, a bit eccentric. Do you remember?'

'Bloody hell, don't I just. I was really angry. The way she looked at you, describing you as a handsome specimen, stroking your arms and going on about your beautiful skin. Anyone would have thought you were a prize racehorse.'

'Yep. I felt very uncomfortable and tried to remember that she probably went on like that because she's an artist, although it also kind of made me think about when folks like me were just regarded as ...' Elsie held up her hands. 'I know, I know ....
I was really embarrassed. And so was Dad.'

'Well, I guess they were living the kind of life they wanted, you know, in the artistic community and all that stuff.'

'Yes, they did. They had some fantastic friends who were very talented. Mum and Dad weren't as successful, despite working damned hard. And I was encouraged to dabble in arty things. I just wanted Mum to approve ...'

He folded his arms, shook his head. 'I understand, you're a talented, wonderful woman. And kind of different. Special.'

'Yes, but you know what it's like when you're young. You want to be like your friends. Anyway, as you know I did end up at art school. I led two different lives, art school during the week and crazy weekends at Maureen's. Mum and Dad didn't seem to mind.'

He raised his eyebrows, 'Yep, until I came along and upset the boat.

She cuddled up next to him; he smiled and held her tight.

She'd never told him that she had been the subject of gossip with some people when it became known that she was one of 'those sort of girls' who enjoyed the company of a coloured man. Girls who were described as being 'common'. You might have thought he and the other Black GIs had dropped from another planet. She always suspected that he was aware of it, but they were both hesitant to discuss it by unspoken agreement.

She raised her shoulders and blew out softly. 'And I've been thinking what a strange Christmas it's been. It will never be the same again.'

'Yeah, know what you mean. Our sweet gal is learning about her family history. That's not a bad thing surely?'

She turned around to face him, 'I'm not sure that she's ready George. After all, in the times ahead, she'll have to be strong in order to deal with …'

'Deal with what?'

'Well, you know – people.'

'Damn right she will, but we can only do our best to answer her questions, however we can.'

'The thing is George she will soon realise that life is not all sugar and spice.'

'Don't worry, she'll be OK, we'll make sure of that.' He touched her face with the back of his hand and raised his eyebrows. 'And – we enjoy our sugar and spice though don't we sweetie?'

She smiled at him and nodded.

Chapter Four

Elsie and Maureen first got to know one another at the table tennis club.

Elsie's parents never really fitted in where they lived. Everyone except them kept their lawns neat and tidy, had proper vegetable plots and carefully tended flower borders, but their garden was overgrown, because her parents believed in allowing wild flowers, plants and weeds to grow and flourish naturally. Elsie loved playing in the long grass when she was little, but as she grew older, it became a shameful contrast between her family and their neighbours.

Her father, Don Taylor, was a painter, and her mother Doris made things using whatever she could find. Don Taylor used a palette knife and thick oil paints to create bold, energetic pictures, mostly of local beauty spots. Sometimes he painted people too, but they weren't very popular, maybe because they generally looked rather strange and dislocated. He sold a few landscape pictures in the small art shop in town, especially during the summer, when tourists visited from up country taking them home to hang in their grand sitting rooms.

During the winter the family mostly survived on a small annuity which had been left by Don's great Aunt Maud, who had been a successful artist as a young woman. History had it that Maud once visited a place in the north of England which had become a magnet for other creative people like herself and decided to stay there.

Doris Taylor's work was much less lucrative; her pieces were built using objects she found in the woods, on the beach – anywhere. On one occasion the rag and bone man stopped outside to feed his horse. It was always exciting to listen as he got nearer, singing out: 'Raggabone, Raggabone', the short tune rising, then fading at the end. Elsie always ran upstairs to watch him from her bedroom window as he passed by. One day he stopped, climbed down from his cart and carried a bag of feed to his horse. Next door's neighbour wandered out to talk to him, followed by a flurry of bright clothes and big hair: Doris Taylor.

Doris started rooting around in his cart and pulled out an ugly lump of metal, held it up high, twisting it about as it glittered in the bright sun. She turned aside to study its detail just as the rag and bone man glimpsed her from the corner of his eye. He approached and shooed her off with a few choice swear words. Looking quite frightened she ran back indoors, the object still clutched in her hand. He grunted, got back onto his seat and trotted off up the road. Their neighbour shook her head and tutted as she went off banging the front door behind her. Elsie stood and listened as the man's familiar call got more and more quiet as he disappeared around the corner. Her parents had a good laugh about the incident that evening over a bottle of Cinzano.

★

Elsie was turning seventeen when her parents decided to move to a small seaside town to fulfil their dreams of becoming part of the artistic community. They were both in awe of those artists who were beginning to become well known in creative circles, and made sure to get involved whenever they could, occasionally arranging supper parties at their moderate home.

Don and Doris Taylor were quite happy when their daughter began to spend almost every weekend back in her old familiar home town to stay at Maureen's house Surrounded by artists and being constantly reminded of Aunt Maud's early success, Elsie had no choice but to develop her own talents, and managed to gain a place at art school as a part time student. She led a double life, trying hard to achieve her parents' aspirations for her, while struggling to keep up with her friends back in the town where she grew up: those whose lives she deemed to be more socially acceptable. Despite his efforts at success, Don Taylor's talent just about enabled him to linger on the social fringes of their artist friends, while Doris struggled to keep up.

Elsie soon learned to be independent, and it came as no surprise when her mother left home for good to embrace the cultural scene elsewhere with an artist who was a family friend, following in the footsteps of the acclaimed Great Aunt Maud.

★

Maureen's mother was often out in the evenings and was very relaxed about her daughter's behaviour, seemingly having little idea nor concern regarding her whereabouts. There was never any mention of Maureen's dad, except a derisive snort from them both if the subject arose. Elsie thought it best not to mention him again, but she enjoyed regaling them both with stories about her own home life and her 'crazy' parents.

Chapter Five

Elsie was staying at Maureen's for the weekend as usual.

'Try this one Else, it's more your shade, the other one's a bit too dark.' Maureen handed her the lipstick; it was almost worn down to nothing and had to be scraped out with the end of an old toothbrush before being applied with a piece of cloth, kept specially for that purpose.

'You sure, Maureen? Looks like it's nearly all gone,' applying it as she spoke, looking in the dressing table mirror with her head to one side.

'Don't worry, plenty more where that came from if I play my cards right!' They locked eyes in the mirror and giggled as they fell backwards onto Maureen's bed. It was Saturday night and they were preparing for a lively night out: both of them seventeen years old and raring to go.

★

Elsie sat up, her face serious for a moment.

'You're really lucky you know, Maureen, to have a mum like yours.'

'What do you mean?'

'Well, at least your mum lets you be yourself. You both seem to get on well. You don't know what it's like in our house. It's bloody bedlam sometimes.'

'Sounds exciting to me; all those weirdos that you talk about – artist types who sit around drinking and all that.' Maureen stood up, started applying eye-shadow, responding as she looked in the mirror. 'It's not as easy as you think, Else. I sometimes worry about my mum; I've stopped asking her where she goes and who with. She either goes cold on me or starts shouting my head off. And of course, we've always got money worries. That's why I've started my hairdressing training. I might even have my own salon one day.'

'Does that mean I'll get free treatment?'

'Course you will, me 'ansum. Your dad doesn't seem to do too badly though, Else. I've seen a couple of his pictures in that little art shop in the alley. Looks quite interestin'. Mind you, I don't know much about all that arty stuff.'

Elsie groaned, 'Yes, all that arty stuff is a bit of a pain sometimes. They were really keen for me to go to art school, said my work is "unique", which probably means it's rubbish.'

Pausing as she applied her rouge, 'Thing is, I actually believed it; I felt that I had to carry on, especially when they started sending me to that bloke for private lessons before I started art college.'

★

Some time later they were sitting in the corner opposite the bar, both of them wearing tight skirts and revealing blouses. They had tried on several outfits from Maureen's mother's wardrobe. They needed to look older than their years, in case the landlord asked them awkward questions.

Maureen, whose hips seemed to have developed overnight, had chosen a long top, to cover the fact that the side zip kept slipping apart, her mother's skirt being dangerously held together by a button on the waistband. Elsie's high heels certainly did not fit the image of the bohemian style so beloved by her own mother. She'd bought the shoes with pocket money she had saved up for a few weeks. The shoes were kept hidden in Maureen's bedroom in readiness to grace their social activities.

Years later it occurred to them both that their warm friendship probably served as a replacement for the sparse parental interest in both their lives.

★

The Jolly Winnard was full of smoke and alive with loud American voices. Coloured soldiers were staking their claim that evening; white soldiers having had their turn the previous night. Following the riots earlier in the year, it was decided that it was safer for everyone.

Maureen scanned the room for a potential victim of her charms.

'Elsie, see that chap in the corner, he's looking at you. See 'im?'

Elsie got her hanky out, pretending to dab the corners of her lipstick as she looked across.

'Oh, yeah, I noticed him the other week. He brushed my arm as I went past to go to the toilet. Apologised like it was an accident.' She looked down at her glass and twisted it around on the table.

'And? Where was I? I don't remember seeing him. Nice too.'

'Yes, he is nice. Thinks he's a bit shy though. But remember, I saw him first, Maureen my dear.'

'Alright, alright. Anyway, where was I that night?'

'You were outside with ...'

Maureen blushed, adding quickly, 'Oh yeah, don't remind me. What a creep he was too. Just because he gave some chewing gum, he thought I was his for the taking.'

★

Elsie was trying to stay cool and relaxed as she sat on her own in the corner, looking at her watch more often than was necessary. Maureen was chatting to one of the soldiers in the opposite corner. A large group of them had taken over the pub that night. Voices were loud, laughter was raucous and plenty of beer was slurped across the bar.

She saw him again; the man who had been there the previous week. He had drifted in by himself and nodded to a few others, but mostly he seemed to be alone. After a few minutes he was approached by another soldier who soon engaged him in deep conversation. She noticed him glancing in her direction over the other man's shoulder as they talked. Would it look too obvious were she to make yet another trip to the toilet? She gulped down her third Babycham and decided to take the risk anyway.

And so it began. Elsie's regular trips to the 'bathroom' as per American parlance was often a private joke between themselves over the years.

Chapter Six

Sunday afternoon: Sarah was drawing and her dad was reading a newspaper article which was sent to him from New York by one of his friends.

'What's the article about, George?' Elsie looked up from her sewing; she was embroidering a cushion. It was to be a surprise, in colours chosen to match Auntie Maureen's newly decorated sitting room.

'Oh, you don't wanna know, honey,' blowing out a sigh and indicating a glance towards Sarah, 'more of just the usual stuff ...'

Elsie put her work aside, 'Let's go for a walk, maybe down the moors this time?'

'Not yet, Mum. Dad needs to tell me about George. His real Daddy George that is.'

He smiled at her, 'Alright, alright little Miss. As I said we loved each other. After I finished being a soldier, I had to go back to New York for a while to see my own mom. That's when I met my Daddy George for the first time. It turned out to be the only time because he died soon afterwards.'

'Wow, you had to wait all those years. That's sad. What did he look like?'

Her dad cleared his throat and laced his fingers together.

'He looked like me, only different.'

'How different? Was he fatter than you?'

'No, he was very sick, and sitting in a wheelchair. He wasn't fatter. But he looked different because he was white. Like Mr Spargo from next door.'

'How could he be white? You're not white, Mum gets really brown in the summer and I'm not white. He must have been someone else's dad.'

'No, he was my father alright. Mom told me. But he had spent most of his life pretending to be a white man.'

'Why?'

Dad took hold of her hands, 'Honey, where I come from, Negroes have a terrible time.'

'What does Negro mean? What is terrible?' recalling her mother's angry words of the previous night.

'Negroes are people who look like us. Folks with brown skin.'

Elsie shifted about and took up her sewing again. George said nothing. They both looked at her.

'Jackie said you were a darky. She said her mum told her that God must have left you in the oven too long.'

Her mother stood up so quickly her sewing slipped to the floor. 'OK, that's enough now, George.'

She took Sarah's arm and started to lead her to the door, 'Let's get our coats and go out for some fresh air.'

George got up from his chair and touched her shoulder, 'It's alright, sweetheart, she needs to know about her history,' his voice quiet, gentle.

Elsie turned back; her eyes wet as she rubbed her sleeve across her face. She slumped back onto the sofa. George got up and shook the coal scuttle. He pushed back the fireguard and put a few lumps on the fire, shifting them slowly around with the poker. It was so quiet you could hear everyone breathing. There was a slight rustle from the corner of the room as one of the paper chains came unstuck and slid down the wall.

'Damn, damn, damn,' Elsie shouted as she rushed to fetch the sweeping brush from the kitchen. George sat Sarah on his lap. They both watched as her mum threaded the broom handle through one of the paper loops and tried to stick it back on. Without success.

'Leave it honey, I'll fix it back up later.' His voice tired and sad.

Elsie sighed quietly, went to the window and stared outside at the quiet road and drew the curtains across before sitting down again.

'What was so terrible for the people like us?' Sarah's quiet voice broke the silence.

'Well, for one thing, white people and coloured people don't usually get married. Not in America anyway.'

'Why not? Even if they love each other like you and Mum?'

'If they do, they can get into lots of trouble and maybe even get badly hurt.'

Elsie had turned to one side, arms folded, staring out of the window.

He ploughed on, 'And other things, there are laws to make sure they don't get together and make friends. Coloureds and whites are not allowed to sit beside one another on a train or a bus or eat together in a café. And there are certain places where Negroes are not allowed to go at all. In America they call it the Negro problem.'

She recalled her mother's angry words of the previous night.

'Are we a Negro problem, Dad?'

'No honey, certainly not. That's why we are happy to live here in this beautiful place called Cornwall. But even here, sometimes people don't understand certain things about us. About our history.'

Elsie shook her head, rubbed the glass with her sleeve and doggedly carried on staring through the window as if she could read words written there: and our history too.

Chapter Seven

A few days later, Elsie was out in the shed trying to paint a picture of two apples and an orange placed beside a flowerpot. George had given her some oil paints and brushes for Christmas and she was doing what she called a 'still life'. It was really cold and she was trying to work all dressed up in her big sweater and a pair of thick gardening gloves, which she said might give her painting an impressionist look, whatever that was. Sarah could understand the 'still' bit, but not the 'life' bit.

Her dad was helping her write thank-you letters to the people who had given her presents. There was a snakes and ladders game and two books from his friend at work. Maureen and her husband Terry gave her a colouring book and crayons and more books. They usually gave her books because they said she was an avid reader; she wasn't sure what the word 'avid' meant but knew it must be something clever.

They were her mum and dad's special friends and they always brought their presents on Christmas Eve. They sat around the fire and made up stories about Father Christmas and how busy he was. Once they had all written their wishes on pieces of paper, George put them carefully just above the smouldering coals and they got sucked up the chimney where Father Christmas was waiting.

And there was the gollywog.

When it was time to write Mrs Spargo's letter, Sarah realised that she hadn't noticed if he was still on the windowsill where she'd sat him propped up against her books. She ran upstairs to check but he was gone. She sat on her bed and tried to remember if she'd put it somewhere else before going downstairs.

★

Elsie was back indoors making herself a cup of cocoa. 'Blow me, it's flipping freezing out there.'

George grinned, 'That's the artist's life for you. Don't they live in garrets, for the sake of their art?'

She didn't reply, just started banging around with the cups and teaspoons. Her artistic skills were a tender issue. She always said that she had dropped out of art school. Sarah wasn't quite sure what that meant. Did she drop out of a window? Who pushed her? Was she hurt?

Although it didn't stop her mum from trying to be artistic, with her knitting, sewing and making weird things out of whatever she could find. There were jars and bottles on every surface in the house, full of shells, stones and twisted bits of wood. There was a tiny bird's skull on top of the bathroom cabinet. She wasn't sure what Mum was planning to do with it, but Sarah tried not to glance upwards when she brushed her teeth because it made her feel a bit sick.

★

'Mum, I can't find my golliwog. Have you seen him?'

There was that look again. George slowly shook his head before Elsie answered.

'Um, I think he must have got mixed up with the rubbish.'

'But how could he get mixed up in the rubbish? He was sitting on the windowsill and smiled at me when I was in bed. Do you think he hid behind one of the books?'

George spoke up then, 'I went around picking up the

32

Christmas wrapping paper that blew out of the bin outside. He must have fallen out of the window and …'

He paused, 'I'll tell you what honey, how about your mum takes you to buy that doll you wanted? Sound good?'

'But what shall I write to Mrs Spargo? I can't say he's got lost.'

'Just say: "Dear Mrs Spargo, thank-you for your kindness, love Sarah," and go put it in her letter box straight away. How's that?'

He took some money out of his pocket and put it in the special milk jug on the dresser.

She didn't ask anymore. She was worried again; she should have been happy about the doll but somehow it didn't feel right. When she'd seen it in Woolworths, the unsmiling lady behind the counter wordlessly held it up to show her as they were strolling past. The doll was chubby and dark, with big smooth curls and long eyelashes which opened and shut when the gloomy shop assistant tipped her upside down. Mum was chatting and laughing with Auntie Maureen and Sarah thought she wasn't listening when she tried to tell her about it.

She decided to call the doll Sarah, because she looked like her, except that her face was a different shade of brown. Her own Baby Sarah would sleep beside her every night.

★

Terry and George had clubbed together to buy an old car. They spent a couple of weekends repairing the engine and re-spraying it before advertising it for sale in The West Briton. The profit was used to buy another vehicle, and so their small business came into being. They decided to keep on their day jobs: George as a mechanic for Western National Bus company and Terry at the electricity board. The added income was a welcome relief and it pleased him to be able to treat his daughter. After a while he was able to buy his own car.

Chapter Eight

It was the day before the new school term. Sarah had just come back from Veronica's house, where they'd spent the afternoon doing colouring in. Veronica showed her a painting book she had found at the bottom of her Christmas stocking. All you had to do was wet the paintbrush and carefully smooth it across the picture and different colours appeared like magic. She let Sarah have a turn. Afterwards Mrs Pearce gave them each a piece of cake and a glass of milk and then said she would walk Sarah back home because it was late afternoon and beginning to get dark.

She insisted on doing up the child's coat buttons, one by slowly one and smiling largely in her face. Talking in her soft Cornish lilt, she tugged gently at the child's plaits before tucking them under her hat. 'Like stretchy black snakes, aren't they dear?'

Sarah was too shy to tell her that she was quite able to dress herself. After all, she would be eight on her next birthday. And the stretchy black snakes thing made her feel uncomfortable.

★

It made her think of what her mum told her if anyone was rude or offended her at school; she should respond by saying, 'I am Sarah and I am special.' She had tried that couple of times but that didn't work. It sounded silly anyway, especially when Tony had said that her lips looked like the tyres on his uncle's tractor, then ran away laughing. Mrs V was on playground duty that day; she marched him over to apologise and sent him indoors to deal with him later. Sarah noticed him grinning even though he did as he was told. The girls were friendly enough, although it got on her nerves when they gently pulled her stretchy plaits as a sign of affection. She didn't mind because they were only being kind.

The children enjoyed the last session of the day: story-time, when everyone sat on the carpet in the book corner. Mrs V would produce that day's special story from what she called her treasure bag. As she read, the characters would leap off the page, each one real and believable. During the week following Sarah's distressing event, Mrs V found a couple of important jobs for her. One afternoon she was allowed to choose her favourite book for story-time, and on another occasion she was sent to the headmaster's room with a special message.

It was a quarter to three the following Friday afternoon. The children began to make their way straight to the book corner, following the afternoon playtime as usual. Mrs V raised her hand, instructing them to go to their desks, sit quietly and fold their arms. They all looked at one another as they followed her instructions. Mrs V went to the front of the room and produced the special story bag from under her table.

She held it up, 'I'm going to put two envelopes on everyone's desk. One will have your name on it and the other one will not. Both envelopes are sealed. You are not to open either of them until I say your name. You will stand up when I give you the nod one by one. First of all, open the envelope with your name on it and read what it says on the back of the photo inside. Then open the second envelope, take out the other photo and read what is says on the back of that one too. You must read the words clearly and slowly so that everyone in the room can hear you. We will all sit and listen politely as you read.'

She stood very still and waited until the whole class was settled. Nobody knew when their turn would come. Mrs V looked around and nodded her head randomly around the room as she chose each child, one by one. Sarah clutched her hands together under the desk and stared straight ahead. It was ages before she got the nod; maybe Mrs V had forgotten?

Finally the teacher nodded at Sarah: her turn.

'My name is Sarah, and I am special.' And in her other envelope: 'This is Malcolm and he is special.'

Tony was the last to be chosen moments before the school bell rang to signal the end of the school day. I am Tony and I am special.' He opened the other envelope and paused for a moment before reading: 'This is Sarah, and she is special.'

Sarah would remember Mrs V for ever.

★

It was really cold when they got outside and held hands as they walked. Mrs Pearce was wearing big mittens and it was difficult to hold on properly, but Sarah didn't want to say so. It was the sort of cold that makes even the inside of your nose feel stiff. The road was quiet, apart from a couple of people going by walking their dogs.

'How was your Christmas, dear? Did you have a nice time?'

'Yes, thank you.'

'With lots of lovely presents?'

'Yes.'

'I expect your dad misses seeing his family in America, doesn't he?'

Mrs Pearce had never asked anything about her dad before. Sarah paused before answering. 'Yes, he does. He used to write letters to his mum and send her photos of me and Mum sometimes.'

'I expect she likes that. Doesn't he write anymore?' We stopped for a minute so she could get her handkerchief out of the other pocket to blow her nose.

'No, because she – she wasn't very well and then she ...'

'Oh, sorry dear, I understand. And what about his dad?'

How could she explain about the two dads; she was still trying to work it all out for herself.

'Cat got your tongue dear?'

'We don't have a cat. Erm … but my dad told me that he used to have one who died and then another one died, because … '

'What's that dear? Two dads? Sounds a bit strange. Never mind, we're nearly there now. There's your mum, looking out of the window for you.'

Elsie opened the front door as they came up the path.

'Oh, there's my gorgeous girl. Give us a cuddle.' She stooped down and held her tight as Sarah looked back at Mrs Pearce over her shoulder.

'Thanks so much for walking her back. Hope she behaved herself.'

'Yes, course she did, as usual. And we had a good old chat on the way down, didn't we, dear?'

Sarah nodded and moved away, taking off her coat and pulling off her hat as the stretchy black snakes tickled her neck.

Black snakes.

She went upstairs and looked in the mirror as she whispered what had been written on the back of her school photo: 'I am Sarah and I am special.'

Chapter Nine

'What does ambitious mean, Mum? Dad always says that about you.'

Sarah was trying to draw a picture of her mum as she sat at her sewing machine, but she moved too fast, using one hand to shift the fabric around to the correct position, while turning the handle with the other. She gave up and instead drew a picture of her parents walking up a steep hill into the sun, with her in the middle holding both their hands.

'What's that, sweetheart?' Mum ran her fingers through her hair. It was pulled back in a ribbon which had come loose while she was working.

'What does ambitious mean?'

'Well, it means having high hopes and plans for your life and then trying to make sure that you do them. Like working hard at your lessons in school.'

The child said nothing. At the end of the previous term she had come home proudly declaring that she was third in the weekly spelling test. But Mum wasn't very pleased. She said that the only way to get on in life was to come top of the class. They didn't talk about it after that. She decided it might be best to tell Dad about school things instead.

'What plans did you have, Mum?'

Elsie stopped what she was doing and turned around.

'Well, as you know, I used to go to art college. We studied drawing, painting, making things … And we learned about all kinds of creative work done by others. Famous people.'

'Is that when you decided to be famous too?'

'Yes, but it didn't happen. I suppose everyone who creates something wants to be well known but it's not easy. There are lots of clever, artistic people that nobody has ever heard of.'

'But, when you think of it, you're famous already. There's me and Dad, Auntie Maureen, Uncle Terry and Grandad think so. We all like the different things you do.'

She put one hand to her chin and smiled. 'Yes, I suppose so, my love.'

'You're more famous than Grandad. Nobody likes his pictures very much.'

She was thinking of his painting of a group of women and men sitting on a beach in the small art shop they walked past when they went shopping in town. The same picture had been in the window for months. Maybe they couldn't sell it because one woman in the picture was making a weird face with her tongue poking out and none of her friends seemed to notice. Sarah felt a bit shy every time she saw it. And his signature in the bottom corner looked like a spider crawling up someone's leg.

'And you read a lot of books; you always say that reading makes you clever.'

'Mmmmm …' Mum leaned forward and touched her arm. 'Sarah, you must remember that there are lots of other places you might want to live in the world. Somewhere else, like London perhaps.'

'I wouldn't want to leave you and Dad though. Why would I want to go and live somewhere else?'

'I'm talking about when you grow up.' Her eyebrows scrunched together. 'You are as bright as a button; wouldn't you want to show everyone what clever things you can do? There are people in the world who … might think … well never mind. You'll understand what it all means one day.'

She turned back to her machine. Sarah noticed the pins which had dropped all over the floor while her mother was sewing. She got on her hands and knees and picked them up, one by one. There were even a few stuck in the swirly rug which slid around the floor if you walked on it too fast. She was thinking about all the things that Mum did.

'And you like reading those magazines that Mrs Spargo brings in and your favourite books by that lady with the animal name …'

'Virginia Woolf? Her stories are much better stories than the ones Mrs Spargo likes.'

'Yes, but you do read them as well. Anyway, Dad says you're brilliant at everything.'

Mrs Spargo insisted on passing on her magazines when she'd finished with them every week. The stories were mostly about shy young women in big hats, who spent all their time looking for the right husband. He had to be tall, handsome, strong and rich and when they met, always in secret of course, he would kiss her hand or gently hold her hair away as he kissed the back of her neck. She had to be slender and pale with long hair, her cheeks flushing in timid delight when the aforementioned man comes on the scene and fulfils his neck-back kissing role where the tender pale wisps of hair lay on her pale skin.

'And you make up good stories.'

'S'pose so.'

Her mum's bed-time tales were full of sadness, happiness, fear, adventure, joy, every emotion you can imagine, the endings always leaving Sarah with something to think about as she fell asleep. Sometimes the stories were a bit too scary.

Chapter Ten

'Hello, my love how was school?' Elsie climbed down from the step-ladder and gave her daughter a quick hug. She had wallpaper paste on her chin, in her hair and all over her hands. Not waiting for a reply, she stood back to survey her handiwork. George had left for the early shift that morning and she wanted to give him a surprise by the time he got home. Her aim was to decorate at least half of the sitting room by teatime.

'Mrs V was home with a bad cold so Mr Tregunna had to take our class. We wrote about our holidays and did lots of sums by playtime, then...'

Elsie was looking away and staring at the walls as she spoke, 'That's a shame, you love Mrs V don't you?'

'So, what do you think then?', stepping forward as she talked, to smooth out some wrinkles in the damp wallpaper.

'It looks all wrong. The stalks are supposed to grow up the walls aren't they? And the flowers are all pointing sideways.'

Mum laughed and rubbed some of the paste from her cheek. 'I did that deliberately you silly-billy. Thought it looked more ... more artistic. Don't you like it?'

'S'pose so ...'

'Think I'll take a break now, I want to finish off something before I get tea ready. That posh lady's coming to collect her dress. You hungry yet, love?'

'Yes, a bit.'

'Alright, tell you what, you get yourself a sandwich and I'll sort out your tea later.'

Sarah went upstairs, took off her school clothes and put on her pyjamas even though it was only four o'clock.

★

Her mum had spent all day before the start of the winter term getting her things ready for school. She liked sewing and made most of her own clothes as well. It all started when Mrs Spargo asked if she would alter her coat, then Auntie Maureen asked her to make a party dress. Before too long, other people heard about it and she was even asked to make a wedding dress which was cut down the following year to make a baby's christening gown.

She bought fabric remnants to make Sarah's summer dresses and blouses and could turn larger garments into little ones. Her new school skirt was made out of one Elsie's old jackets. The skirt was gathered around her middle with straps which crossed over at the back and buttoned onto the waistband at the front. The fabric was quite thick and stuck out around her like a bell. Mum said she looked like a real Cornish girl when she tried it on, because the fabric was Cornish tartan: a yellow and black squared design with pale blue lines running through it. The only thing was she never ever felt like a real Cornish girl. And she didn't want to tell her mum that Jackie said she looked like a painted football on the way home from school the first day she wore it.

Chapter Eleven

George had come home from choir practice earlier that week, full of excitement. He was talking about it at teatime.

'I've listened to lots of different music in my time, but this was unlike anything else. I could have cried when Jason, the new conductor played us some of it. He brought his record-player in specially so we could listen to it all the way through.'

'Oh, yeah, is it like that that other stuff you like with the soprano swinging up to the rafters?

'What the Pergolesi? No, this is different. It's a big choral piece by Elgar. We don't usually get to listen to the stuff before we start rehearsing, but this is ... well, just wait 'til you hear it. It will be the most ambitious thing we've ever attempted since Ted retired. He was keen on popular songs and carols, but this new man has high ambitions for us.'

Elsie smiled, 'Sounds exciting. Why don't we go and buy the record tomorrow, so we can all get to know it before the next concert? What do you think, Sarah?'

★

She remembered the day her parents came home with the record player; it had been a special treat for their wedding anniversary. They went all the way to Plymouth on the train and didn't get home until evening. Mrs Spargo looked after Sarah because it was the school holidays. She let her bring some of her toys and sat with her for 'Listen with Mother' on the wireless after dinner. Nobody called it lunch in those days. Except posh people that is. Mrs Spargo didn't know that Sarah and her mum always joined in when the presenter said, *Are you sitting comfortably? Then I'll begin,* before they cuddled up and listened to the story.

She spent the rest of the afternoon playing with Mrs Spargo's puppy Cogan, who was named him in honour of Mrs Spargo's favourite singer, Alma Cogan. The Spargos had bought a new television and invited Sarah and her parents over to watch one evening. Alma was on, resplendent in a dress which was tight at the top, the skirt like a gigantic birthday cake bouncing around her hips while she swayed and sang in a broken sultry voice. Mrs Spargo said she was so rich that she never wore any of her dresses more than once. Sarah and her mum wondered where she kept them all.

She wasn't too keen on going outside with the Spargo boys, Derek and Andrew, who were much bigger than her. All they wanted to do was race up and down on the pavement on their trolley, shouting a lot. Although it was a very impressive vehicle: a plank of wood with old pram wheels and a rope handle. She only had one go. Fell off and grazed her knee. But later, at teatime they offered to take her to Saturday morning pictures with them every week after that.

Elsie came to collect her afterwards and put her hands over Sarah's eyes as she led her into the sitting room for the surprise. There it was: the Dansette, in all its pristine glory on the sideboard: a box in dark red, which Mum said was properly called maroon, with a grey lid and grey mesh across the front where the sound came out. The man who sold it recommended a record shop in the town, so they also bought a few records. Well, five to be exact. They played those five over and over again until they knew every scratch, every note of the sparkling improvisations and the names of all the musicians. The player soon became known as the Dancing

Dansette because they sometimes enjoyed jiving to the upbeat numbers. Dad would twirl her around and then it was Mum's turn.

A few weeks later, George saw an advertisement in *The West Briton* for a double bass on sale. The man who was selling it said it was left to him by his uncle who used to play in a band 'up country', which meant/could mean anywhere north of Plymouth. They never did find out where. George and Terry went off in the van to collect it. She and her mum were so excited as they watched the two men bringing it up the front path. A huge violin for a giant. Her dad was tall and strong, but even so she wondered how he would ever be able to lift it and play. She helped Mum move the armchairs about to make room for it in the corner.

George used to go to the library every week; he and Elsie read everything from history, to politics, to great stories. Their evenings and weekends were busy making things or having discussions about issues that Sarah didn't always understand, although she knew they were important.

Sometimes George received a magazine/article through the post, which his friend Richie sent him all the way from New York. The stories in it were completely different to those in Mrs Spargo's magazines. They were mostly about people who looked like Dad: coloured people.

★

George borrowed a beginner's music book from the library and practised on his double bass most evenings, until he had mastered a couple of the basic scales, mostly G and C major. After studying at the theory for a while, he would try to play alongside some of 'the greats', as they called them. His favourite was playing along with Slam Stewart at the beginning of 'Yardbird Suite', because it sounded as if Slam was playing the same note for most of the tune. He sent away for quite a few music books after that, including one called Easy-to-Play Jazz. Easy to play? Hardly… the title didn't make any sense, but he was determined.

They used to listen to music on the wireless too. It was often difficult to tune in and find the right station, George had to keep turning the knob on the front slowly and carefully until all of a sudden, a deep American voice would resonate around the room: 'This is the Voice of America', and they were treated to sounds and songs which would enthral their young daughter for the rest of her life.

Chapter Twelve

Elsie used to go and visit her father occasionally. He still lived in their old house in Back Road East in St Ives. It was one of a row of fishermen's cottages, opening onto the narrow street, with steps on the outside leading up to the loft where the fisherman once kept his nets. The loft was always full of painting things: brushes, old squeezed tubes, folded at one end with crusty bright colours stuck on the sides, rolls of paper, discarded half-finished pictures and stiff bits of canvas lying around on the floor.

It was Saturday morning; Sarah and her mum were on the train from Truro to St Erth. George stayed home, said he wanted to catch up on his music. He would switch from Charlie Parker to Pergolesi, to Elgar and countless others all in the space of a day.

Sarah sat near the window watching the fields rush by, trying to count the cows before getting bored, while her mum was reading. They had to change trains at St Erth to get the branch line to St Ives, then walk among the narrow streets to her grandfather's house.

Elsie usually carried a book in her bag, wherever they went, even if there wasn't an opportunity to read it. Sarah recognised the cover; it was white with a couple of yellow streaks across the front and a brown design all around the edge of strange-looking circles with squares inside. It was one of her favourites: *To The Lighthouse,* by Virginia Woolf. At the bottom was written 'The

Hogarth Press' and underneath that, in smaller writing the name 'Vanessa Bell'. It was her most favourite book. When she and her parents moved to St Ives she loved the fact that someone as famous as Virginia Woolf used to spend her holidays there with her family.

Elsie enjoyed telling her daughter about Virginia and her sister Vanessa Bell, the painter. When they got off the train they often strolled along pretending to be the famous pair: Sarah wanted to be Virginia, calling herself Ginnie and made up silly stories as they went. Elsie's role of course was to be Vanessa. When they reached Grandad's house, she would create a picture to go with 'Ginnie's' story using a selection of some of the plentiful art tools from her father's collection.

Elsie decided to go and see her father on her own a few weeks later. Feeling relaxed she took her time to walk through the town, sometimes pausing to stop and look at the shops along the way. She finally arrived and hunted around in her pocket for her father's spare key. Her anxiety grew as she banged on the door and tapped at the front window for several minutes, calling out his name.

Don Taylor's neighbour stepped outside, wondering what could have happened. She opened her door, saw Elsie's face, red with fear and invited her in. A woman of few words, she opened her kitchen drawer, handed Elsie a short note and stood back as she watched Don Taylor's short note to his daughter, informing her that he had decided to visit s distant cousin in Australia and would get in touch.

She never heard from her father again.

Chapter Thirteen

Mum was upstairs reading. Sarah and Dad decided to see what was showing on TV. The set stood in pride of place in the corner, with the double bass leaning beside it. She switched it on just as a big brassy introduction as the curtain rose on the evening's entertainment: *The Black and White Minstrel Show*. Dad got up and turned off the television.

'Can't we watch it Dad? Mrs Spargo said it was fantastic.'

It was a fairly new programme and came highly recommended by Dot Spargo. She had been talking about it with Elsie a few days before and kept going on about the beautiful women and their gowns: the lovely singing, the men with their faces painted black, all of them acting like 'true gentlemen'. She carried on talking while Elsie made a quick dash back indoors.

★

George hesitated before turning back to sit beside her on the sofa. On the screen, a parade of blonde women sashayed across the stage dressed up to the nines in bonnets and frills. The 'true gentlemen' in black-face with thick white makeup around their eyes and lips, wore striped trousers, tail coats, white gloves and top hats. They made huge gestures, tipping their hats and dropping to their knees as they tried to court the fair maidens who pretended to peep out shyly from behind their parasols.

When that didn't work, they assembled and broke into songs about their coal-black Mammies and the joys of the cotton fields back home.

George's face was a mask. When the singing was over he turned down the volume and gave Sarah an enquiring look. 'So, what do you think? Do you like it?'

'I don't like the way they paint their faces, do you, Dad? Makes them look silly.'

'Do you think the people who make them dress that way want them to look silly?'

'I don't know. I feel sorry for them, don't know why. But the singing's um, quite nice.'

He stood up and started pacing around the room. It was beginning to make her feel uncomfortable, even a little bit scared. He was usually so quiet and kind.

'Dad, what's wrong? Why don't you sit down? We can watch something else. Or play snakes and ladders ...' She trailed off, feeling tears throbbing behind her eyelids.

He sat back down, put his arms around his daughter and held her tight. She started snivelling, her head on his shoulder.

'Oh, I'm sorry, sweetheart, I didn't mean to upset you. It's just that there are things we've never talked about properly before, but I think you're old enough now to understand.'

'Understand what?' She looked up as he rubbed her face with his handkerchief and then gently pulled her plaits. He kissed her cheek and she felt the comforting brush of his moustache across her face as he drew away.

'You remember me telling you that back where I come from, lots of people don't have a very nice time because ... because they look different to a lot of other people.' He paused, 'They are often treated badly and there are rules which are unfair.'

Even so, she had an idea of what he meant: 'Like when I go to Saturday morning pictures with Veronica and all the others?'

Lots of children from their estate went. It was the highlight of the week, when they weren't outside playing. Most of the films were about cowboys and Indians.

'Like when the Indians get shot and fall off their horses, and everyone cheers and shouts?'

'Yes, they only do that because nobody's told them that it's unkind and cruel.' He paused. 'Do you cheer too?'

She didn't know how to respond. If she said yes, he might think she was a bad person. She didn't know how to explain her mixed-up feelings. 'Only sometimes.'

She wanted to tell him that she didn't really want to join in, but didn't know how or why she did. Nobody seemed to care about those poor people being killed or injured. Once an Indian was dragged along behind a horse, the whole audience shouted even louder and some of the boys laughed. She came home one day and asked why all they did that, but when she tried to ask Mum about it, she told her to go upstairs to fetch her slippers.

The minstrel men on the show were still singing bravely. One of them stepped forward to the prettiest lady and pretended to cry when she flapped him away with her lacy gloves. He turned his mouth down and the white make-up around his lips made them into a big upside-down letter 'U'.

Then she remembered.

'Those men on TV look like my gollywog. The one that got lost in the rubbish, remember?'

'Yep, sure do.' He shook his head and grunted.

★

Dad's response made her think about something which had happened a few weeks before, when the ice-cream man's tinkling song was ringing outside the gate.

Mum took out her purse, 'Here you are lovely, go and get yourself an ice-cream before he drives off again.'

There were several children waiting to be served, Derek and Andrew from next door and a few others. When it was Sarah's turn, the ice-cream handed over her cornet with a big smile and two chocolate flakes stuck on the top. 'And how's our little piccaninny today?' she smiled back, saying, 'Very well thank you.' Andrew sniggered. She wondered why. She didn't know what was so funny about Mr Kelly being friendly. She sauntered up the path and had eaten one of the flakes before she reached the door. Next door's puppy Cogan came out and jumped up, trying to get a lick too, and she shooed him away.

Elsie sat reading, looking quiet and relaxed. She was so often rushing about doing things, making things, changing things. Creating her world. She was hunched in the corner of the sofa with her knees up. She glanced across as Sarah came into the room. 'Oh, that looks nice. I should have asked you to get one for me too.'

'Do you want a lick of mine?'

'No … oh, go on then.' Sarah watched as she bit a tiny bit off the top of the flakey chocolate and bits fell down her cardigan.

'The ice-cream man called me his little piccaninny. He was kind and put an extra flake on top. I ate it on the way indoors.'

Within a flash Elsie wordlessly threw down her book, opened the front door and ran down the path. She was barefoot, her hair swinging around about. Sarah rushed to the window. Most of the children had wandered off, except Andrew who was sitting on the pavement with his ice-lolly. The man was closing down the hatch on his van before getting ready to drive off. Elsie grabbed hold of the collar of his white jacket and put her face up close to his. She couldn't hear what her mum said to him, but she watched as he flushed and stared, straightened his jacket and drove away quickly. She marched back indoors and returned to the sofa, saying nothing about the incident. He never called her a piccaninny again after that day, and served her politely without catching her eye or even smiling.

The incident was never referred to again.

Chapter Fourteen

Mum and Dad were so proud when I passed the eleven-plus and got a place at the Trebean Grammar School for Girls on the other side of town. When we got the news, Dad went out and bought a bottle of wine to have with our tea that evening. Talk about pushing the flippin' boat out … I was even allowed a drop. Mum got the best glasses down from the top of the dresser and gave them a good polish; that usually only happened on Christmas Eve when Maureen and Terry popped in for a glass of sherry.

The day me and Mum went to the uniform shop to buy all the stuff I needed was shameful, to say the least. Mum said the whole lot would cost a good bob or two, so she had to make sure to buy everything in big sizes so it would still fit by the time I reached sixth form. Told me that was why Dad had been doing extra overtime for a few weeks. Plus he and Terry had been lucky enough to sell three cars recently.

★

'There now, don't you look smart.' The man in the shop was a slimy git; he knew I looked like the flippin' Michelin man when I had all the gear on. I felt like a prize prat.

'There's just one more item on the list madam, the regulation jersey. He stroked his chin as he looked me over, as if he was sizing me up to take my photo. He took out one he thought would fit from under the glass counter and handed it to Mum.

'Chin up and arms out, there's a good girl.' She held it up to my chest, making sure that the side seams stretched right across and down under my arms. I thought at any minute she would take out her hankie, spit on it and wipe my chin.

'Yes, that looks about right, madam, I'll put it in the bag with the rest of your items.'

She hesitated and then said, 'No, that won't be necessary, I could make one myself for a third of the price, thank you.'

'Are you sure, madam? I know they have quite strict uniform procedures at Trebean.'

★

'So, Miss Sarah, you're all set. Well, almost – let's just pop into Wally's Wools, so I can get the things I need for your jersey.' She patted my cheek, right there on the street. 'I'm so proud of you, my girl. You could go anywhere in the world after a decent education. There's more to life than dear old Cornwall. Wished I had been given the chance.'

Yeah, don't I know it, I was thinking. She'd kept on about it ever since we got the letter.

'Shall we go and have a cup of tea and a bun at that new place in Chapel Lane afterwards? Might as well make an afternoon of it.'

I nodded. She was in such good spirits I didn't have the heart to say anything about the jersey.

In Wally's Wools she got the stuff she would need: a few balls of black wool and one ball each of red and blue to trim the v-neck and the cuffs. She got thick wool so it would keep me warm out on the hockey pitch. I swore to myself that I would never wear it no matter how cold I was. The regulation school jersey cost twelve and six. I was sure I had more than that in my piggy-bank. I could just go and buy one myself on Saturday and hide it in my satchel every morning.

Chapter Fifteen

M e and Veronica arranged to walk together that first day. We hoped that we would both be in the same class group. It was the beginning of the autumn term, and the weather was still quite mild. Poor old Veronica turned up wearing the complete works: the regulation school jersey, the blazer, plus the gabardine mackintosh to boot. Her top lip was beaded with sweat just from walking the hundred yards from her house down to ours.

We were nervous as hell by the time we'd walked across town, up the hill, past the railway station and along a fancy-looking road to the school. There were a few sixth formers waiting outside to welcome us and show us into the great hall. Some of them looked very grown up, with an air of brisk efficiency, breasts and hips straining to escape their uniforms.

All the new girls had to sit at the front of the hall. Miss Goddard the Headmistress hobbled onto the stage, looking like the wicked witch of the west, all done up in her academic gown which had obviously seen better days. Everyone stood up until summoned to sit down again, which even included the teachers sitting along the walls, poor sods.

Miss Goddard welcomed everyone, especially us new ones. She rabbited on about the wonderful history of the school building that was a 'spawning ground of academic greatness'. I got a fleeting image of the tadpoles we used to catch from a stream down the moors near our estate. Veronica and me had left ours out in the sun that spring in a rusty wheelbarrow at the bottom of her garden and forgot all about them. When we went back to look a couple of weeks later, the water had all dried up and the tadpoles had turned into hard black squiggles. So much for spawning.

I nudged Veronica and widened my eyes. She nodded and whispered behind her hand,

'Just like the tadpoles.'

The Deputy Head then read out the form lists for each year group. The first years were in either One A and One B, and so on until the fifth year. I wondered what the difference was, but it became apparent as the school year trundled on. The six-formers were *Six One* and *Six Two*. The lists took ages, before we were led away to be spawned.

The posh girls were in the A class. Out of about two hundred and fifty girls in the whole school, only a small percentage of us were from the council estates as far as I could see as time progressed. We were all plonked into the B class from day one along with other odd types who must have come across as such when they were interviewed. Veronica and me were the only two estate girls in our year. The A girls were distinctly different. Most of them came in by coach from outlying villages or were dropped off by their parents in fancy cars. They sported expensive satchels, well-groomed hair and their uniforms looked as if they were replaced every year.

Chapter Sixteen

I was standing on the stool, trying to look down as Mum adjusted the hem of my gymslip.

'Keep still, Sarah. Every time you bend down it goes skewiff.' She was on her knees, her mouth full of pins.

'Yes, but I don't want it to be too long. I'll look stupid and anyway the mark from last year will show.'

She was getting really pissed off now, started to speak and the pins dropped out and stuck in the carpet. 'Look here, you can't go to school showing your knees. You know how fussy they are. Anyway, I can press out that mark.'

We both knew that the hemline would still show no matter how many times she went over it with a damp cloth and a very hot iron. The pale line from first year was still there for heaven's sake.

★

The dining hall was more relaxed than usual. Miss Lister, one of the new young teachers, was on duty, blissfully unaware of the strict rules usually enforced by the Deputy Headmistress, Miss Jowell. Consequently, there was more chatter than usual and the table monitors, those unfortunate enough to sit at the top end of each table, conveniently forgot their duties of ensuring that all plates were scraped clean and passed along for collection by the lowly canteen staff.

The food was even more inedible than usual that day. The mashed potato was full of grey lumps, the meat, of unknown provenance, was stringy, and the green vegetables swam listlessly in their own dank water. Nobody was able to finish their food. One girl even got up from her place and wandered about talking to a couple of others on nearby tables.

That was Julie Penrose. She was in full flow as usual, making us all laugh. She produced a brown paper bag from her pocket and stood at the top of her table, briskly scraping the mess from each plate into the bag before scrunching it between two plates and pressing hard. Bits of food squirted out from the sides and some ended up in Veronica's hair. We squealed and laughed while Miss Lister stood, vainly clapping her hands in her efforts to maintain control. Miss Jowell appeared at the door. Table by table, the room grew quieter. Julie slowly sauntered back to her seat.

★

Julie had deliberately tied her pony-tail to one side in the school photo the previous year. It so happened that she was positioned right in the middle of the picture, grinning coquettishly with her head slanted alongside the errant hair. It was one of those long photographs where the photographer walks slowly along to capture the whole school: teachers and pupils.

The teachers sat either side of Miss Goddard in the front row, hands in their laps and their ankles neatly placed to the left. The first years sat cross-legged in front of them, their gymslips respectfully pressed down in the middle to hide their young thighs and navy-blue knickers, while the rest of us stood to attention in the rows behind. Except for Julie. It was only after every parent in the school had ordered a copy of the picture to stick at the back of a bedroom drawer, that Julie's misdemeanour came to Miss Goddard's attention. It was rumoured afterwards that Julie's parents were summoned to her office to discuss their daughter's commitment to the school. Apparently a large donation was contributed to the cost of refurbishing the sixth-form block later that year. Miss Goddard announced the generosity of the anonymous donor in assembly.

Julie smirked.

Chapter Seventeen

A fter I twirl you around, I'll pause while you slide your hand all down my arm. Then we carry on. Got it?'

Saturday afternoon. Veronica had brought down her transistor radio so we could listen to Alan Freeman playing the latest pop songs. We were practising our jiving. We'd seen a couple doing the slippy-arm thing on *Top of the Pops* and it looked really cool.

Thought we might try it out at the youth club next time we went. The only trouble is I always had to be the boy, because I was taller than her, which was annoying. Plus my hair didn't really help, adding about another two inches to my height. It was sticking up like a toilet brush. Minutes before Veronica turned up I'd run outside to help Mum take in the washing because it had started to rain. I didn't have time to tidy up before Veronica knocked on the door.

★

My hair was always a cause for concern. Mum decided that it should be cut short as I got older, she said my plaits looked too babyish. Getting my hair tidy for school was a daily trial, gathering it together into a neat bun or a French pleat took too much time, plus it sometimes came undone during the day. Auntie Maureen was summoned to the rescue. As a hairdresser, she knew, or thought she knew, all about hair, but it soon became clear that cutting mine would present a challenge.

She arrived with her professional scissors and a magnifying hand mirror one Sunday afternoon. The operation took place in front of the hallway mirror. Mum sat in attendance nearby, handing me the small mirror every so often so that I could check how short it was at the back. Auntie Maureen was smiling rather too broadly, her hands shaking slightly as she approached each stage of the process. Dad wandered through every so often, ostensibly to pick up his newspaper or fiddle with his double bass. The atmosphere was charged with a quiet anxiety, denied by us all. When Auntie Maureen had finished to everyone's satisfaction, he offered to sweep up after I brushed the tight curls off my shoulders.

Dad put on his latest favourite: Tubby Hayes and the All Stars, playing a tune called 'Lady E'. He called out, 'This is for our very own Lady E', clicking his fingers along at the beginning and pretending to dance with the sweeping brush. His eyes appeared to be glistening as he moved about. I stared at him: it was all very embarrassing.

Mum and Auntie Maureen went to put the kettle on. Heaven knows what they were thinking while they fiddled about in the kitchen.

A few weeks later I was at the table doing my homework in my hair rollers: a constant addition to my indoor wear. Mum had sent me up to the local shop earlier because we had run out of milk. It had been raining and still felt damp outside, meaning that my frizz immediately stood to attention and I had to rush upstairs to put my rollers in when I got back. I could complete the process in about three minutes, without even looking in the mirror.

'Just remembered, I've got you a present sweetie.' Dad went out into the hallway to hunt around in his coat pocket. He came back with a paper bag. Inside was a metal comb and a jar of Vaseline.

Mum put her head to one side and raised her eyebrows, 'I have to say, your dad is full of surprises, isn't he? What's that all about, George?' She smiled.

'I remember my mom using one like this when I was a kid. She used to heat it up on the stove. While it was getting hotter and hotter, she would take a clump of hair and put grease on it, then straighten it with the comb before going on to the next bit.'

Mum screwed up her face. 'Sounds rather dangerous to me. Why did she do that?'

Dad groaned, 'Because she wanted to have "good hair"', emphasizing the last two words and rolling his eyes. He paused, 'Anyway, I thought this might make your life a bit easier, Sarah. What do you think?'

I turned the comb over in my hands; it was heavy and industrial looking, with a wooden handle and the teeth very close together. I could never have imagined being able to run a comb like that through my tight kinks without suffering considerable pain.

'Sounds ideal. But where did you find it? There's nobody else who would need one of these. Only me.'

He grinned, 'Well – erm – I bought it in the pet shop. It's meant to be for grooming dogs.' There was a pause – until we all started laughing. 'Thanks again Dad, woof, woof!'

And so it began: it had to be used on dry hair, causing a strong singed smell throughout the house. Mum said nothing but opened the windows with a tut, occasionally commenting that it would ruin my hair one of these days, but she didn't try to stop me. I burned the top of my ears a few times, but it was well worth the pain. The straightening was then followed by rollers to add natural looking waves. Just like all the other girls. Like Veronica's.

★

Little miss–oh–so–petite–and–dainty Veronica's slick blonde curtain of lazy curls fell obediently about her shoulders as she danced.

'Like this?' She made a half-hearted attempt to do the sliding bit while maintaining the hip wiggle which we agreed had to continue all the way through the song.

'Not really, 'Ron. Let's just forget it. Do you want some orange juice?'

'Yes, alright'. She sat down, looking a bit cross as I went out to the kitchen to fetch our drinks. She turned the volume up loud and Neil Sedaka's voice flooded the room, '*Happy Birthday Sweet Sixteen. Tonight's the night, I've waited for …*'

★

I went back in with our drinks. We slurped away for a few moments, both of us sensing that our friendship had subtly changed. I suppose it was after I became more friendly with Julie and got an invitation to her barbecue. Veronica started going to the church social most weeks, instead of the youth club. She was getting seriously religious, wearing longer skirts and talking about the lovely people she met at church.

'OK, how about a different tune then?' I went over to Dad's record player and found 'Swingin' Shepherd Blues'.

Veronica raised her shoulders and folded her arms; anyone would think I was about to slap her or something. 'Is it that, erm, jazz stuff that your dad likes?'

'Don't looked so flippin' scared, 'Ron; it's music, just a bit different from our usual stuff, that's all. And it's not actually proper jazz, it's more- kind of …oh, just listen to it. It's fab.'

She slumped back on the sofa. I lifted the arm and put the needle carefully on the first grooves of the disc. We sat quietly as a flute began swaying and sliding across the main tune, accompanied by gentle accompaniment of the other instruments. Veronica watched in silence as I stood in front of her, smiling and moving from side to side in time with the swinging rhythm. I pulled her to her feet, held both her hands and tried to lead her into joining me. She was as stiff as an ironing board, her eyebrows squeezed together. When the flute broke into a tender improvisation, she let go and sat down. I went across and lifted the needle back up so roughly that it slewed across the grooves.

'Oh, damn, damn, damn … Dad won't be pleased if I've scratched it.'

I swivelled around and stared at her, 'What's your flippin' problem anyway?'

She sunk into the cushions, 'It's just the music, Sarah. Don't you think it's a bit too – a bit too – sexy? A bit rude? I know you and your parents enjoy that darkies' music but …'

'Darkies' music? Darkies' music? What do you mean?'

She rubbed her eyes with her knuckles, 'It's what my mum calls it. She said it's because your dad …'

'My dad what? Oh, OK I get it.' I slowly shook my head and felt my shoulders drooping.

I stared at her. 'So you don't think Neil Sedaka's song is too sexy though, do you? Have you ever thought about what the words are all about?'

'What do you mean? It's just a pop song.' Her voice shaky and quiet.

'It means that some dirty dog can't wait until his girlfriend is sixteen. Sixteen. Old enough to have sex. Old enough for him to …is that sexy enough for you? Is that rude enough?'

She got up, picked up her cardigan, slid towards the door and into the hallway. I went after her and tried to touch her shoulder. But it was too late. She quietly opened the front door and walked down the path without turning around. I went upstairs and put my rollers back in.

Who is it who declared that when people decide to make a noticeable alteration to their appearance it marks a significant change in their lives, albeit unconsciously.

Chapter Eighteen

Julie had her own horse in the paddock at the back of their contemptuous house. She grandly invited her whole alpha class: I was the only one from the beta lot. The occasion was her fifteenth birthday. I spent days worrying about what to wear, knowing that the well-off girls would have exactly the right things. They knew how to achieve that carelessly casual yet expensive look.

Mum suggested that she would help me to think of something. It was Sunday afternoon and the party was the following Saturday.

'After all, my love, it's no use trying to look like the others, because you don't.'

'Yeah, s'pose so …'

She continued, 'It's nice to be different from everybody else anyway. It means that you're special.' She squeezed my shoulder, 'And there's nobody more special than you, me 'ansum.'

'Yeah, yeah, yeah … thanks Mum.'

I didn't tell her that I had recently got in the habit of pursing my lips in class or pretending to be thinking by leaning on my elbows and covering my nose.

'Hang on, I've just had an idea.'

She went to the cupboard where she kept her sewing things and drew out two pieces of velvet: a long length of emerald green and a smaller piece which was black.

'How about we make a cape out of this? It's left over from when I made that evening outfit for that woman down the road a few weeks ago.'

'Mum, sorry, I can't wear that, can I? I'll look like a flippin' witch.'

'You could wear your jeans with a bright blouse underneath. You'll look really cool. Much more stylish than the others; you might start a new fashion.'

I shrugged my shoulders; maybe she was right; I couldn't think of anything else. She whizzed up the cape that afternoon. It was quite short and swung around my hips, to show off my long legs in tight jeans. That evening we cut the black piece into little squares, and I spent the rest of the week sewing them randomly all over the cape by hand. I had to admit, it did look quite fashionable, in a kind of arty-farty style. Much like some of the patterns in her Vogue catalogue. She even let me use some of her dark eye-shadow and bright lipstick.

I soon realized that Mum's idea of high fashion had been a mistake. I was so embarrassed when I noticed a few girls tittering behind their hands when I turned up. Three small squares of black velvet with a few ragged bits of thread hanging off them was all that remained of our design by mid-afternoon. I took the cape off, stuffed it into my bag and tried to ignore the fact that my arms were freezing cold by the end of the day.

★

I was surprised and a little shocked that Julie's parents had gone out and left us to it. An older boy was there; well, a young man really. Apparently, he was her boyfriend. I had sometimes seen her getting into a red sports car after school and noticed it parked in her parents' driveway. He smoked dark cigarettes and throughout the afternoon they sometimes wandered off behind a huge rhododendron bush at the bottom of the garden if they thought nobody noticed. I followed them once and caught a glimpse of what they were doing. He was touching her in places that made me clench my thighs together.

Shortly after that, I knew that I wanted to do it. I met a boy at the youth club the following week and laid it on the line. Johnny. He was a bit of a loner as I recall and was usually on the edge of all the action. I had a tiny bottle of rum in my bag which I had poured from Dad's big bottle before going out. I sneaked off to the toilets and drank it in one go. Then I went straight up to him and asked him to come outside where I mumbled my request in the small alleyway beside the cinema. He was up for it of course and started to squeeze my breasts; it made me think of how Mum made pastry. Within minutes he groaned and slumped against me. I was confused and hurt. I gave him a chewing-gum and we went back inside. After that, he started to come around to my house on Friday nights when my parents went to meet Terry and Maureen.

The thing is, I didn't even like him much. His breath came hot and sour, and he kept poking his snaky tongue against mine. But I tried to ignore all that because I liked how his clumsy, sweaty fumbling made me feel. Afterwards we would sit in awkward silence and watch the TV for about half an hour. Then I usually made some excuse about being tired because I wanted him to go so that I could get into bed to rewind what had happened.

Chapter Nineteen

Miss Duckworth was doing a lesson about Australia. It was clearly one of her favourites; she relished telling us about a holiday she had spent there once with her chums from university, at least a hundred years before. She wrote the names of all the weird and wonderful places she'd visited up on the blackboard and blathered on about them all before getting on with the lesson. Places with names like Hippo's Yawn and Lake Magic, her most favourite being Wave Rock in somewhere called Hyden in Western Australia. She said it was particularly beautiful because it looked just like human hair and waxed lyrical about the colours of the rock, all blonde and brown, sweeping down to the ground. She chose a few girls to stand up and asked them to swish around their own gorgeous tresses. I lifted the lid of my desk and fiddled about inside.

'Everything all right, Sarah?' Her voice sharp, the question accompanied by what looked to me like a smirk.

'Yes, Miss, I was just looking for my geography text book,' I mumbled from behind the lid.

'I expect people to be prepared for all their lessons, Sarah, you know that. Perhaps you need to keep your lesson timetable somewhere more visible so you can refer to it quickly.'

A couple of the others sniggered. Miss Duckworth stood very still as she glared and waited for silence.

Daphne from Five Alpha had been telling us all about what to expect at morning break. Her class had endured the same lesson the previous day. We were hanging around by the fence next to the road, hoping to catch a glimpse of the rugby team from the nearby boys' school as they boarded the coach before going off to what would doubtlessly be a winning match against the local Secondary Modern boys.

'Yeah, just remember to look excited and interested when old Ducky passes her flipping photos around.'

Julie giggled, 'Oh yeah, the famous photos, I've heard about them before. Apparently, she does it every year. All the pictures are labelled on the back with the place name and date that she visited. Sad cow.'

Daphne pitched in again, 'My aunt said she remembers the pictures from when she was at Trebean and she's really old; she's about thirty-five. She said Ducky's probably been showing them since she graduated back in the olden days. Just remember to say ooh and ahh at the appropriate time.' We all had a good laugh before going back inside.

We duly made the required responses to her boring photos and Veronica was chosen to collect them all up afterwards and put them back carefully in the box on the teacher's desk as Miss Duckworth continued talking.

I was gazing at the huge world map along one wall, hardly listening and completely unprepared for the next part of the lesson. She stopped talking for a moment and wrote three large capital letters on the black board: W.A.P.

'Put your hand up anybody who has done their prep and can tell me what these three letters stand for.'

No hands went up, not even Goody Two-Shoes Veronica.

'No one? Well, I did ask you to read chapter four from your geography textbook for last week's homework.'

There was still no response. A couple of girls, including Veronica looked in my direction.

Miss Duckworth came out from behind her desk and took a couple of steps forward.

'W.A.P. stands for the White Australia Policy. Does anyone know what that means?'

Silence. 'Surely some of you have read it?' accompanied by a theatrical sigh.

Then took on that sharp edge again. 'Well since nobody can tell me, the White Australia Policy means just what it says. The Australian government decrees that people who do not originate from Europe, especially those from Asia or the Pacific Islands are not allowed into their country.'

'You mean brown people?' I couldn't help it. I hadn't even put my hand up. The words just flew out. The room fell silent.

My mouth was dry, my armpits began to sweat as I struggled to stop my voice from shaking. 'Brown people are not allowed into the country?' I moved back in my chair, linking my hands behind my head and stared at her.

Some girls started whispering; I heard my name rustling around the room. Miss Duckworth's face flushed as she stepped back behind the safety of her desk.

I stood up and folded my arms. Although my legs shook, I was past caring. 'Aren't there brown people living in Australia already Miss Duckworth? The Aborigines?'

The whispering stopped.

'Well, yes, they already lived there so …erm … the Australian government decreed that they could be regarded as white citizens.'

A girl from the back of the room stood up, 'But they aren't white, are they? And if they were already there, was that before other people came? I don't get it, Miss.' I glanced around and saw nods of agreement.

Trembling with anger, fear and humiliation, I stuffed my things back in the desk just as the bell rang.

Everyone else stood up, one by one, without waiting to be dismissed; chairs scraped in anguish across the floor and desk lids banged as Miss Duckworth vainly tried to declare the lesson over and give her permission for us to leave the room.

★

I waited outside Miss Goddard's office. It could only be about the stupid geography lesson. A couple of the teachers swept past, glanced at me and tutted to one another as they walked on. Miss Goddard herself had come to find me in the dining hall and summoned me to see her at lunchtime. It had to be important, since she usually spent most of her time fiddling about in her room with her poncey title of Headmistress painted in loopy golden letters on the door. That had been a bit of a joke between us ever since Julie once declared that the poor old dear had probably never been lucky enough to be anyone's mistress.

Miss Goddard was rarely seen around the building and only visited the classrooms on the odd occasion, when she was showing a visitor around; some bigwig from the town hall or the education department. She would gush into the room like a grand dame and we all had to stand up including the teacher who was in mid-flow imparting her wisdom. I'm surprised we weren't expected to curtsey.

I was thinking about how I would respond when faced with her stern accusations: upsetting Miss Duckworth and causing mayhem during the geography lesson. There was no doubt it would be seen as my fault. I reflected on the different ways I had learned to cope at Trebean since starting four years previously. But oddly enough I realised as I sat waiting that I wasn't frightened.

In my first year I suppose I was too overawed by everything. The imposing granite building set on the top of a hill, a million miles away yet only about a twenty-five-minute walk from the other side of the town where I lived. The school had been built at the end of the nineteenth century and stood proud with the attendant trappings of grandeur, as the first select girls' grammar school in town. The dark wooden curlicues, panelling and stained glass windows in the main hall, the impressive balcony which ran along one side where the worthy sixth formers were allowed to sit on chairs when the lowly first to fifth years had to sit cross-legged on the floor during assembly. The teachers' chairs were set along both sides where they sat with their feet demurely crossed at the ankles as per usual. God forbid any of them should cross their legs and show too much flesh.

★

My outsider status sat perched on my shoulder like a giant crow during all my waking hours outside my home, for as long as I could remember. A giant crow ready to peck my earlobe if I said or did the wrong thing. It was important not to let anyone know if I was upset, angry or embarrassed with regard to any allusions about my appearance, or lifestyle: my hair, my skin, my mixed family background, or any ill-informed ideas some of the girls had about people like me. I wanted to be liked and accepted just like everyone else, and for some crazy reason it was vital not to make any of them feel uncomfortable, regardless of my own discomfort.

There were things I could do if anyone said or did anything offensive, whether consciously or unconsciously.

– Be shy and say nothing: I did that when I was a small child. That didn't work and made me unhappy.

– Laughingly go along with it, as if it is of no importance. That didn't work and made me unhappy.

– Act the fool and make fun of myself before anyone else does. That didn't work and made me unhappy.

★

I cringe when I think of one example. I was in my second year, aged about twelve. It was a hot day. A small group of us had tucked our skirts up into our regulation thick navy knickers and were lying around in the long grass at the bottom of the playing field, enjoying the sun with our eyes closed. We'd been chatting away, then everybody relaxed and became quiet when I piped up,

'You lot will never catch me up. I was born with a ready-made suntan!' A few girls sniggered lazily.

I don't know why I said it.

Perhaps I felt uncomfortable because it was too quiet.

Perhaps I felt embarrassed at showing more of my skin.

Perhaps I felt the need to draw attention to myself. But why?

Rosemary stood up. I didn't know her very well; she had a lot to say for herself even though she'd only recently joined Trebean, having moved down from somewhere 'up-country'.

'C'mon, let's play leap-frog.'

Before too long the silence was broken as we played, cheering one another on and generally enjoying ourselves. As we took turns to leap over one another it was clear that Rosemary was by far the best at jumping higher than the rest of us.

She leapt over me, calling out, 'Hey, I was just thinking, who can think of another word which rhymes with frog?'

We all looked at each other. None of the others had a clue what she was talking about, but I knew what she meant. My head began to feel hotter; I sank into the grass and made a big deal of picking at the daisies. It looked as if everyone had tired of the game anyway as they stopped playing and sprawled about.

'Nobody? OK, watch me again and think harder! Come on Sarah, bend over again so I can do another jump.'

I hesitated for a moment, not for very long, then looked up at her and grinned.

I kneeled down onto my hands and knees.

She leapt over my head, squealing and giggling.

And I laughed.

Chapter Twenty

I was sitting down with my back to the door when I heard the handle click. I turned around and instead of Miss Goddard it was the PE teacher who opened it. Mrs Lister was one of the more popular teachers, often seen about the school wearing her long, pleated shorts, white aertex shirt and encouraging smile. Our PE shorts were of the same design: navy blue linen which irritated your inner thighs until they'd been washed several times, big box pleats and most importantly long enough so that the hem was no less than three inches above the floor when we kneeled down in order to maintain our feminine modesty.

'Come in Sarah,' she almost sang out, so hearty was she, in her hockey pitch voice. She raised her eyebrows and touched me gently on the forearm as I went inside.

Miss Goddard sat behind her desk and waved me to one of the chairs near the window with a tight smile. Mrs Lister sat down beside me. She gave me a quick wink, her grin as wide as a canyon.

Miss Goddard stood up and cleared her throat before speaking, 'Just a couple of things, Sarah. As you can imagine, we're very committed to ensuring that every girl in our care has the opportunity to fulfil her full potential.'

I was unsure how to respond until Mrs Lister gave me a slight nudge.

'Yes Miss Goddard, but I thought you were going to…' I tailed off as Mrs Lister started to speak over me.

'Do you mind if I tell Sarah the good news, Miss Goddard?'

Miss Goddard plonked herself back down, rested her arms on the desk and laced her fingers.

'Yes, please do Mrs Lister, you'll be able to explain it far better than I can.'

She started fiddling with things on her desk, picked up a piece of paper, folded in half, then half again, and again, and again until it was a small hard lump before moving on to put her pens in straight lines, equidistant from one another.

'Well, the thing is, Sarah, I was telling Miss Goddard just the other day how talented you are on the hockey pitch. You demonstrate such speed and awareness of the game.'

I understood the speed thing, because I was a fast runner; I'd run a hundred yards in eleven seconds the previous year and Mrs Lister told me I had beaten the school record from as far back as she could remember. But awareness of the game? Hardly. I never understood the rules of hockey and usually spent the whole time running up and down on the edges of the action, pretending I could fathom what was going on. I cheered when my fellow team members cheered and groaned when they did too. Mrs Lister knew that, so what the hell was she talking about?

We both looked at one another as she continued, 'So I was thinking Sarah, how about you enter the county championships next spring? You would be representing our school and running alongside many other runners from across the county. Athletes like yourself.'

Athletes? That was overdoing it.

Several girls came up to me afterwards, wanting to talk about it and asking what Miss Goddard said when I was summoned to her office. There was much nudging and discussion about the meaning of the W.A.P. I'd never been the subject of so much interest. I didn't want to talk about it and tried to tell them so;

after a while they all sloped off. Julie had been at the edge of the group, saying nothing. She stood quite still as I tried to recover myself and approached me after they'd all gone.

'Thought you were brave in class, Sarah. You OK?' Touching my arm as she spoke. My throat constricted and my eyelids fluttered. I tried to shrug her away and started to move off towards the outside toilets, but she followed me.

'Leave me alone. No more questions. It's all rubbish.'

Then I started running.

Running and shouting.

Running and crying.

Running and dying.

But she caught up with me and held me, right there beside the fence as I died in her arms.

Chapter Twenty-One

Hope you're hungry my love. It's stewpot day ...' Mum had her back to me as she spoke. She was cooking up some weird smelling stuff in the big pot she only used when resources were running low. Stewpot days usually meant chucking in whatever she could find in the cupboard, adding salt and pepper and hoping for the best. Her questionable creative talents were also reflected in her cooking.

I went into the hall where Dad was hanging up his coat; we grimaced at one another in recognition of the meal that awaited us. I listened as he went back into the kitchen, 'Do you want me to take over, sweetie? I've had a stinker of a day and a bit of cooking will make me feel better.'

'OK, you're welcome to it. I can finish off that dress I'm altering for Mrs Whatserface, or whatever her name is.'

She went back to her sewing machine in the living room. I threw my satchel in the corner and hung up my mac, the navy blue gaberdine I'd had since the first year. Underneath the collar was still navy blue, the mac itself having faded to a greyish dusk.

★

'So how was your day sweetie?' Dad had managed to resurrect our meal and we were all sitting down to eat. 'Better than mine I hope.'

I was buttering a few slices of bread as Mum cut each piece and put them on the big plate in the middle of the table. I took time arranging them as I wondered how much to tell.

'Yeah, it was alright. Usual boring stuff.'

Dad shrugged his shoulders and Mum rolled her eyes. 'Usual boring stuff ...', repeating my words in a monotone.

'Oh, and Mrs Lister asked me to join the running club. Me and Julie.'

She beamed, 'That's hardly boring stuff. How did that come about?'

'Don't know. Mrs Lister asked me to come for a quick chat after school in Miss Goddard's office.'

'Miss Goddard's office. Well, aren't you the lucky one. I wonder why they chose you.'

Dad joined in, 'Because she's the best, that's why isn't it, sweetie?' as he patted me on the back.

'Yeah, s'pose so.' I paused, 'And they said that Julie and me will be taking part in the county championships in the spring term.'

'Champions eh. Think that deserves a tot, don't you, George?'

Dad duly got up to get the rum bottle. He even gave me a tiny dribble at the bottom of a huge glass. We guzzled our way through the stew accompanied by the fat slices of home-made bread; it didn't taste too bad after all.

And we all stood up to toast my consolation prize. I rolled my eyes: what a joke.

★

I sloped off upstairs for a while after our celebration drinks. An hour later I was kneeling on the sofa staring out of the window. Maybe I should have told Mum and Dad about the geography lesson. They were so pleased that I had been selected for the athletics tournament, I didn't have the heart.

I was determined to try and put the day's incidents aside – at least for a while. As the evening wore on it became more and more difficult.

Mum swept in with her bag of sewing stuff; her latest project was to make a quilt covered with embroidered replicas of things she'd found: a couple of empty snail shells, some lumps of rock and a twig which had grown into a twisted shape resembling a small, humped figure. Dad was leafing through the newspaper.

'You alright Sarah? You look like someone who's drawn the short straw instead of ...'

'Not at all, I'm fine, Mum. Just a bit bored.'

Dad put the paper down. 'Well, you gorgeous gals, it's time we had a good old boogie to some hot music this evening. I've got something you might like.'

'What a good idea, darling.' Mum stood up, wiggled her hips and started waving her arms about.

★

Another musical evening in the Hodges household. Dad would put on a slow record to start with and invite Mum to dance, while I stood by sniggering. Then he livened things up by finding some bebop jazz. The days when I used to dance with him perched on top of his shoes as a little girl were over.

It had been difficult to get hold of the kind of stuff he liked. He often went into the small record shop in town and asked for particular jazz artists, but their collection was limited. After several visits, Pete the proprietor suggested that he could order records for him. Of course, they cost more because they were sent from London, or even occasionally the USA.

Pete and Dad became friends and before long were borrowing records from one another, swapping notes and records. They followed the careers of jazz musicians they'd read about in *The Melody Maker*, including such names as saxophonist Dick Morrissey, pianist Michael Garrick, trumpeter Henry Lowther and many, many others. Pete's jazz collection grew and subsequently, so did ours. Neither of them were as keen on what was known as 'trad jazz' which was more commercial and popular, including such talented musicians as Acker Bilk and Chris Barber. Over time, a few jazz lovers heard about the shop and came in from other towns and villages across the county.

I occasionally joined Dad down to the record shop on Saturday afternoons. We would squeeze into the sound booth and take turns on the head-phones to listen to the latest musicians he'd read about. I thought I was pretty smart hanging around with the other jazzers and tried to dress accordingly. The velvet cape which Mum had made for Julie's barbecue finally suited the role, especially as it looked rather scruffy. Some of the squares I had so carefully sewn on had fallen off which added to the style. Mum said I hung about thinking I was 'the Queen of the May', as I sauntered down the front path.

★

'I borrowed this record from Pete. I'd like to know what you both think of him he's a saxophonist who came here from Jamaica a few years ago. A guy who reckons that he's as good as Charlie Parker.'

Mum shook her head. 'Shouldn't think so, George, after all, Charlie's one of our favourites, isn't he?'

'I've read about him before in the *MM*, but only got to listen to this today.'

I shook my head. Dad went on, 'Yep, he has a saying that people have often quoted.'

He pretended to be holding a sax to one side, creasing his brow and lowering his voice;

'*Parker? There's them over here can play a few aces too.*'

He went over to set up the record player, throwing a few words over his shoulder.

'Just take a listen. I'm going to put on two versions of the same tune, and you need to tell me which one is Charlie playing, the first one or the second one … close your eyes and don't peep over my shoulder. Or better still go and wait in the kitchen.'

Mum and I grinned at each other and went out to clear the table; she turned around and whispered, 'Your dad's just checking that we've done our homework.'

'Oh yeah, I'd better get a pen and paper.' I scrabbled around in the kitchen drawer and called out, 'We're ready, Dad.'

'OK, coming up.'

The first few notes of 'How Deep is the Ocean' drifted into the hallway as we crept back in. By the time the second saxophonist was halfway through the song, I had started scribbling. I glanced up at Mum; she raised her shoulders, opened her hands and made a funny face.

★

Dad turned around grinning, 'Well who wants to go first?' I shrugged my shoulders.

'My colleague and I would like to listen one more time', announced Mum in a mock serious voice.

I nodded sagely, 'Yes, I think you're quite right, Elsie, being asked to analyse two pieces of important music is not to be taken lightly. I think we need time to listen once more, and we will then confer together before making any hasty decisions.'

'My pleasure, ladies.' Dad bowed low before lifting his head with a wink in his eye; he carefully placed the needle on the first disc, which was quickly followed by the second one. Mum and I whispered together when his back was turned:

'What did you think of this evening's stewpot? Did you ever finish that abstract painting you started last week? Look at your father's hair, do you think it needs a trim?'

I stood up grandly with my piece of paper and referred to my notes. 'Having listened carefully to the two renditions of a beautiful song, my colleague and I have compared both pieces.

Disc one sounded very familiar as a well-respected, talented musician with whom we are all familiar.'

'And the second?'

'In my vast experience of listening to jazz ever since I was in the womb and …' Mum interrupted me with a snigger and I paused. 'As I was saying, the musician on the second disc did two things very reminiscent of Mr Parker.' I ruffled my papers,' … namely what I call the swoop, in which Mr Parker tends to swoop up into a note sometimes, and secondly he often includes short in-between riffs as he plays the tune.'

Dad was nodding and rubbing his chin. 'Anything else, Miss Sarah?'

'Yes, as far as I have observed in studying this music, improvisation is a kind of flowery way of playing with the tune, usually placed after a straight version of the verse, and then some of the other musicians join in and …'

Dad put his hand up: 'Thank you, my dear. Very well said. Lots of other things happen at the same time, but I appreciate your observations.'

I quickly added, 'That's not to say of course, that jazz follows a strict formula, the very nature of this music is the creative greatness.' I sat down again; we all looked at one another, nodded and smiled.

Mum piped up, 'So George, do you think this man can really play like Charlie?'

Putting his head on one side, Dad responded, 'It's not so much playing like Charlie, but being able to refer to his style; he's certainly an extremely talented musician. And from what I've read, he's moved on since then and has created a style which he describes as abstract.'

'Abstract? Like your painting, Mum.' I patted her on the shoulder.

She concurred, 'Ahem, yes s'pose it is. Us creative types like to experiment you know.'

Half an hour later we were still thinking about what we thought jazz improvisation meant.

Dad was thoughtful and paused a while before speaking: 'I think jazz improvisation is having the ability to immediately create music to which the untutored listener might consider merely as a collection of sporadic notes floating about. However, if you listen you will hear that those 'flowery' notes still adhere to the chord structure and shape of the tune.'

Ruffling my hair, Mum nodded. 'Wow, sounds pretty serious, don't you think? It means being able to make things up really quickly as you go along.'

'Yes, when I'm writing an essay or you're painting a picture, we can always scrub it out and start again, but improvising on a tune has to be done on the spot.'

'Yes, and you're certainly spot on.'

★

It was yet another occasion when we came together as a family making the most of what we loved best, and I managed to put aside my sadness for an hour or so. But after lying there in the quiet dark, the pain loomed before me again. The pain of having to think quickly and use protective strategies when encountering comments or activities which reinforced my outsider status was all too familiar. In fact, you could say I improvised. It was hard going and left me feeling alone, misunderstood, resentful ... and unhappy. I was so tired. For the first time in my life, I had voiced my real feelings in front of my classmates that day. And in front of the teacher.

The teacher:
Someone who holds privilege in her hands is
Someone who cares
Someone who listens
Someone who enables

Whose aspiration is to guide, educate and support
The lives of young people
A precious gift indeed.

★

My silent weeping grew into a painful moan, a wail of misery, a rough blanket about to suffocate my mind and body as I rocked from side to side. Two pairs of strong arms came to hold me as I tried to explain.

Eventually I slept.

Chapter Twenty-Two

It was almost ten forty-five. Dad had 'phoned the school early the following morning, demanding a meeting with Miss Goddard and Miss Duckworth. Miss Goddard had royally agreed that she could 'fit us in' at ten thirty: mid-morning break time. Mum, Dad and I sat outside her office at exactly the appointed time. We were still waiting fifteen minutes later as staff and pupils walked past on their way to their next lessons before lunch. A few girls from my form strolled by, raising their eyebrows in question; I responded with a small shrug each time I caught someone's eye, but mostly I pretended not to notice.

Eventually, Mum rapped on the door and Duckworth herself opened it, a slimy apology on her equally slimy face as she apologized for keeping us waiting because time 'just seems to run away sometimes'. She and Miss Goddard had clearly met up beforehand so as to get their stories right, while we sat outside like three lemons. Not a good start. Mum was ready to go into full throttle and opened her mouth to remonstrate until Dad quietly squeezed her arm. Nonetheless when we were invited to sit, she loudly plonked herself down on the nearest chair, sighing as she pointedly tapped on the face of her watch.

Miss Goddard got up to approach the door, 'Nice to see you, Mr and Mrs Hodges, and of course you too, Sarah. I'll nip along to the kitchen to see if Cook can bring us some tea ...'

'That won't be necessary thank you I think we've waited long enough,' replied Mum.

Dad gave her 'the look' and she went quiet.

He began the discussion by saying how proud he was of me and my achievements at school, both academically and how glad he was that I had been chosen to represent the school at the athletic tournament. Mum mumbled something about the running thing being a 'consolation prize'. Dad was being as nice as pie. What was he playing at? Both women nodded, looking smugly contented with themselves. Confident that they were in control and had the upper hand. Mum frowned as we glanced at one another.

Duckworth grinned and folded her arms as she watched Miss Goddard getting into full flow about how proud she was of the school, the high standards expected of all pupils, blah, blah, blah.

'As you are no doubt aware Mr Hodges, Trebean is very highly respected.' She gestured towards an embroidered picture on the wall behind her. 'This is a copy of our school crest.' Speaking in an almost theatrical tone she read, '*Nil satis nisi optimum*. It means …'

Dad held his hand up to stop her in her tracks, 'Yes, of course I know what it means: Nothing but the best is good enough … Very impressive.'

Her mouth fell open as he continued. 'So – nothing but the best is good enough … hmmm … tell me, does that also apply to the teaching standards here?'

Duckworth's smile headed towards her chin; a red flush slowly bloomed upwards from her neck as she looked helplessly at Miss G. She crossed her ankles neatly and smoothed down her skirt.

In contrast, Miss Goddard's face went white, she clenched her hands together and began mumbling about the expected code of conduct from all pupils and it was part of her job to ensure that … then Dad stood up.

The room fell silent, except for the chirping of joyful birdsong. The Janitor had finished pruning the roses which surrounded

Miss Goddard's private outdoor area and was sitting on a low wall with his back to the window, smoking a cigarette as he surveyed his handiwork. This was where Miss Goddard could sometimes be seen entertaining special visitors as they drank tea and discussed the important educational issues of the day. She always wore her academic gown on those occasions, just in case she forgot who she was.

We watched as Dad slowly crossed the room to where a huge leather bible lay open on a small table, made of dark wood with a shell shaped design around the edges and one heavy looking central stand, similarly embellished.

'What a beautiful bible. It looks very old.' He opened the first page and pressed the rusty looking mechanical musical box which emitted a tinny sounding rendition of All Things Bright and Beautiful.

The quiet.

The listening.

The waiting.

By this time Duckworth looked as if she was about to slide onto the floor, her eyes big, beads of sweat hanging precariously along her top lip. Mum gave me an almost imperceptible smile. It was our turn to fold our arms.

Miss Goddard started gabbling away, her voice about an octave higher than usual, 'Yes, it's been passed down through my family's generations. Ermm – I like to refer to it sometimes.'

Dad continued turning the pages as he talked. 'Good idea Miss Goddard, your bible must be of great comfort to you. After all, maintaining professional standards of teaching in such a reputable institution must be challenging on occasion. I would hope that every member of your experienced staff must surely include the importance of considering the wellbeing of all pupils when they deliver their lessons. And I should imagine that the education department would be very displeased should anything untoward have to be reported about Trebean.'

The page turning stopped as he came across what he had been looking for:

'Ah, here it is: Acts 17, verse 26. Do you mind if I read it aloud Miss Goddard?'

'Yes, please do,' she responded faintly.

He looked straight at Duckworth for what seemed like several seconds and cleared his throat before he began.

Slowly, surely, confidently, his deep voice filled the room:

'God hath made of one blood all nations of men to dwell on all the face of the earth.'

Chapter Twenty-Three

That was Saturday mornings sorted then. Mrs Lister asked Julie and me to be at school at ten o'clock every week for the rest of the term. What she hadn't told us was that apart from us two, there were only another five other girls in the running club. And as far as I knew, they weren't exactly brilliant at running anyway. It only occurred to me much later that the so-called running club had only been invented on what Julie and I called Ducky's Downfall Day. No wonder I'd not seen it on the activity noticeboard.

Julie's dad dropped her off just as I reached the gate. He was about to drive away but stopped when he saw me. He wound down the window.

'Hello, you must be the famous Sarah.' He put his hand out and gave me a handshake which just about broke my knuckles. 'Hello, Mr Penrose, nice to meet you.'

Julie stood beside him, smirking. 'I was telling Mum and Dad how we've become friends, and how fab you are.'

'Well, have fun, you two.' He kissed Julie on the cheek, winked at me and drove off.

★

'What are spikes anyway?' Mum's voice also spikey as she turned over the sausages and tried to mash the potatoes at the same time.

I didn't immediately realise why she was in one of her moods, but I had clearly chosen the wrong moment to have brought up the subject. We were about to have tea. Dad had just got home, looking tired, and slumped in his chair leafing through the newspaper. He was obviously fed up too.

'Spikes are, well, kind of special shoes for running.'

'So, what's wrong with your plimsolls?'

'Mrs Lister said that if we were to do well at the athletics tournament next term, we would need to have the proper shoes. Like you see them wearing on TV.'

'Why are they called spikes?'

'They are proper running shoes with pointy bits underneath to dig into the grass as you run. Helps you to go faster, or something like that.'

'Oh, right. Well, it looks as if you'd better have some if they're going to help you to win the race. Winning is the main thing.' Dad looked up from his reading, rolled his eyes and shrugged his shoulders. Mum looked daggers at him, 'And before you say it, George: I know it's the taking part that matters.'

'Well yes it is … but you're quite right, honey … as always.'

Chapter Twenty-Four

The coach finally drew through the main gates after a treacherous lurch along a bumpy lane. The athletics ground was quite far away, probably more than thirty miles, as we had to pick up more people from outlying villages. It was an early start; those from our area met outside Woolworths dead-on half past seven, and most of us had eaten part of our packed lunches before we got to the stadium.

The noisy lot from the swanky boys' grammar school spent the whole time braying loudly at the back of the bus. Half a dozen other boys from the secondary modern in town nudged one another and looked at the girls. Apart from Julie, Mrs Lister and me, a small number of our fans from school were on board, even though only Julie and I had been selected to represent Trebean. They had come along for the ride and to cheer us on. Suppose it was something different to do on a Saturday. A handful of village-type girls from their posh houses near the river climbed aboard on and kept themselves to themselves, as they loudly tried to out-talk one another. Julie had managed to find a space for us both right in the middle of the back seat, between the boys. The girls were outnumbered anyway, so we had no choice. We sat down and grinned as Mrs Lister gave us the look.

Penfold Park had the only proper running track in the county and looked quite fancy with rows of seats either side like those you see in films. Julie raised her eyebrows and poked me in the ribs The long jump was to one side and further in the distance were the tennis courts and the pitches for hockey and other games. The staff stood around in matching outfits: black trousers, with bright red shirts. The main building was large and white, its windows gleaming in the mid- morning sunshine.

We gathered our things together and climbed out of the coach to assemble in school groups near the hedge. Mrs Lister's chin bobbed up and down as she did a quick headcount; you would think we were about six years old, instead of nearer sixteen.

'Please listen, girls. Today promises to be fun as well as particularly challenging for Julie and Sarah. And I know you all wish them well.'

She duly waited for the half-hearted well wishing to begin, which took a couple of seconds longer than it should have done, while Julie made a silly face and wiggled her hips from side to side.

Mrs Lister continued: 'The spot just to the left, inside the main gate will be our meeting place. I'm quite happy for you to explore the wonderful facilities here, secure in the knowledge that you will behave appropriately at all times. Remember that your school badges are easily recognisable as being from Trebean, and we certainly don't want any negative gossip about our school. Everywhere is well signposted, so there shouldn't be any problems.'

Daphne put her hand up. 'Do we have to meet back there for lunch? And what time?'

'Good point, Daphne. Thank you for reminding me. I expect everyone to meet at exactly half past twelve, so that we will have time to eat and then be ready for the girls' under sixteen races at two o'clock. It would be nice to sit together as we cheer on our very own athletes. Now off you go. Sarah and Julie, a quick word first please.'

The others drifted away in twos and threes and Mrs Lister started walking ahead show us where the changing rooms were.

★

That's when I saw him. He was coming out of the building just as we were going in. He was laughing and talking with another, shorter chap with a similar complexion. They were both dark-skinned and as they spoke I heard an accent which was different from any I had ever known. They stood aside politely as we passed by; he paused speaking for a moment, looked across at me and nodded slowly before moving on. Mrs Lister smiled graciously as she thanked them and proceeded to talk about the School of Mines, approximately fifteen miles from our town, where students from other countries from across the world came to study their skills, many of them being from West Africa. I turned around a moment later and saw him looking back at me.

★

'Come along everyone; how about a round of applause for Julie and Sarah?' Mrs Lister sang out as the coach began to pull away along the lane. Julie and I looked at one another and sank into our seats. I was nearest the window and tried to concentrate on the bushes as we scraped by. Julie groaned. It was almost teatime and we were all tired and hungry

Our race had been gruelling; we were beaten by two girls from a school which was quite nearby the stadium. They both had legs like gazelles and looked a bit too sexy in their shorts, which were much skimpier than ours. Julie and I decided that we hated them at first sight. We didn't have a chance. Confidence oozing from every pore, they made a big deal of doing some show-off exercises at the edge of the track before we were summoned to our places. They grinned at one another quickly as the starting gun went off, then they were away. They easily took both first and second places. Julie reckoned that they had only won because they probably had the benefit of using the proper running track for regular practice.

After enduring the flimsy clapping and a couple of mumbled 'well dones' I closed my eyes and pretended to fall asleep.

'Wake up, Sarah, we're nearly there. Can't believe you've been asleep all this time,'

I shook my head and tried to look as if I'd just woken up.

'Sorry Jules, I closed my eyes for a second and must have dropped off.'

'Yeah, yeah, don't give me that. You've been in a funny mood ever since we all met up again. Crikey, it's hardly worth getting upset just because we didn't win the bleddy race.'

'No, it's not that, it's just been a long day, that's all.'

Julie rolled her eyes, sighed and looked away. I turned back to the window. The coach was quieter than it had been in the morning, apart from some of the boys, who were laughing and nudging one another about heaven-only-knows-what.

Julie poked me with her elbow. 'Oh yeah, wanted to ask you – did you get to talk to that chap that we saw on the way this morning. Think he fancied you.'

'Which one?'

'You know – that chap and his friend who we saw on our way to the changing rooms. The one who looked, umm, you know … foreign.'

'Oh, him. Can't remember, oh yes, I do. I said hello a bit later on and we talked for a bit. His name is Kofi. I only went off because you were sizing up those boys from that school near the stadium. I didn't know what to say and felt a bit silly, standing there like a lemon.'

'Yeah, you disappeared for quite a while. Wondered where you were.'

'Dunno, just had a look around; that place is huge. I went exploring, there are some beautiful trees behind the main building. I looked around some of the other areas, the buildings and the woods …' Pausing for a moment, I carried on, 'When I came back, I didn't want to interfere because you seemed to be having a great time.'

'Didn't I just! There's one boy, his name's Colin, he was telling me all about when he and his friend once…' She prattled on as I kept on gazing at the passing hedgerows.

There was a large hawthorn tree towering above the other bushes, which hadn't been trimmed back. Generous bunches of its tiny white blossoms weighed wantonly along its branches. May blossom. It reminded me of something Mrs Spargo told me once about may blossom. I had brought a few branches home one day for my mum and she saw me carrying them up the front path.

'Hello Sarah, those lovely flowers for your mum? Can't take them indoors me 'ansum. They bring bad luck.' Then she swept on.

When I took them indoors, Mum agreed that they were indeed very beautiful, but even so she put them in a big pot just outside the back door.

The coach wound its way through the country lanes, dropping people off at outlying villages. By the time we arrived back in town there were only a few of us left. We said our goodbyes and went our different ways.

I walked up the hill, swinging my bag and listening to the early evening birdsong.

What an eventful day.

Chapter Twenty-Five

The usual crowd were lounging about in the grass at lunchtime: me, Julie, Daphne, Fiona, Diane, Pam and a couple of others I can't recall. We were playing with our nail varnish, swapping colours, holding up our smooth and lovely hands to show one another. Except we didn't know we were smooth and lovely then, youth being wasted on the young and all that. Daphne had brought some nail varnish remover, but it tipped over into the grass, so we had to try and wipe off each application quickly before it dried hard. The trick is to put more varnish on top to soften the underneath layer and then rub vigorously with your handkerchief. No way could we go back into class sporting brightly coloured nails.

There was a lull and then Daphne produced some scraps of paper and a few fat pencils from her pocket, which looked very like the soft ones used in the Art Room.

'OK girls, let's play a truth game.' She gave everyone a piece of paper and pencil, being well prepared like a proper Girl Guide.

She continued, 'I want you all to write yes or no on your piece of paper. I will then collect them in to see what the results are. Oh, and you must write your answer in capital letters, so we don't recognise the handwriting.'

'Yes or no? About what exactly?' Julie wasn't too happy when Daphne took the lead; after all, she was the one usually in charge.

'Yes or no if you've done it or not.' Daphne's voice deeper, measured.

'Done what?'

'You know … it.'

We all went a bit quiet. Then someone else piped up, 'You mean S.E.X? You are aware that boys always know if you're easy?'

'Yeah,' said Diane, 'they can tell by the way you walk.'

Daphne was getting fed up by this time. 'Look, shall we do it or not? Who's too scared?'

We all set to and duly wrote down our answers, folded our papers up small and handed them back to her. She walked away a few paces to check the results and then came back where we all waited. By this time everyone was sitting up, some of us gazing into the distance or fiddling about with bits of grass. It's an odd thing but most of us had assumed the sitting cross-legged position by the time Daphne came back. She stood up, waving the papers around in the air, standing with her back to the sun, presenting a dark silhouette against the sulking sky.

'And the results are: ta-da! One yes, six no's … and one half.'

'Half?' said someone and started giggling. Everyone looked at one another. Julie got up and started to walk away, throwing over her shoulder as she went, 'Come on, it's time to go back in. Stupid game anyway.'

★

The last day of the summer term. Almost home time. I went to the toilet and came across Julie. She had been unwell and had spent the afternoon in the sick bay. The sick bay was just a little camp bed surrounded by a hospital screen in the corner of the balcony overlooking the school hall.

I had once spent most of the afternoon there when I started my first period, back in the second year. Thought I was going to bleed to death up there alone, with my stomach clambering over itself in knots. Even worse, after the pains had finally stopped, I fell asleep. When I woke up it was about six o'clock and getting dark. The teacher who sent me to the sick bay had forgotten I was there. I was so scared. I got up and ran about the building trying to find a way out, but every exit door was locked. Fortunately, the janitor was still about, and he heard me sobbing in the cloakroom. He let me out and I ran all the way home, sweating and bleeding.

★

Julie was looking sideways at her stomach in the mirror.

'You feeling alright now Julie?'

'Not too bad. You don't look too good yourself.'

'Yes, I've been feeling dizzy and sick. Be glad to get home.'

Ponderous reality tilted towards us both as I murmured: 'It was you that wrote yes?'

Julie nodded. Slowly. Then she grinned, 'And you wrote half? You soppy cow.'

It was my turn to nod; perhaps it had not been half after all.

★

The next few weeks were a blur of shouting, shame and shock from Mum, and a sad quietness from Dad. Apart from Terry and Maureen, my mother told people that they had decided to send me to London to stay with a relative for a few weeks so that I could check out what job opportunities there were in the big city. God only knows what story Julie's parents concocted for their elevated social circle.

I mostly stayed in my room, although Mrs Spargo no doubt saw me through her kitchen window one afternoon when I dashed out to use the outside toilet. I tried to be sick as quietly as I could every morning into the bucket that Mum shoved around the door without speaking. Said bucket would disappear and reappear the following day.

Chapter Twenty-Six

'In, over, under, off. In, over, under, off.' We were sitting on Julie's bed, two sixteen-year-old girls shut away from the outside world. I was showing her how to knit, chanting the words to accompany each action just as Mum did when she showed me how to do plain stitch when I was seven years old. I used to whisper the words to myself every time I made yet another doll's scarf to add to my collection: *in, over, under, off, in, over, under off,* feeling my breath whooshing softly across my sweaty sausage fingers. I often ended up crying; it didn't help that the wool was so old and re-used it was wiggly and the fibres kept coming apart. Plus the needles were big and wooden, like flipping telegraph poles. Mind you I would cry at the drop of a hat, especially when me and Dad listened to Billie Holiday singing a sad love song. Her voice was beautifully sad; I loved a bit of melodrama even then and I still enjoy a good cry.

Mum would be sitting at her sewing machine and I was supposed to be helping by picking up bits of material and tidying up the cotton reels. One Saturday afternoon when I was hanging around Dad out in the shed, he found four little nails and hammered them in around the top of an empty cotton reel. I used it to do French knitting, making long woollen snakes. Me and some of the other less adventurous girls all sat on the wall at school playtime comparing lengths. Lot easier than proper knitting believe me. And safer than going into the middle of that scary space where the boys shouted and ran into each other.

'God, this is hellish! The bloody stitches keep sliding off. You and your fancy ideas, Sarah. Can't we just sneak out and have a fag instead? I've still got a couple hidden at the bottom of my bag.'

It didn't take much to get her going. Guess she was always used to having her own way, what with living in a big house and all the rest. I was trying to be patient and took the knitting from her to put the dropped stitches on again before handing it back.

Julie sighed, 'Does it matter if a few slide off along the way?'

'Well yes, if we leave it the whole thing will have holes in it and the jacket will be all the wrong shape. Here give it to me, I'll do a few rows for you. Then I'll show you how to do purl-stitch as well if you like.'

She went over to the window. 'OK, go on then, Goody Two-Shoes.' She looked down at her belly, 'Although I don't suppose Baby Boo will be bothered, poor little chap.'

She turned back grinning, pausing for a moment and looking at me in that familiar, challenging way which always reduced me to a dull-witted, fat sloth. Even with her swollen belly under a lumpy sweater she managed to look somehow poised, glamorous, sexy. She flicked back her shining dark wave of hair and pouted. I hated her at that moment. She sauntered across, sat back down beside me on the bed and squeezed my shoulders.

'Anyway -Baby-Boo might turn out to be a girl; she would probably like a few holes in it: sexy-looking, know what I mean?'

Then I loved her again.

'Oh, you're so naughty – what if Matron hears you using the S.E.X. word?' Trying hard to sound matey, intimate, in a we're-all-girls-in-it-together way.

'She'll only be jealous, poor cow. Don't suppose she's ever had any action in her whole life.'

We laughed so much that the all the stitches really did slide off the needle.

★

Spending a few minutes alone every day with Julie was all that kept me going during those months. We always tried to finish our chores quickly, so we could spend some time chatting before supper and evening prayers. It was seriously rubbishy there. All the floors had to be scrubbed every day so that 'you could eat your dinner off them', to use Matron's words.

As if any of us wanted to eat the dinners anyway, but we had no choice. You should have seen the crap they gave, us including lots of stodgy pies, the pastry turning into cosmic dust when you stuck your fork in. Maybe Julie was right when she used to say that the women who worked there were probably just frustrated old witches. She certainly had a mouth on her, but she was a laugh even though we were locked away like criminals.

Some people have a knack for cheering people up, and Julie as certainly one of them. She was one of the only two girls at Brightview who had her own bedroom. Her parents had insisted on it, having made a hefty donation together with the promise of more to come. It reminded me of the 'anonymous' donation made at Trebean regarding an issue involving Julie. It makes you wonder. The other own-bedroom girl Wendy had the sense to keep herself quiet and didn't mix much with the rest of us. Spent most of her spare time praying in the chapel, riddled with guilt as she polished the altar rails.

Julie's rebellious spirit sometimes got her into trouble with Matron though, but she didn't care too much. She thought of so many ways to be annoying, by tying her ponytail to one side for instance, so lingered sensuously over one shoulder as she had done in the school photo. We were shovelling up yet more greasy stew one suppertime when Matron walked by to check if any of us had our elbows on the table. She noticed Julie's hair and stopped, stood behind her chair with her hands behind her back, perhaps fearing that she might have landed Julie with a clip around the ear if she didn't restrain herself.

'Would you step out into the hall and tie your hair up properly please Julie?'

'It is tied up Matron. Don't you see?' She shook it about.

'You know the rules, it's about hygiene and decorum.'

'But it is hygienic Matron. It's quite clean and look it's not falling in my food so that's OK.' She demonstrated, leaning over the bowl of steaming brown stuff. 'And I'm afraid I don't know what decorum means. Is it some sort of medical condition?'

Matron clicked her tongue and hurried off. Julie could get away with murder compared with the rest of us, thanks to her parents' largesse.

★

Some girls took the opportunity to go for a walk around the gardens if they had a few minutes before supper. There was a high hedge all around because heaven forbid anyone living in the village should catch a glimpse of any of us sinners. If we went outside the gates, we had to wear dresses made of dark brown serge. They were loose and pleated, the pleats gradually opening up as the months progressed, looking suspiciously like school gymslips: a kiddy fiddler's dream. Still makes me shudder. But I suppose people didn't think of the dodgy connotations in those days.

It's conflicting: the sixties was a time of contradictions: one minute it was all about love-ins and give-peace-a-chance, juxtaposed by the wickedness wrought on any young girl who 'got herself into trouble'. After all, wasn't it our generation that invented sex? Men and boys got off scot-free of course, with the throw-away comment that 'boys will be boys'. What kind of rubbish was that?

After lunch we had an hour and a half to spend on 'activities'. That's when you could go to the village shop if you needed anything, or take a walk around the grounds, write letters home, whatever. If you needed to go to the shop or post office, you had to be accompanied by another girl and chaperoned by a staff member. Julie commented that chaperoning was hardly appropriate, after all the horse had already bolted the stable door. She even said it in front of Matron once and was locked in the cellar to consider the grossness of her behaviour. Those of us who giggled when we witnessed the affront were sent to sit in the chapel for a whole hour with our hands on our heads. Julie's mum and dad didn't get to hear about that one.

And that's the time of day when any personal post is handed out. Mum wrote to me every week, usually full of something or nothing and ending with a resentful, 'love from Mum' in her swirly writing at the end. The letters were always much the same.

Dear Sarah,

Just a few lines hoping that you're keeping well and taking care of yourself. Remember that you're not just responsible for yourself now. Your father and I are busy as usual. He's decided to build yet another shed in the back garden to keep his tools in. So, what with getting home from the late shift at work and having his tea, he disappears for the evening until it's time to go to bed. I've been sent a big bag of alterations from Thomas and Sons, you know, the gents' outfitters in Duke Street. So, I've had to slow down on some of my other dressmaking for a while since this will be regular work. But putting new zips in trousers which have not seen the dry-cleaners for God only knows how long, is a horrible job. Needs must after all. We must save up for when you get the opportunity to complete your education as we planned before the other issue came up.

Talk about laying on the guilt. She always said that too, referring to my condition as an issue, no pun intended of course. Mum didn't do puns. And she always found a diplomatic way of reminding me that I could go anywhere and achieve anything I wanted in life when 'it' was all over.

There were a few more lines about the road being dug up outside, and a neighbour's lost kitten, before signing off.

Julie never mentioned any letters she received, and I never asked her. I don't think she received many. She usually went for a little walk with one of the others while I read mine.

Chapter Twenty-Seven

We were getting our boxes ready. Time was passing and Julie's baby was due within the following two weeks and mine shortly afterwards. Those of us who were 'near our time', as it was so quaintly put, were expected to make our preparations during the last month or so. Worthy members of the local church would save their shoe-boxes, and bits of fabric, card and crayons to donate to Brightview. Every girl had to prepare a box, which Matron called Baby's Layette. It was to be sent away with the baby when she or he was taken away for adoption at six weeks old.

At home, our house was strewn with the evidence of Mum's various projects including sewing. I was a dab-hand at hemming and button-holes, which is how I earned my pocket money before getting a Saturday job. Creating and decorating our baby boxes was relaxing; I enjoyed embroidering the fabric and devising interesting designs, but the reason for such activities were heavy with sadness. We knew this would be the only thing we could do for our babies.

'It's nearly half past two. Shouldn't we tidy up and go for birthing class now?' This was a weekly lesson which got more horrific as months passed, dependent on your stage of pregnancy. I hated to be late. Anything was better than being on the receiving end of Mrs Choat's spiteful tongue. Julie was struggling with her sewing, but I didn't want to keep butting in to help her. She so wanted to do it herself.

'Yeah, OK. I'll just finish this bit off.' She couldn't find the scissors, so she bit off the thread and shoved all her stuff into a pile. I said nothing but surreptitiously tidied up while she rushed off to the toilet again. She was doing that a lot lately and often complained of feeling tired.

★

The black and white pictures stuck around the walls in the birthing class room should have been enough to put anyone off sex for the rest of their lives. Diagrams of babies in the womb, at various stages from looking like scrawny little fish right up to full term babies all scrunched up with big heads and starry fingers, and seemingly all of women with only one leg. The idea of actually seeing images up close of another person living inside you was creepy. Mrs Choat walked up and down and pointed at each picture, describing it in horrifying detail. But worse was to come.

'This week, I thought I should tell you about torn labia. I'm not saying that it could happen to any of you, but it's just as well to be prepared.'

'Holy shit', Julie whispered. I said nothing but held her hand under the table for a moment.

'Of course, some women sail through delivery without a care in the world. They know that God will protect them and their little ones.' She had to mention the God bit. I suppose that those of us who didn't sail through were doomed to be ripped to shreds for our sins.

'Who can remember the items which need to be on hand during delivery? Wendy?'

'Um, clean towels, Miss?'

'Pardon me?'

'Mrs Choat.'

'Yes, thank you. Well done. Anyone else like to offer any suggestions? Wendy? What do you think? We haven't heard much from you lately.'

'Um, plenty of hot water, Mrs Choat?'

'Yes, would anyone like to think of anything else that might be needed?'

Julie put her hand up, 'A stick to bite on when the pain gets too much. Like for torn labia or something? Like the stitches afterwards?'

Mrs Choat winced. 'Well, yes, I must admit some people do need a little help in dealing with the pain.'

The room fell silent and a second later Wendy's head fell forward onto the table with a thud. Her friend was sent to fetch her a glass of water and helped shove her head down between her knees. She seemed to be alright after a few minutes. Mrs Choat flushed and flew into a flat spin when trying to deal with it. When it was quiet again, she took on a smarmy, reassuring tone,

'But of course, since you are all healthy young women with strong muscles, you will probably be fine when your time comes.'

But the damage had already been done.

When we got outside the room even Julie was less talkative than usual. We all looked at one another as we shuffled out and went to the next lesson. Small group work took place on Tuesdays and Thursdays, following birthing class. This was to prepare us for 'life after baby'. The groups were allotted to whatever or whomever Matron considered worthy or needful of certain subjects. The chosen few, usually those whom she favoured, had lessons in shorthand and typing once a week, from a lady from the Pitman College in the nearest town. Most of us had maths and English, and a couple of the poor girls who could hardly read or write were given yet more menial tasks to do, such as polishing cutlery, wiping around the skirting boards, or cleaning around the taps with old toothbrushes dipped in vinegar.

'Matron, do you mind if I ask you something?' Julie was back on form after a short rest following English lesson. Matron was chatting to Mrs Choat in the corridor who was probably relating what had happened earlier in the afternoon. No doubt trying to cover her back in case there were any complaints.

'Only if it's important Julie. I'm very busy at the moment.'

'I can see that.' She grinned at me, and I pretended to look for something in my bag. She continued, 'We had English earlier on and I thought maybe …'

'Yes, I know Julie. I'm quite aware of what happens at Brightview every day, thank you very much.'

'I'm sure you do, Matron. I only wanted to suggest that perhaps some of the other girls could attend English and Maths lessons too? Instead of doing extra cleaning duties?' Her voice rising up at the end of each sentence: little Miss Innocent.

'And what do you mean by that, may I ask?'

'Well, surely if you are a person who has difficulty in reading or writing you would need it more than say, some other people would. You know … for life after baby.'

I lingered by the wall. Matron started fiddling with a long piece of thread which was dangling from one of her cuffs. She began to wind it round and round one of her fingers until it was quite tight. Her flesh bulged out on either side and turned red. Julie stood still and waited.

'Don't you think so, Matron?'

By this time, Mrs Choat was listening too, as she began to straighten some posters on the wall. One was advertising the village fete, another about how much money had been raised towards the upkeep of St Jude's Church and the third one proclaiming the virtues of the sterling work of the lifeboat men. All things which held little or no interest to us, invisible and sullied as we were. Well, that's not quite true. There was a photo of one of the lifeboat men that Julie and I would pause to look at whenever we passed by. We agreed he was certainly tasty. And very interesting.

'Would you like to come into my office to talk to me please?'
Matron hurried off followed by Julie who winked at me as she
passed by.

★

'Yeah, go on. Spill the beans. What did she say?'

We had a few minutes to spare before supper and got back to
our boxes. I got on with my knitting and sewing and Julie with
bits of card and sticky paper. She was very creative and made
cut-outs of two babies dancing in spiky grass across the front of
each box, surrounded by flowers and stars. Because we didn't
know if we would have a girl or a boy, there was one of each and
they were holding hands. I thought of something else I wanted
to add to my box. I measured a piece of heavily patterned fabric
to fit the underside and embroidered four alphabet letters, one in
each corner before pasting it on. We thought we should write a
message too so that when they learned to read they would know
that we loved them, even if we had to give them away. I chose:
Good luck little one. I will always remember you. Julie wrote: *Have
a lovely life deario. Think of me sometimes.* We both had a little cry,
just before the supper-bell rang.

I never did find out what the conversation was between Julie
and Matron about the English and Maths lessons, but I read in
the local paper a few months after I left that an anonymous donor
had made a large donation stipulating that it should be used to
'enhance the life chances and learning for the young women at
the Brightview Home for Unmarried Mothers.'

Chapter Twenty-Eight

'Wake up Sarah. Wake up. I'm not feeling very well. Oh, dear God.' Julie was standing by my bed.

Shaking me. Hard. By the shoulder. I shoved off the blankets, sat straight up and watched as she slid to the floor clutching her back. She was making kind of animal noises and her face was slicked with sweat.

The dormitory where I slept with a large group of others came awake. Someone turned on the lights. Supper had been quieter than usual. There was a new cook whose culinary abilities ran into minus figures. She had prepared a dish with some fancy name, which looked like yesterday's leftovers bound together with egg and deep-fried in lard. Accompanied by the usual mess of slimy green stuff. And nobody was allowed to leave the table until they finished what was on their plate. A few of us started retching, until one of the kinder kitchen assistants quietly gathered up our plates which were mostly still half covered with food. No wonder Julie was feeling unwell.

'What's wrong? Have you got stomach ache?'

'No, I think I've started. Oh God, it's agonising.'

'The baby? Are the pains bad?' I was pulling on my dressing gown as I spoke and gestured to one of the others to fetch someone.

'Of course, it's the bloody baby…what do you think it is…wind?'

Within minutes, Mrs Choat heard the commotion and came racing up the stairs.

'Flipping heck, she's wet herself. All over my slippers.' I don't know who said that; it was all chaos. But dear old Julie just lifted her head and called out, 'To hell with you and your bloody slippers.'

Mrs Choat took control. 'Now, now Julie dear, no need for that kind of language. God is here to help you along the way,' trying to be all nicey-nice. 'Now get back into bed the rest of you.'

'Can I do anything, Mrs Choat? Julie's my best friend and we said we would help each other when the time came.' I was trying to sound sensible and responsible, but heard myself all squeaky and breathless. Julie was moaning, clutching her belly and coming out with swearwords I wouldn't dare repeat. You'd have to have been there to know how bad it was.

'Yes, run downstairs and tell Mr Potter to call the ambulance. Straight away. Hurry now.'

I dashed off to find him. He was the janitor and usually hung about in the stockroom smoking, when he wasn't mowing the lawn or fixing things. Sometimes he hung about in the garden shed in the evenings, even after his working day had finished. I ran about shouting his name.

He came in from the garden after a couple of minutes. Glancing down, I noticed that his flies were slightly undone. I quickly glanced back up to his flushed face. Why he was roaming around outside in the pitch dark was anybody's guess. I recalled something one of the girls had said about him. She thought she saw him peering through the toilet window one night when she was in there. We all laughed and told her she should be so lucky: as if anyone would want to see her swollen belly and fat backside lowering onto the toilet. Come to think of it, it might have been Wendy. Can't remember now.

★

Julie had been carted off to hospital and we were all back in bed; there was another tap on my shoulder. This time it was her. Wendy. She was the only one who hadn't got out of bed earlier, but lay rigid and quiet while the pandemonium went on.

Once again, I sat up; my eyes felt dry and big. 'Flippin' 'eck, Wendy, not you as well? Shall I call Mrs Choat again?'

'No, no, please don't do that. I just wanted to talk to someone. I'm really scared, Sarah.'

I shoved over, patted the bed and she got in beside me. 'What are you scared of?'

'You know, that thing that Mrs Choat told us about this afternoon. That thing about your bits getting torn to pieces and getting stitched back up. Do you think Julie will need to have that? Do you think I will?'

Mrs Choat and her nasty mouth. I didn't know what to say to the poor little cow. She was trembling like a kitten, and holding onto my arm so hard it hurt.

'No, I shouldn't think so. You're healthy and strong ... and everything.'

She started to cry then. So I did too. For the second time that day. Flippin' 'eck.

Chapter Twenty-Nine

One for sorrow, two for joy. I was looking out of the window of Matron's office watching a lone magpie as it stalked across the lawn. Every so often it stopped to nibble at something in the grass but didn't look around or above. Magpies mate for life, but this one seemed unconcerned that its mate was nowhere in sight. I started counting inside my head; if I got to twenty and the other one did not appear, then – then what? I started to count more slowly, trying not to move my lips and staring hard through the glass.

Matron's hands shook as she poured the tea. Mum and Dad sat on the other side of her desk, while I had been relegated to a corner seat.

'Would you like sugar?' her voice trembling, but still with that slimy tone which she reserved for visitors.

'Yes please, two for me and one for my wife.' Dad's voice slow and deeper than usual.

'And what about you, Sarah? Would you like some tea?' Giving me a look which dared me to accept.

'No thank you, Matron.'

My breasts were full and sore, having given birth to my beautiful boy three days before.

I glanced down, horrified to notice two small wet patches on the front of my cardigan, and quickly crossed my arms, holding my hands up high to my shoulders. I thought if I had any more fluid inside me I would probably burst, and my milk would splash across the shiny floor and trickle towards Matron's bulbous ankles. I couldn't resist a tight smile as she glanced across at me.

Julie was gone, her parents having been anxious to hasten on the adoption process. She left within a couple of weeks of having her baby girl and wrote me a card to say that she had been sent away for a while. She promised to write a proper letter, but I was still waiting and had no idea of her address. It was upsetting to discover that she'd left her baby box behind.

The birth had been as terrible as Miss Choat had warned us all; clearly God had decided that I didn't deserve any leeway for my sins. Whereas the sweet Wendy smiled like the Virgin Mary when she came back from hospital, sanctimoniously cradling her bundle of joy. All that cleaning and polishing in the chapel had obviously paid off.

Mum was getting impatient. 'Thank you for your letter, Matron, but what was the problem you mentioned? My husband and I would like to see our grandson before we go home this afternoon.'

Dad shifted forward in his seat: 'You said he is fit and healthy, so we don't quite understand the reason for your concerns.'

'Of course, of course, I understand … umm … I think perhaps your daughter may not have been quite honest with you when she … well … when she became pregnant. Sarah, would you like to tell your parents anything?'

'No thank you, Matron. I'm feeling rather tired. I think it would be much better coming from you anyway,' my face blank as I looked at her. Couldn't resist it. I glanced out of the window as I stood up and noticed that the magpie had gone. Don't know whether he found his mate or not.

'Why don't I take you down to the nursery now then. Although, you've not yet finished your tea.' Matron's chair scraped across the floor, Mum and Dad got up from their seats and I followed on behind as we walked down the corridor.

★

A few minutes later we were all looking in the crib, where my tiny brown baby lay, his smooth face in sharp contrast to the white knitted blanket wrapped around him.

I stepped back for a moment to study the expressions on each of their faces. Matron's arms were folded. Dad was rubbing his chin and Mum wore a puzzled look, her head to one side.

After a few moments Dad looked across at me with a puzzled frown before slowly nodding.

Chapter Thirty

I lay in the dark, turning from one side to another, my body heavy as lead. My back was aching as I sat up slowly and reached out into the dark for my baby's box and a pen from the small table beside my bed. I limped along the hall into the toilet. Getting back in bed, I tried to concentrate on the flickering leaf shapes on the ceiling, reflected through a gap in the curtains.

Earlier in the day I'd asked Matron if I could feed my son one last time. My breasts were engorged; it would be my last gift. We were expected to breast feed for the first few weeks anyway, no doubt to ensure that we made a motherly bond before he or she was collected, and to add to the pain we so rightly deserved. Collected. Like a parcel.

My son: seized from my breast.

My son: carried away to a new life.

My body: limp and broken.

My son: who will learn to feel alone.

★

Matron tapped me on the shoulder. Gently, gently. She even gave it a little squeeze, her face too close to mine. I saw a look in her eyes that I'd never seen before. I hadn't heard the alarm bell and when I opened my eyes, the room was quiet. All the others had already gone down for breakfast.

I sat up quickly, 'I'm sorry, Matron, I didn't realise the time, I'll get up now.'

She nodded and produced a tray, with a bowl of porridge and a mug of tea. There was even a small banana carefully placed to one side. She said no more, placed her finger across her lips, shook her head and crept out of the room.

★

I slept on until late afternoon and woke up to hear voices outside, speaking softly. My back aching and my legs weak, I crept to the window. The sky glinted cruelly, and shards of bright sunlight bounced off a gleaming car on the drive. A man stroked the head of a tiny baby before handing him into the back seat and his wife's open arms. My baby.

As she took him, I watched how tenderly she patted the warm, rounded shape clinging to hers. Her smooth hair draped across him, claiming him as her own. Before stepping into the driver's seat, her husband glanced up, acknowledging me with a slight nod before climbing inside.

The rhododendron blossoms trembled as he moved off, the sound of the engine fading away into nothing as the car glided along the gravel.

★

Supper was over. Matron quietly closed her office door and sank gratefully into the armchair near the window. She looked out at the lawn and the evergreen bushes which sloped down towards the drive. The gardener always made sure that they were not clipped too low, on her instructions. It was not seemly that outsiders should catch a glimpse of a pregnant girl taking advantage of the sun during her afternoon break.

She had been at Brightview for thirty years.

Thirty years of reminding young mothers how sinful they were. Thirty years of watching the agony as their babies were taken

117

from their arms. As time wore on it had become increasingly difficult to witness their pain and to maintain the strict rules she herself had put in place. She often wondered what lay ahead for them all. And what kind of life awaited the little boy she had seen off that afternoon? She admitted to being shocked when he was born, knowing full well that it would be difficult to find a home for him. The girl's parents seemed like very decent people. She felt guilty for thinking otherwise when they had turned up with their daughter and wondered how her initial reaction related to her Christian values.

It had been a tiring day. There was a lot to consider and by the time the child was due to be collected her head was pounding. She was still unsure whether or not she had seen the tall, dark figure of a man stepping out from the bushes as she waved goodbye to the adoptive parents and firmly closed the front door.

Just then the phone rang: 'Good afternoon … yes of course I recall what you asked … erm, it's not usual practice, but … yes I understand …I will have to think about it … erm … I will write to you within the next day or two … yes, she's absolutely fine. I'm sorry I really must go now. Thank you for calling.'

She sat back in her chair and folded her arms. She must be getting soft in her old age. Perhaps it was time to retire.

Chapter Thirty-One

Things had been noticeably different between George and Elsie for a couple of weeks after they'd been to visit Sarah and her baby. Her brown baby.

Elsie began by saying very little when they first got in the car. George was trying hard to engage her in conversation; how beautiful the baby was, how healthy he looked and thank God that their daughter had seemingly survived the birth without any complications. Elsie grunted in assent until: 'Is that all you can say? Don't you see what this means?'

She broke down in tears, not crying but wailing, thumping at her thighs, shaking her head, mumbling incoherently, coming out with language he'd never heard her use before. George briefly looked sideways at her as he was trying to negotiate a narrow lane. He pulled over onto a patch of grass beside the road and held her.

'Honey, that little boy is our grandson, whether you like it or not. Life's not going to be easy for him.'

'He's not our grandson and never will be. He's nothing to do with us. He will soon have a proper family. And as for easy? How easy do you think it will be for Sarah when it becomes common knowledge that …'

She stopped, blew her nose and they continued home in silence.

★

Another quiet evening at home. Elsie was spending more and more time out in the shed painting; her pictures now slashed with stark angry colours, storming among the trees before disappearing off the edge of the canvas. George didn't know how he could comfort her. He brought the bass out from the corner, but didn't feel the motivation to try and play it. He put the instrument aside and sat down to listen to some relaxing Billie Holiday, her warm yet anguished tone flooding the room. He sat back, eyes closed.

★

Elsie had come indoors and began scrubbing her hands at the kitchen sink, her painting frenzy over – at least for the time being. She had been thinking about her outburst when they first saw the baby. There was so much from her past that had boiled over that day. Ever since they had met and fallen for one another, a cloud had hovered above them. An issue not of their own making but was nonetheless tacitly unspoken between them. There were things they needed to discuss and they both knew that the time would come when they would have to face it. And that time was now.

She slightly opened the door of the living room and studied her husband for a few minutes. He was in the far corner, with his back to her. She watched as he moved about with his instrument, plucking away at the strings for a moment before putting it back.

Moments later Billie's tender voice pondered over the fate of young lives in 'God Bless the Child'.

'Oh, for goodness sake, George!' His eyes flew open as he turned down the volume and got up to face her. Elsie knelt on the sofa, facing the window, her body shaking, her head bent low.

He was a strong, patient and kind man and she knew that their love for one another would never fade.

'I'm sorry, I'm so sorry.' She didn't turn to face him but continued to apologise, almost as if he wasn't there. Not knowing how to respond, he tenderly turned her around and lifted her chin. She looked down at her lap, stretching and clenching her fingers together.

'I know, honey. Don't think I haven't been pondering on your words over the last couple of weeks. I know what you meant.'

The silence was palpable, neither of them knowing how to start the conversation which they had managed to avoid for so long. George leaned back in the seat beside her and thought about his life now as compared with his home in Harlem.

★

He had been living in the beautiful south west of England for several years. Even so some of his work mates still made the occasional inappropriate, or even offensive comments. He would laugh it off or shoot back with a witty retort which he considered was probably wasted on those of a certain mentality anyway. Sometimes he would pretend he hadn't heard or simply walk away, maintaining his dignity and leaving them confused or embarrassed. By the end of the day he might receive a cringe-making apology about the fact that it had 'only been a joke' or other snide remarks about the supposed 'chip on his shoulder.' When he came home to his family after work, he never mentioned it. What would be the point?

When he was a small baby, his mother took him to work with her. Her job was to take care of Frankie, a boy the same age as him, for a couple of classical musicians, in their grand house in Manhattan. He and Frankie played and sometimes fought together as kids do and spent their early years together like brothers. Mom was no longer needed when Frankie was enrolled at a private kindergarten, and before long both boys would be starting elementary school.

He remembered going straight into the kitchen to his mother as soon as Frankie's parents got home after playing a concert or attending rehearsal with the highly esteemed New York Philharmonic Orchestra. His mom didn't have to tell him to leave his games with Frankie at that moment, and he never asked her. Even at the tender age of five, he knew that the expectations of people like himself had no social place in their lives. He would sometimes cuddle up on Mom's lap and listen as they played beautiful music on the phonograph in the sitting room, or Frankie's mother would sing alongside her husband on the violin, her soprano voice soaring high and pure up to the sky. That was when he first learned that classical music was as beautiful as jazz.

As he grew older he would talk about such things with Mom and Aunt Flo. Both women had suffered severely at the hands of racism, but their responses during such discussions were quite different. Where Aunt Flo would fly into a rage, Mom would quietly repeat what her own mother had told her as she was growing up: 'there were good people out there who wanted to help, and God would save them ...' Mom was loath to add that unfortunately his grandmother had run out of positivity in the end and hanged herself on the beam of a barn when she and her family were fleeing from the South.

★

Elsie went to bed early and a while later George joined her. He crept about in the bedroom, so as not to disturb her, but saw that she was still awake, staring into the dark when he lay down beside her.

'Tell me everything, honey. There's nothing you can say which will upset or shock me.'

He sighed, 'Think about where I was born and brought up.'

They were awake until the early hours of the morning. George tried his best not to comment as Elsie poured out her soul and talked about the barrage of insults and threats she endured once it became known that she was involved with a 'coloured man'. He occasionally sighed or groaned, but gently encouraged her to continue talking. He knew it had been a tough time for her, but not to such an extent.

As a GI, he remembered that black and white soldiers were segregated, and only allowed to visit the local pubs on alternate nights, as decreed by American officers. There had been some skirmishes and even small riots between black and white soldiers, so the very fact that she and her best friend Maureen had met him and his friends in the pub was sufficient for them to have been considered as 'cheap tarts'.

Elsie wept into his shoulder. He wondered how to say what he had long wanted to ask her, 'Why?'

'Why what George?'

'If you knew what people would think, why did you and Maureen make life so difficult for yourselves? I just don't get it …'

She went on to tell him that she was impressed by his polite ways, his gentle voice and how he spoke to her so differently from any other chaps she had met. 'We were young and, well, you know how it is, wanting to be rebellious I suppose.'

She paused. 'I loved you from day one anyway, so …'

'Me too honey. And what did your mom and dad think?'

'They weren't like my friends' parents. I suppose they were rebels too, in their own way. Being artists, they saw things differently.'

He grunted in assent, 'Yeah, I remember our first meeting. The way they looked at me anyone would think they were checking me out to see how fit I would be to do hard labour.'

'Hell, yes, I remember that day. I was so embarrassed when Mum even used the word …?'

He finished her sentence: '… exotic. Yep, that word.' He gave a tight laugh and shook his head. 'Mmmm … call it artistic licence I guess.'

'The thing is, they didn't seem to care what people thought, or so they said. People pretended not to see me in the town when word got around about Maureen and me being seen going to the pub. Mum and Dad told me just to ignore them and what they thought. Mum even grinned and called them all idiots. But they'd already moved out to live near their artist heroes by then, so they didn't realise how it was for me.'

She paused, 'And now they're both gone ...'

George said nothing, but held her tight before speaking again. 'I know honey, I know.'

He continued, 'And this is why you're worried about Sarah right? Afraid of what people might think?'

'Yes. I don't want her going through that. Things have not changed as much as they should have done. We'll bloody well show the lot of them. Let them watch and see how our girl is going to make a success of her life.'

George nodded and said nothing. GI soldiers knew that the US army had an agreement that 'No negro soldier or sailor will be given permission to marry any British white girl.' It was common knowledge among he and his fellow soldiers that commanding officers would refuse permission. That's when he returned to the US to see his mother and organise the procedure for leaving the army while Elsie waited for him.

★

Elsie told him about the responses from friends and neighbours. Their opening gambits were usually one of three:

'I don't have any problem with it, but what about the children you might have?'

'Is it true what they say about coloured chaps?' – usually accompanied by a little laugh, a wink or a nudge.

'I think you're so brave and kind for taking on a coloured chap.'

The community was such that she couldn't be out in town without coming across someone who knew her and her arty parents. An offensive name often left their lips as she passed by.

She and George acknowledged that they overheard the odd comment when they were out together. They usually raised their eyebrows at one another, said nothing and never discussed it afterwards. If Sarah asked questions as a small child, she was told to ignore it and carry on.

'Do you think we've done the right thing all this time George?' Elsie leaned across, turned on the bedside light and turned to face him, her eyes big and questioning.

'What do you mean?'

'All this time, we've told her to dismiss the nasty things that people sometimes say.'

He paused, 'Well what else can we do? It's no use getting riled up every time and …'

She patted his arm, 'No, no I agree. That's what my parents told me to do, but it didn't really help. In fact, I eventually realized it was no point telling them anything. I was alone.'

'Yes, I guess you're right. Maybe we should help her think about a few responses she could make while maintaining her dignity. There's no point in allowing people like that to upset your equilibrium and spoil your day. It would only come across as the 'chip on the shoulder' thing. I wouldn't give them the satisfaction.'

They finally fell asleep, little knowing that their daughter had devised her own tactics years before. Strategies which, as her life progressed, she would consider and amend as necessary in her adult life.

Chapter Thirty-Two

It was almost the end of two long years. I was wandering along the corridor after a rubbish day at college. I hadn't made any real friends although there were a few girls I sat next to in the canteen occasionally. I always made an excuse when they talked about going to the coffee bar around the corner after lessons. In the end they stopped asking me. The latest outings they talked about were about a pub quite nearby, where there were older students. Apparently, most of them had come from abroad to learn about the mining industry. The girls giggled a lot when they talked about their pub trips but the conversation usually faltered to a stop whenever I sat down to join them; I wondered why they were so reticent to continue and what it was they didn't want me to know. I put it aside anyway.

After 'the big mistake' I couldn't go back to school to do my A-Levels. Instead, I was enrolled at this miserable place about ten miles from home. I caught the train every morning and the bus back in the evenings, because the bus ticket was cheaper. The journey took forever, followed by a twenty-minute walk back home. Maybe it was just as well I had little or no social life.

I saw Veronica occasionally, to go for a walk, but our jiving days were over. She usually managed to steer the conversation towards God's forgiveness for those who sinned. People like me. We chatted a bit about some of the girls from school, but it meant little since I had left that life far behind when I became a mother. I often thought about my baby and wondered whether I would ever see him again. Matron told Dad that the couple who adopted him were from London. I wasn't supposed to know but Dad told me anyway on the proviso that I didn't tell Mum. I would always be that little boy's mother, no matter who brought him up. Sometimes, during the night, that thought brought me some comfort.

At least I had my student place for teacher training in London to look forward to. The offer had been on condition of satisfactory results. The heat was definitely on at home; it was tiresome having to pretend how much I was enjoying studying and all that blah-de-blah. I was doing French and of course Art. Whether either subject would be useful in a career which entailed coercing innocent children into reading, arithmetic and leaping over wooden blocks at PE was beyond me. But I had learned to take it on the chin and get through whatever was necessary to take me into the next chapter of my life. Although, I did quite enjoy the art classes. Mum was delighted and pressed me for all the details. My latest project was screen printing.

We spent lots of sunny afternoons at the weekends exploring the gentle hills and the beautiful coastline just a few miles out of town. Dad sometimes took off for a drive by himself on those days when Mum was stuck into her latest art project and I was studying up in my bedroom. He would take a flask of tea, the latest copy of *The Melody Maker* and find somewhere to read and be alone with his thoughts.

We often went to quiet coves along the river which were sometimes frequented by the sailing community. It was interesting to study those more affluent types as they sailed by: pulling ropes, which I learned later were properly named 'lines', and steering the boat this way and that as the wind playfully taunted them to respond. They would have to swing across from one direction to another, which I discovered was known as 'tacking'. The skipper, usually a 'him', would steer and call out to his obedient crew members as they slid from one side of the boat to the other in order to keep the boat, always called a 'her' – properly balanced.

The him and her thing made me think about who is usually in charge in the world. When I said as much to Dad, he gestured towards Mum as he spoke, stating that it wasn't always the case. Mum took it well, as she gently punched him on the shoulder.

I decided to use a sailing theme for my screen print as part of my final art exam. It was covered in slashes of colour: bright red, orange and pink boats, large and small, not one of them correctly drawn, but as Mum so wisely said, 'art has its place and creativity knows no bounds.' The 'creativity knows no bounds' phrase henceforward became a password for dodgy and incorrect renditions of my artistic attempts. Mum used the fabric afterwards to make curtains for the bathroom.

The French lessons were quite another thing; I was pretty good at pouting my lips as I foolishly thought that would make my accent sound more authentic when it was my turn to read aloud in class. I only did it a couple of times until the French teacher told me off. I enjoyed the conversational stuff but studying the old poets and writers did little for me.

Although there was one poem, by Victor Hugo entitled 'Paroles Sur La Dune'.

We had to learn the whole thing to recite in class, but I will never forget the first verse because it was so wonderfully sad that I vowed that maybe one day someone might read it at my funeral. On reflection, these were very dire thoughts for a young girl, but I found the melodrama of the words very appealing. I whispered the words to myself as I walked.

'Maintenant que mon temps décroît comme un flambeau,
Que mes tâches sont terminées,
Maintenant que voici je touche au tombeau,
Par les deuils et par les années.'

Chapter Thirty-Three

I had almost reached the college gate one afternoon and saw Maureen outside. She was leaning against the wall smoking a cigarette with her little finger cocked up to look stylish. I must have looked like a wet rag, sauntering along. Alone as usual. She took one look at me, quickly stamped out her cigarette, gave me a big hug and we linked arms. She would sometimes just turn up out of the blue like that. She always seemed to know when I needed her most. And that was one of those times.

I didn't always believe what she said about her reasons for appearing as she did, but neither of us felt the need to talk about it. I knew she did home hairdressing for people who were house-bound but thought it rather strange that they couldn't find a hairdresser in their own locality. But none of that mattered. That day was different.

As we strolled along she told me that Terry had work to do in the town. She had decided to come along and we would meet up with him after tea. She always made a point of telling Mum to expect me home later than usual on those occasions. We usually went for tea and cake. She very diplomatically asked how I was 'really' feeling, rather than accepting the usual stock answer of my declaration of being 'fine'. Whatever fine was.

We stayed longer than usual in the tearoom as we waited for Terry to come and take us home. After the usual surface chatter, Maureen took on a more serious expression.

'I really enjoy our times together, Sarah.'

'Me too – don't know what I would do if I didn't have you to talk to. Mum doesn't always get it and …'

She patted my hand, 'I know that, but you do understand that it's not always been easy for her. She had great ambitions for becoming a well-known artist and then when she fell in love with your dad well – everything changed.'

'I appreciate that, Maur, but passing her disappointments onto me feels unfair sometimes. Anyway, she and Dad really love one another. That's something I suppose.'

'I know, love.' She paused: 'I don't quite know how to say this, but it wasn't easy for your mum. Erm, during those days, people took a dim view of local girls dating an American GI. People said that girls like that were …' Her cheeks grew flushed. She picked up the teaspoon, and began stirring her tea over and over again, the brittle sound seeming louder and louder until I put my hand over hers to make it stop. 'What do you mean?' I frowned at first.

I couldn't say the words, which reinforced again and again,
incidents
comments
ignorance.
And pain.

★

Forty minutes later we were sitting in a pub a couple of miles away. Terry had turned up while I was in the toilet trying to reset my face. He and Maureen were talking quietly together as I approached the table. He stood up quickly, declaring that he'd had a helluva day and would appreciate a quick beer before we went home. He began telling us about the fusspot he'd been working for while Maureen and I picked up our bags. The tale which continued on the drive home, his voice stilted and louder than usual.

We sat in a quiet corner of the pub. Terry declared that since

I was nearing the end of my college days, it was only right that he treat me to a cocktail to celebrate my achievements. He came back from the bar, carrying a tray with a pint of Cornwall's best cider and two glamorous-looking cocktails for me and Maureen, complete with paper parasols and bits of unidentifiable fruit floating on top. Terry insisted that we drink to 'Little Miss Cleverclogs' as we raised our glasses.

Just at that moment, the door opened, and three young men walked in, chatting and laughing. They were all black, probably students from the mining school nearby. They were greeted warmly by the bartender who immediately started pouring their drinks before they had time to order. As they chatted at the bar, one of them turned around a couple of times and caught my eye wearing a puzzled expression.

It was time to leave; we finished our drinks and the student who had looked at me nodded and smiled at me as we passed by. Terry and Maureen glanced briefly at one another as they passed by.

Chapter Thirty-Four

One Saturday afternoon Dad came across a special place quite by chance. He had stopped along the side of a quiet road to look at the sea and smoke a cigarette. He couldn't wait to tell us all about it when he got home and promised he would take us there.

I was upstairs studying and came downstairs when I heard voices in the kitchen. I had spent the afternoon struggling with dead French poets and was ready for a break and something to eat. Mum had just come in from the garden, her apron pocket full of flower petals. She tipped them all out on the table with a flourish. She had bought an old flower press in the flea market a few weeks previously which had obviously been lovingly used for many years, one of the screws was missing and the wood was stained and smudged. Once pressed, she would use the petals to create pictures.

Dad was washing his hands at the kitchen sink; he turned around with a big grin on his face. Mum raised her eyebrows, followed by an inquisitive smile,

'Well, get you, looking like the cat who got the cream. Where have you been?'

'I'll tell you all about it over dinner. Let's see what we can cook up this evening.'

★

He had even brought home a bottle of wine to accompany our meal. We were all hungry and didn't have much to say until we'd had a glass of wine, mine in a small glass as per …

'So, tell us all about this special place, me 'ansum,' Mum was in good spirits and flushed with the joy of spending time in the garden.

Dad was in full flow. 'Ok, I know Cornwall is a beautiful place but where I went today is – I don't know – kind of magic …. I think this will be one of our favourites from now on.'

'What's so special about it, Dad?' He was in one of those 'let me tell you a story' ways of talking.

He leaned back in his chair, crossed his hands on top of his head and sighed.

'I just got in the car and drove. I didn't know where I was going, but it didn't really matter. I came off the main highway and went down a narrow road. I was heading for the open water, there were hardly any houses along the way. I pulled into a grass verge beside the road to stop for a while and enjoy the quiet. There was a gate to a large field and a few cows standing about; beyond them I could see the water. Looking across to the opposite side of the field the lower branches of the trees at the edge leaning forwards as if they were paying homage to the beauty around them.'

He paused for a moment, me and Mum looked at one another with raised eyebrows, and he carried on.

'So quiet was it that as I leaned over the gate, I could hear the cows munching the grass while a few birds sang out their call and response beneath the sky.'

I butted in, 'Call and response – like music Dad? Like one of those tunes you play, what's it called again?'

He smiled, 'It's called "Moanin". That's right sweetie, just like music: nature's music.' Mum nodded sagely.

'A young couple turned up and parked a little further ahead of me and we nodded at one another. They took a couple of rucksacks from their car and headed for a little path in the hedge nearby. They disappeared behind the bushes for about twenty minutes before emerging at the top of the cliff further in the distance. I realized there must be steps there and I watched as they slowly made their way down onto the shingle below.'

'And then what – did you go down to the beach, Dad?'

'Of course. I waited a few minutes more because I didn't want them to think I was following them. There were some farm outbuildings beside the path until I reached a stile over a little stream. Up ahead was a hill and yet more cows. They glanced at me as I strolled by before continuing with their afternoon snack.'

Mum piped up, 'They must have been having a Cornish cream tea. I hope the scones were just right and the cream was on top of the jam, not underneath.'

Being a real Cornish maid, Mum knew all about such things. Her home-made pasties were delicious even if the shape didn't always fit the norm.

'After safely navigating across the meadow without disturbing the cows, I stood for a moment to gaze at the stunning view. There was a small wooden bridge and the path continued between some bushes and towards the cliff edge.'

'Sounds exciting, Dad.'

'Yes, it was and very different from parking up in some little car park, buying an ice-cream and joining the hordes of trippers.'

Mum joined in again, 'You mean all those emmetts who come here from up country and leave their litter on our beaches? They think …' she broke off; 'Well you know what I think.'

'Yes Mum, we do.' She grinned and shook her head.

Dad continued, 'The walk down the steps cut into the cliffs took me some minutes, some of them were sloped and narrow but it was well worth it. The beach was all shingle and almost deserted, apart from the two people I'd seen who were lying in the sun quite far away to my left. I sat on a large rock quite near the edge of the water and watched as the tide drifted as slowly as an old man going for a stroll.'

Chapter Thirty-Five

The beach became our secret sanctuary; we went several times that summer. On the busiest day we might see maybe two or three local people walking their dogs, or a few small groups who nodded as they passed by before walking away into the far distance. Maureen and Terry often joined us, and we went well equipped. Terry would bring a few beers, which he set into a small pool in the shade to keep cool until needed, and we had pasties and tea to keep us going until sunset. Maureen and Mum were both adorned in fancy straw hats, as if they were disporting themselves on the French Riviera, until Mum proudly pointed out this was the Cornish Riviera. Sometimes we swam in a natural pool surrounded by rocks away from the tide, collecting stones and shells and dipping into tiny rock pools to feel the sea anemones wrap their tentacles around our fingers.

The last time we went was a couple of weeks before I set off for London. We knew it would be our last visit for the summer. It was early September and not quite as hot as we would have wished, but we still followed our usual ritual. After lunch, Dad and I wandered off to find more cowrie shells.

You had to look carefully among the shingle to spot their tiny oval shape. Pink and translucent, some of them with a couple of pale brown dots on top and, when turned over, the little slits underneath looked like tiny smiles. We found hundreds of cowries between us that summer. We often discovered small gatherings of them at the edge of the high tide line; it was a race to see who could find the highest number by the end of the day. When we got home, Mum added to our collection in a tall glass which took pride of place on the sitting room mantelpiece. Maureen and Terry saved theirs in tiny glasses in every room of their house: talismans of happiness on every windowsill.

Dad and I wandered off in the soft breeze, going further along the beach than usual. We took our time to climb over the rocks, slippery with seaweed. Sometimes one of us would stop to point something out: an oddly shaped stone, a long strip of seaweed waving gently at the edge of the water, or the living creatures lazing about in small pools. If a boat passed near enough to see the people on board we usually waved and they waved back in acknowledgement of a shared joy.

Apart from that there was little to say, knowing that our lives would soon change. A grey cloud shuddered gently above the pleasure of the afternoon. We sat down on a sloping rock and watched a passing yacht, but so wrapped up were we in our own thoughts that we forgot to wave.

Dad took out a handful of cowries from his pocket and jiggled them about in his hand before laying them out on the smooth rock, carefully placing each one into a straight line.

'So, my girl will soon be a Cornish exile then, hey?'

I paused for a moment, then and shook my head. 'I'm not really a Cornish girl though, am I, Dad?'

He patted my hand, 'Well I guess you are sweetie – you were born and brought up here.'

'And you were born in New York, so you must be American.' I hesitated: 'But somehow it doesn't feel as straightforward as that, does it, Dad? After all, even if that makes me Cornish, I don't look like anyone else, so ...'

He began to re-arrange the cowries into a circle before he spoke.

'I've told you a lot about life in America, about the way that some people are treated and …'

I nodded as I recalled some of our discussions.

'Let's walk a bit further before the tide comes in too high.' He gathered up the shells, ten in all. He took my hand, turned it over and placed five of them in my palm before closing my fingers around them 'Five for you and five for me, because that's only fair.'

★

'I know you've taken a lot of interest in my stories about America. And, just like your Mum, I love reading and always have done. When I was younger, I came across the work of a very clever man, named W. E. B. Du Bois. He was a black man, a social scientist and an educated person of great wisdom and knowledge. When we talked about you not really feeling Cornish because you don't look like any of your friends or neighbours, it reminded me of something he wrote way back in the last century. I was so impressed that I learned one of his statements off by heart when I was about sixteen years old.'

'Wow, I've never heard you mention this before, Dad. Can you still remember it?'

'I think so. Of course, the language sounds pretty antiquated, but it was written sometime in the 1890s:

"It dawned upon me with a certain suddenness that I was different from the others; or like, mayhap, in heart and life and longing, but shut out from their world by a vast veil."'

We both stopped and looked at one another. 'That's just it, Dad, isn't it? It's all about feeling as if I don't belong here.'

We continued walking, both silent for a while until he spoke again.

'Du Bois described that feeling as "double consciousness". For black Americans, it meant being part of their country and yet not a part of it, because they were, and still are in fact, treated differently from the rest of the population. Remember, they had been forced to leave behind their own beliefs and culture behind when …'

I finished, '…when they were enslaved.'

'Exactly.'

'But how does that relate to my life?'

'Think about it, sweetie. It's about navigating your way in accordance with particular situations and – well, it's kind of complicated. We'll talk about it another time. Meanwhile, I think we should head up that path ahead, and make for that field before the tide cuts us off. The others will think we've been washed away. We can walk across there and find our way back down.'

Dad watched as I shuffled the shells from one hand to the other before putting them back in my pocket.

'Cowrie shells were used as currency in many parts of the world at one time. In West Africa, they were widely accepted as legal currency until about the mid-nineteenth century as part of the Atlantic slave trade.'

'Would that have included Ghana?'

He nodded. I decided not to make any further comment as we retreated from the shoreline and made our way up the cliff. My throat felt dry, and the back of my neck began to sweat as I tried to process what he'd told me.

★

We stopped and looked back as we reached the top. A faint, grey cloud was hovering above the horizon; it was getting late in the afternoon, soon it would be time to pack up our things and head home.

Dad stood quite still, his hands in his pockets, 'Mr Du Bois died years ago. He died in Ghana, then known as The Gold Coast.'

'How come he was there?'

'He returned there and the USA refused to renew his passport so he couldn't get back. He lived there for a couple of years and died in Accra.'

He spread his arms and looked up at the sky, 'Mr Du Bois went home to Africa.'

Chapter Thirty-Six

Dad started whistling as we pulled into the station, always a sure sign that he was feeling nervous. I quickly got out of the back seat to help as he fiddled about getting my things. I squeezed his arm and gazed at the side of his face while he pretended to look about, as if searching for something else. The whistling stopped and he gave me a hug so hard I thought my ribs would crack.

Maureen and Terry were parked nearby: a proper send-off. Maureen patted Mum on the shoulder: the worst thing she could have done. Mum went into overdrive and began quietly weeping, her thin shoulders heaving up and down. Terry and Dad stood about looking like two bookends. Flipping 'eck, you might have thought I was going off to join World War III. We all trudged across the bridge to get to the opposite platform to wait for the train which would transport me away to my new life. The men slouched behind, Mum and Maureen were both linked up, and I was trying to look as if I wasn't over-the-absolutely-flipping-top-excited.

We stood about waiting for an agonising fifteen minutes. Dad was glancing at his watch and Mum was wittering on about – well – nothing really. The farewell tea-party the previous afternoon had been anything less than fun. Three bottles of wine were imbibed, and she completely lost it. The usual words came into play namely: opportunity, ambition, new chapters and all the rest.

Maureen and Terry didn't linger long after that; apparently because Terry had to see some bloke about a car. Mum went to bed early. During the night she crept into my room and climbed into bed with me. We didn't talk, but simply held one another tight and both cried for a while until we fell asleep. Dad woke us in the morning with tea and toast on a tray.

Then came all the goodbyes, take care and work hard stuff from everyone; Mum with her head on one side as she smoothed down my recently straightened hair.

'You know how much I love you don't you, me 'ansum?'

'Course I do, Mum. I love you too.'

The three of us hugged together as Maureen and Terry stood by watching.

The train rolled to a stop. Dad got on to help find my seat. He put my suitcase up on the luggage rack, helped me take off my coat, gently folded it and put that up too, before giving me a quick hug before returning to the platform with the others. I rolled down the window. Maureen stepped forward, winked at me and slipped a small bulging envelope into my hands. I nodded, stuck in my pocket, and stood there as they waited to see me off. I looked at them, their arms all linked together. The train began to slowly move off; we all waved and carried on waving as I watched their figures get smaller and smaller until the track turned a bend and they disappeared from sight. I returned to my seat, put my head back and cried silent tears.

Four wonderful people cared, sustained and cherished me:

The complex, passionate mother who bore me with courage, love and aspirations, where her own hopes had been dashed.

The loyal friend hiding her solitary, secret desire for a child of her own: a dream unfulfilled.

The staunch, generous man who gave and supported with rough love, his calloused hands as witness to a life of toil.

And my dad: strong, loyal, committed, with a heart as big as the moon.

Huge banks of purple rhododendrons rushed by the window. They gradually dwindled away as we left Cornwall behind. I poured some tea from my flask, sat back and opened the envelope which Maureen had thrust into my hand. Inside there was a short note and a small lumpy package inside a drawstring bag with a strange looking symbol embroidered on the front.

Dear Sarah,

I hope that you find all that you are searching for as you begin the next chapter of your life. You will make a wonderful teacher. Perhaps these precious keepsakes will help you along the way.

Lots of love, Maureen.

A handful of cowrie shells fell into my hand as I opened it.

Chapter Thirty-Seven

I knew what the main building looked like: I had found some pictures of it in a library book entitled *Great Educational Institutes of Britain*. The librarian had kindly photocopied a couple of the pictures during her lunch hour, even though it was against the rules. I picked them up the following day and added them to the direction leaflet which had been posted with my acceptance letter.

There were several cars parked all along the drive as I struggled past with my suitcase and my new shoulder bag. Students and their parents were chatting away as they unloaded their cars. There were many voices calling out with excitement, warnings and declarations of undying love. It hadn't occurred to us that it was probably usual for parents to accompany their offspring as they were shunted off to university.

I kept my head down and trudged on, only stopping to look up when I caught sight of the huge white pillars of the main entrance looming before me. It was certainly very grand, surrounded by carefully manicured lawns and flower beds with a few smaller buildings to one side. A couple of older students were strategically placed in the corridor to accompany us to the reception area and give directions regarding student accommodation. They wore the stamp of confidence as they politely helped everyone, a couple of them adding gushing praise for one of Britain's sacred institutions of academia.

I looked and listened to the people around me. Could this really be London? I had spent months reading about this great city and its inhabitants, people from all over the world lived here, I had checked out pictures and information about the important buildings and popular tourist spots. I so wanted to visit all the different areas I'd read about, and to have the opportunity to go and listen to some live jazz. I imagined making a circle of new friends with similar tastes and interests.

I stood and gazed around and for a moment; I suppose crestfallen would be the word: my crest certainly fell to my feet as I thought I would probably be the odd one out again. I took off my shoulder bag and made a pretence of searching for something, so that I didn't have to catch anyone's eye. Someone tapped me on the shoulder. I turned around to see a couple and their daughter a few feet behind me. None of them said anything, but they all smiled; the daughter and her mother gave me a little wave and the father nodded. Perhaps I was not alone after all.

Chapter Thirty-Eight

Angela and I struggled through our first term. We knew early on that we would stick together; it didn't have to be said. But we soon realised that other students may have assumed that we didn't want to join in, so we occasionally sat near them at lunch and dinner times. Navigating within that community took on a whole new set of considerations for me.

Angela and I were placed in the same tutor group from the start of the course. There were fourteen of us in our seminar meeting for one of the modules. We all had to introduce ourselves on the first day, giving our names and thoughts about what it meant to become a committed teacher.

It was the summer term. We had just come out of a seminar meeting and decided to stroll about outside to enjoy the sun for a while. The gardens were beautifully maintained, including manicured lawns, neat flowerbeds surrounded by proud trees. A few wooden benches were placed around, some bearing carved memorials to respected academics of the past, the steadfast harbingers of the proud education establishment.

Angela sighed, closed her eyes and held her head up to the sun, 'I can't believe that we've been students here for almost a year and Miss Hunter still gets our names mixed up. I'm sick of it.'

I nodded in assent, trying not to feel too annoyed, 'Yeah, me too.'

We both went quiet for a while before she opened her eyes and quickly stood up.

'I know, why don't we do the same next time and call her by the name of one of the other tutors! That would be a laugh.'

I wasn't so sure. Angela had more confidence than me, probably because she had been brought up in London.

The day came. I was hoping that she had forgotten. The meeting was well under way; Miss Hunter had opened the discussion about the previous lecture and asked students to make their contributions. A few of them spoke before Angela nudged me. I pretended not to notice and looked firmly ahead.

She put her hand up, 'Just a thought Miss Miller, erm … Hunter. I really enjoyed today's lecture, especially when Mr Russell spoke about the importance of being aware of the differing needs of the pupils we teach and how to help them develop their confidence and self-esteem.'

Miss Hunter frowned, folded her arms and didn't answer for at least three or four seconds.

'Well Sarah, I would have thought by now that you would address me by my proper name and …'

Angela held her hand up and interrupted her from finishing her sentence, 'Yes, I was thinking the same about you, Miss … erm … There are only fourteen of us in this group and we've been meeting regularly since September of last year.'

Some of the other students began to grin as she continued, 'My name is Angela and sitting beside me is my friend Sarah. It appears to me that one glance in our direction indicates that when you see us, you only see one thing. We don't even look alike.'

She paused … 'And I suspect that everyone knows why.'

She rolled her eyes and the grinning stopped.

★

Angela's parents had decided that it was best for her to stay in student rooms during the week, so she could make friends and take part in social activities. They and her younger brother Johnny lived in south east London. She sometimes went home at weekends and came back telling me about her family and extended family, who were not too far away. I couldn't imagine how comforting that must be. She described where she lived as a different planet compared to our grandiose surroundings.

Lectures finished a bit earlier on Friday afternoons. We were in Angela's room and I was listening to her transistor radio as I watched her stuffing a few overnight things into her bag. She was leaving early the next morning to go and visit her family.

'So, what you doing this weekend, babe?'

'Erm, nothing planned ... I might make a few notes on that stuff about child development ... or ... might have a lie in and go for a walk or something. Dunno yet.'

She stopped what she was doing for a moment, 'Hey, why don't you come with me? You can meet Mum and Dad and my cute little brother. I've told them all about you.'

'Wow, are you sure, Ange? I must admit it would be great to get away from here for a few hours.'

'You can stay all weekend, they won't mind, they'll be pleased. Go and get your stuff ready and I'll meet you by the phone box down in the hall in about half an hour. We can tell them that you're coming.'

I went back to my room and looked about, wondering what to wear. I decided to go casual after considering that one of Mum's creations might not go down too well (sorry Mum!). When I got downstairs Angela was already speaking to her mother. They chatted for a while and then she handed me the phone to say hello. The voice at the other end was deeper than I was accustomed to with an accent that sounded like warm music as she told me how pleased she was that was coming to visit.

As we walked toward the bus stop, I realised that for the first time in my life I was going to meet another family like mine.

Chapter Thirty-Nine

Two bus rides and one underground trip later we finally arrived near the railway station. I looked about as Angela strode on ahead towards the open market. There was a large clock tower ahead and what looked like a long street virtually covered in street stalls, with rows of shops on either side.

I could not help but smile as we strolled along. I noticed shoppers who clearly came from different parts of the world, some of them speaking in languages other than English, or dressed in traditional clothes representative of other countries.

★

It was early evening and Angela was fumbling around for her door key. Her brother Johnny had been looking through the window as we approached; he rushed off and within a couple of minutes Mrs Williams opened the door. Having only seen her briefly on our first day, I couldn't remember what she looked like. She was wearing a wrap-around apron and her hair was piled high under a headscarf. She hugged me tightly before stepping out wearing a smile,

'Welcome Sarah, it's so good to meet you properly at last.'

Angela stood by, beaming, 'So, how about a hug for me too, Mum?'

We all laughed as I followed them into the hallway. Thirteen-year-old Johnny lingered at the doorway of the sitting room, waiting to be introduced. He was taller than I thought he would be for his age. He shook my hand and whispered a shy hello, before turning away towards the stairs.

Mrs Williams grinned and patted his shoulder, 'Excuse my boy, Johnny. He's a bit shy aren't you, my love?' Her son groaned theatrically and rolled his eyes before turning away.

Angela and I picked up our bags and followed her upstairs, as she explained the sleeping arrangements. I was to be honoured by having Angela's bed, while she would sleep on a camp bed which had been set up in the corner. I tried to explain that it would not be necessary, but they both insisted that that was the plan. I was their guest after all.

★

Dinner was ready. Mr Williams had got home from work a short while before, and greeted me just as warmly as his wife had done. Johnny was persuaded to come downstairs, and we sat down to eat in the kitchen. It was a large room, with a huge sofa in one corner and a TV. The dining area reminded me of our kitchen at home but instead of being decorated with shells and pebbles, interesting looking herbs and spices lined the shelves which I hadn't seen in any of the local shops at home. There were three large bowls of food on the table for us to share. Before we sat down, Mr and Mrs Williams insisted that I call them by their first names: Sonya and Clive.

I helped Angela to lay the table; when gathering the cutlery and plates from the cupboard, I noticed a couple of strange looking vegetables; Sonya told me they were yams and sweet potatoes bought from the local street market. I decided there and then to visit the market before Christmas, so I could buy some things for Mum and Dad.

I wondered what my parents would be doing that evening. Dad would be home from work, having taken off his overalls and washed up. Mum had probably cut the sewing cotton on the last seam of a dress she'd been working on all day. They were no doubt cooking a meal together, listening to one of their favourite records or watching TV as Mum told him about the film she was going to see later with Maureen.

★

'So, Miss Sarah, what a pleasure to have you come spend the weekend with us. You must tell us all about what life is like being a country gal.' Clive was clearly in good spirits the working week was over and it was family time.

I didn't know where to start, I was more interested in their own lives and stammered a bit as I tried to tell them something about my school experience, my friends and my parents. Everyone listened attentively; Johnny's ears perked up when he learned that my dad was American. He probably thought that he would be like those actors he had seen on screen. I told them a little about my parents' backgrounds. After a while my words dwindled to a stop, not knowing what else to say. How would I explain the narrative of my life over one dinner conversation as compared to theirs?

Sonya began to ladle food onto my plate, explaining each dish as she served.

'I don't know if you've ever had chicken served like this, Sarah, we call it jerk. It's a way of making the meat more tasty. I seasoned the chicken pieces up last night, rubbing special spices all over it so that the taste could seep in before being cooked.'

Clive joined in, 'Yep, this is traditional Jamaican food – the best!'

Sonya went on to explain that the rice looked pink because of the juice of red kidney beans mixed in it and the taste was enhanced by the addition of grated coconut, as well as salt and a little pepper. 'Yes, and my boy prepared all the vegetables for the coleslaw before you got here.' Johnny sunk into his chair as his sister playfully squeezed his shoulder.

Things quietened down for a while as we enjoyed our meal. The food was delicious. I could taste the spice all mixed up with some coconut sweetness. Johnny's coleslaw was a success. I didn't know that raw grated vegetables could be so tasty. Sonya kept filling my plate until I asked her to stop. Politely of course.

I looked around at Angela's family. Johnny had relaxed and began telling us about the day he'd had at school, with some persuasion from his sister. In turn she tried to tell everyone about our lectures, the long reading list and how much she missed eating what she called proper food. As we were about to finish the meal, Clive got up from the table and took a bag of carrots and a grater from the pantry. We carried on chatting as he grated all the carrots into a large mixing bowl. I wondered what was next on the menu; I certainly couldn't have eaten another mouthful.

Johnny leaned back into his chair, as if waiting to hear a familiar story. 'You grew up in the countryside too, didn't you, Dad? Why don't you tell Sarah about your boyhood days in Jamaica.'

Clive paused for a moment and shook his head. 'Well, I can tell you this, Sarah. I can tell you my life was very different from yours. Me and my friends had fun even though our folks didn't have much money. You know what I mean?'

But he had friends who looked like him. He wasn't alone.

Despite the warmth and welcome of the evening, my eyes began to fill. I didn't know why, but I knew then that I was not prepared to spend the rest of my life as an outsider. Sonya was the only one to notice; she quietly passed me a tissue and nodded.

'I have an important job to finish first, Sarah, then I'll tell you a little about country living in Jamaica.'

The carrots were grated and Angela was instructed to get a tin of condensed milk from the pantry, while her dad pressed the carrot juice through a piece of muslin into a jug. He caught my eye as I looked on, wondering what was coming next on the menu.

'Don't worry, dear, my hands are quite clean.' He laughed as she handed him the tin.

'Alright everyone, let the operations begin. Tools please.' He rolled his sleeves up with a theatrical gesture and called out to his assistant. 'Tin opener!' Angela scrambled across to the cutlery drawer to find it as he stretched out his arms and wriggled his shoulders about as if preparing for a heavyweight championship.

He opened the tin and poured in a small amount of the thick creamy liquid, before calling out again; 'Large spoon!'

Once again, his daughter was at his side with said tool as requested. She winked and curtseyed quickly before returning to her chair. Sonya was trying hard to contain her laughter, as she dabbed at her eyes with her apron. By that time Johnny was balancing on the back two legs of his chair; this was clearly a familiar family performance.

The next couple of minutes seemed to take ages to pass as we watched Clive adding the milk, little by little, tasting the contents of the jug as he went. Finally, he stood back and nodded.

He threw the muslin cloth into the kitchen sink and sat down. 'My job is done.'

Johnny got up and added a sprinkling of cinnamon powder on the top before dutifully filling our glasses. 'Sorry to remind you, Dad, you didn't add the cinnamon.'

Clive grinned, 'Oh yeah, I forgot that – proper carrot juice needs a bit of spicy kick.' He raised his glass and tasted, 'Mmm, mmm, sweet and nice, just like your beautiful mother. Here's to you, my dear.'

Sonya simpered as we clinked our glasses and drank a toast.

Chapter Forty

After clearing away the table we all retired to room next door, except Johnny, who mumbled that he homework to do. So far, I had only seen the bedrooms, the bathroom and the kitchen. As we passed through the hallway into the sitting room, Angela whispered in my ear that I was certainly very honoured to be invited into what was clearly a very special place, used only for entertaining visitors or other special occasions. Apparently, they usually spent most evenings curled up on the sofa, watching TV, or up in their bedrooms.

The room was decorated in a style which I discovered later was traditional in many Jamaican homes of the time. What first struck me were the family photos all over the house. I didn't want to appear rude and tried not to make it look obvious that I was fascinated by the variety of faces on display, old and young, and of varying shades from light brown to dark. Most of them had been taken in Jamaica; the sun was shining and I noticed the branches of what might have been a mango tree. The photographs bedecked most of the wall space and right across the mantelpiece.

The floral three-piece suite was large, with hand-embroidered antimacassars across the arms and velvet cushions. An important looking radiogram commanded the view from its position in the corner and a large coffee table in dark wood with curlicued legs stood proudly in the centre of a deep pile carpet. In the middle was a large display of flowers surrounded by a collar of stiff netting in a variety of colours, sewn onto a mat of white linen with hand embroidered place mats placed to one side.

Sonya watched as I took it all in, 'I expect this reminds you of being at home. You must be missing your mum and dad.'

'Yes, I do miss them. There are certainly things which remind me especially of Mum. She's very artistic and likes sewing too, but she usually makes clothes and curtains on her sewing machine, doesn't do much hand sewing. And she likes knitting.'

I didn't tell her about Mum's wallpaper hanging and about her bits and pieces collection. Everyone would think she was bonkers, whereas Dad and I knew that it was because she was an artist. She was unique.

'Sit yourself down dear.'

Clive opened the lid of the radiogram and started rooting around in his record collection in the cupboard below.

Angela spoke up, 'Don't put your music on yet, Dad, you promised to tell Sarah about life back home.'

He turned around, 'Yes, you're right, so I did.'

★

'Wow, where do I start? I was born in Kingston, a busy, bustling place. My father did odd jobs for people and my mother used to sell fish on the street. I was a lively boy; I suppose you could even say I was not very well behaved. I had two older sisters who went to school every day and helped Mum on the market. But as for me – well I got into a lotta trouble and took advantage of the fact that my parents were so busy trying to make a living that I was often left to my own devices.'

Angela shook her head, 'I remember you telling us about some of the stuff you got up to, Dad ... like that time when ...'

Sonya touched her arm, 'I think Sarah might be more interested about what happened when your father went to live out of the town. Is that right, dear?' I nodded.

'Yes, I was sent to live with my grandmother who lived in the countryside, in Clarendon, one of the parishes of Middlesex. I don't need to tell you why there are so many English place names in Jamaica.' He sucked his teeth.

'My grandpa had passed away and my parents thought it would do me good to stay with her. She was getting old and needed some help around the house. I was about seven, eight years old.'

He paused, 'Man, I'm telling you my gramma was a strict old lady, who didn't believe in holding back if I misbehaved. I loved her though, and soon learned what the boundaries were. I felt like a big man when I helped out in the house. I had to get up early, prepare the breakfast and sweep the yard before I walked the two miles to school.'

He looked at me and Angela, 'You see how you gals have it good?' He gave a wry smile.

'It wasn't all bad, me and my friends would sometimes go down to the beach after school and go for a swim, or talk to one of the old fishermen. He sometimes let us row a likkle way out in his boat. Happy days.'

It was interesting to note how his Jamaican accent became more pronounced as he reminisced. He went on to talk about how he and his grandma spent the evenings. She would sing and tell him old Jamaican folk tales. He talked about 'duppies' and 'the rolling calf' and other tales which had been passed down the generations.

Angela was grinning happily, 'One of these days, we're going to write down all of Dad's stories. There's enough for a flipping book!'

★

A couple of hours later we both went upstairs. Sonya and Clive stayed downstairs for a while. I heard the clatter of dishes and plates in the kitchen; they had insisted that they didn't want us to help clear up. It had been a long day. Angela was soon quietly

155

snoring on the camp bed and I lay in the dark thinking about all the things I had discovered during the day.

I thought about all that Dad talked about regarding the black American experience: the Jim Crow laws, the inequality, the blatant racism, the search for their long lost African background and traditions. Yet that evening, I was made aware of Jamaica's own rich culture, one which had grown and developed over the years since slavery. No doubt it was impregnated with ancient African folklore, but nonetheless real and robust. Could it be because it is an island, whereas the American slaves had been spread over a much larger land mass, surrounded by the default population on all sides? Although, my dad spoke fondly about black American dishes and of course the history of jazz, our favourite music; we called it American Classical Music. I couldn't wait to get into conversation with Mum and Dad when I went home for Christmas.

I turned over and was just falling asleep when I was sure I could hear quiet music playing downstairs. Music that sounded familiar. Or perhaps I was mistaken.

Chapter Forty-One

Sonya had been upstairs knocking on Johnny's bedroom door, to make sure he was up in time to do his newspaper delivery. 'I love my sweet boy, but he could sleep all day if I didn't wake him.'

She came bustling into the kitchen. 'Don't forget you've got an appointment today, Angela. You asked me to book up with Cherise the other week, remember?'

'Thanks Mum, I'm looking forward to getting my hair sorted out.' Angela looked at me across the table, 'How about getting yours done, Sarah? I'm sure Cherise can fit you in. Let's try and get there a bit earlier.'

I noticed that she had worn a silk scarf to bed the previous night and kindly lent me one too. I'd never done that at home and usually woke up with a stiff kinky lump to one side of my head every morning. Sonya began delving her fingers into my scalp. My neck felt hot. I had to steel myself not to wrench my head away because it reminded me of what some of the other children did when I was in primary school, teasing me and saying that hundreds of nits must be stuck inside my plaits, and they couldn't climb out because my hair was so thick and nasty.

She quickly drew back, 'Hope you don't mind me touching your hair, Sarah but last night I thought that you might like to have yours done too. What do you use at the moment?'

'Erm, my dad found a metal comb when he went shopping –

you know like the ones they use to groom dogs and ...' I couldn't say anymore, so embarrassed was I in having to confess the shabby details of my personal care.

Sonya sucked at her teeth and frowned, 'Well, we can't have that, can we, dear. We'll sort it out. And don't worry, it's my treat. Get your coats then, girls, and we might just catch the next bus.'

★

A burning smell together with something chemical greeted us as we stepped inside. Although it was quite early in the day, there were already half a dozen women in the various stages of treatment and another woman waiting. Angela and Sonya went straight up to one of the hair stylists: Cherise and both gave her a hug as I lingered near the door. Sonya gestured towards me as they were talking. Cherise nodded sagely as she looked across at my hair.

I didn't have to wait too long. I spent the time studying the variety of creams, gels and oils lined up on the shelves as well as watching the process of black hair styles taking place. Most people, including Angela were having cream rubbed into their hair; I was about to find out what it was for shortly afterwards. A young teenage girl was having a long wig woven into her own curls.

The only person seeking something more distinctive was a mature looking woman having her natural hair plaited and twisted into an intricate series of concentric circles around her head, every strand being carefully selected so as to ensure that all plaits were of the same width; it was a work of art.

Cherise invited me to her chair. She chatted away as she draped a black gown around my neck and began parting my hair into sections.

'You ever had your hair properly straightened before love?'

I shook my head and thought I would have to go into the whole dog's comb explanation as she began applying greasy stuff to my scalp, ensuring that it was all covered, including the edges around my neck and face.

'Don't look so scared, dear, this grease will stop the straightening cream from hurting.'

Hurting? I wondered if it would be any more painful than the hot comb touching the top of my ears at home. Mum would rush for the Vaseline and rub it carefully over my tender skin. Cherise took a big tub of white cream from the tray beside her. No doubt that was what had been applied to Angela's hair. Cherise was trying hard to distract me as she rubbed it in, starting at the scalp and working it outwards.

'So, you're a good friend of our Angela then? I hear that you come up from country. Nowhere in them places to get a proper hairstyle, eh?' I was afraid to shake my head as her fast fingers worked away. Within minutes I sensed a slight burning sensation, but I didn't say anything, after all she surely knew what she was doing. She combed it through to the ends and left the cream to process.

'Right, there you go, sweetheart. This needs to stay on for twenty minutes. Keep an eye on the big clock up there and give me a little wave when your time's up in case I forget.'

She was about to move off to help someone else when a large woman pushed the heavy glass door open. A child came trailing behind: a beauty of a girl about eight years old. Although the day was cloudy, the girl was all done up in orange satin and lace. Her hair a fuzzy halo, swayed in the breeze, her face brown and shiny. She quietly sniffed as her mother called across the salon with a voice that could cut through steel.

'Hey, can you do anything about this? We're in a hurry.'

Cherise raised her eyebrows and went across to the mother and daughter, professional diplomacy in her every step.

'Good morning, Mam. And hello my love, don't you look pretty.' She touched the child's shivering hair. The woman pushed her forwards. 'Nicky, tell the lady what you done.'

A small voice, ragged at the edges, 'Maisie stayed over and we were dancing.'

'Tell her everything.'

'It was that Stevie Wonder song. We got all sweaty and – and my hair must have got a little damp.'

'Yeah and tell her what happened after the goddam dancing.'

Cherise shook her head. I gazed at the child, my eyes shot through with compassion.

Everyone in the salon went quiet, but I had to say something, 'You look lovely. Going somewhere special?' The child looked up at her mother before responding.

'My friend Maisie's birthday. And – and also to celebrate because me and Maisie both won top reading prizes in school,' with an apology of a smile.

'Well done, clever as well as beautiful.' I looked at her mother, who responded by sucking her teeth.

'Yeah, go on, you still haven't said what else you done.'

'We ran outside in the rain. Because we felt happy ... then my hair got all wet.'

'Happy, yeah, and you're supposed to go to the party looking like that.' Her words sliced through the air.

She stared at Cherise, 'Look can you do something with this mess or not? We only got one hour.'

Cherise looked away before putting her arm around the child, 'Sit down, darlin'. We can sort you out in no time.' She started up the blow drier and began to part the child's hair, one clump at a time.

Grumpy mother stood nearby, watching her every move. 'Needs pulling out completely straight. Like mine.'

I looked in the mirror at the little girl, seeing her fear and trying to show her some comfort. Again, there was that tentative smile before she closed her eyes, wincing with every long pull of the hot brush, hands clenched, knees twitching, mouth tight.

Her mother rapped at her hand, 'And don't bother with no cryin' neither, like last time.'

Cherise stopped what she was doing. 'Would you like to help yourself to coffee, Mam? Machine's right over there. Make yourself comfortable.'

The miserable woman slouched away. Poured her coffee and sat watching.

Twenty long minutes passed in a sad rhythm of pain. Bunches of frizzy curls, gathered up, straightened to perfection, then set aside. I watched as Cherise with tears in her eyes as she gently squeezed Nicky's shoulder each time, after every stroke of the hot brush.

She glanced at the clock and looked across at me; by this time, I felt as if my head was on fire, 'I haven't forgotten you, love.' She called out to one of the other stylists to 'do a cold rinse and towel dry'. It was certainly a relief. That done I went back to my chair and smiled at the child beside me. Her hair was done. The beautiful curls of a half hour ago were gone, replaced by a long curtain of stiff looking straight hair. She shook it about as she gazed at herself in the mirror.

I leaned over and touched her hand, 'Enjoy the party, Nicky.'

Everyone in the salon had seen and heard what was going on and clapped when they saw the finished result. Someone took a chocolate bar from her handbag to give her.

Even her miserable mother managed a smile as she took her daughter's hand.

'Now that's how good hair s'posed to be – you looking good, girl!'

★

I realised how much the care and maintenance of their hair means to all black women. It is an ongoing issue which brings to mind so many feelings about what is considered to be a potent symbol of feminine beauty. Why do we believe that the pain, the trouble and the cost it takes to make us feel beautiful is so vital to us? I thought of what it signified as the child's mother declared, 'That's how good hair s'posed to be.' Good hair? What effect would that have on her daughter's vision of herself as she grew up?

I was relieved when the treatment was over: my tight curls had been wrenched from their tender growth by harsh chemicals, followed by big hair rollers under the drier to create large natural looking waves. Natural to whom? Even so those thoughts did not deter me from continuing the process for many years.

I felt a strong kinship with every woman in that little salon in south east London.

I was not alone.

Chapter Forty-Two

We wandered through the market for a while and I helped Sonya to carry home the vegetables for the following week. She pointed out all the different vegetables on the way: yams, plantains, green bananas, sweet potato and so many others which I didn't recognise. She promised to cook a big brunch for us the following day.

Some of the street traders called out their wares as people passed by. Their south London accents were so different from those we heard among our fellow students. We paused to look at a tray of oranges; the trader caught my eye, calling out: 'Get yer oranges 'ere sweetheart – tuppence each, an' every one a glassa wine.' We smiled and walked on. Every time Angela and I had oranges after that, we would giggle and chant his words aloud.

Angela and I went to the park later and spent the afternoon disclosing our secrets. I ended up telling her everything – I mean everything – about my life. All about Dad's life and his love of music. She was somewhat perplexed by the description of my mum and her bohemian background. I promised to take her to meet both my parents one day. Finally, I told her about my baby boy and we both cried before walking home.

★

Another delicious dinner was over. Clive kept us all amused as he related so many stories about his childhood back home, proudly stating that his Jamaican home was indeed a very special place.

Things became more serious later in the evening as he began to relate the events of his arrival 'inna England' in 1954. He had to leave Sonya and the children back home with their grandparents and promised to send for them as soon as he was able to find a job and accommodation for his family. When he left, Johny was a small baby and Angela was about five or six.

'Man, that was something else. The boat took about three weeks. After we docked, we all scrambled onto the trains known as boat trains. Sitting there I looked out of the window and my first thought was: but – wait – why they have so many bakeries in England?'

Angela giggled, 'I love this bit, Dad. Tell Sarah why you thought that.'

'Ok, ok, you've heard it all before, but likkle Sarah here want to find out, innit gal?'

I smiled and nodded.

'Well, that's because you only see chimneys in Jamaica where there is a bakery – you know – for the bread ovens. I never knew these people needed to have fires in their houses to keep warm during the winter.'

He shook his head and sighed, 'But I tell you I soon found out when winter come a few months later.'

I couldn't imagine anyone leaving their own country to travel thousands of miles without knowing where they would stay when they arrived.

'So, where did you sleep that first night?'

'I hailed a taxi and when the driver asked me where I wanted to go I had to think fast. I didn't know what to say at first and then I tell him 'jes drop me off where all the black people live.' We all laughed, even though this was no doubt a story that had been repeated many times over.

Johnny piped up, 'Yeah and tell us where you ended up, Dad.'

'He took me to Brixton and stopped right in the middle of

the main street and wished me well, 'This is the place mate, good luck. He took his money and drove away fast.'

'You still haven't told us where you slept Dad.' Johnny was well away, as he rallied his father to keep talking. Not that he needed any encouragement.

'Well now, that's the thing. There I was walking along the street, carrying my cardboard suitcase and looking around me. The taxi man was right, most of the people walking by looked like me. I looked in shop windows to see if there were any cards asking for tenants, but there was nothing.'

'There would have been no chance of that, Dad,' said Johnny grimly.

'I didn't know what things were like then. Anyway, long story short, I hear a man shouting my name from across the street and waving like he wanted me to cross over, so of course that's what I did.'

'Was he on the boat with you?' I asked in all innocence.

'No, it turned out he was an old friend of my father from way back who had come over here for a short while many years before. He let me sleep on the floor in his rented room above a shop for a while, until I get my first job and find my own place.'

I recalled what my father had said about the Jamaican man who helped my grandfather, George Hodges, when he first pitched up in New York City way back in 1923. The comparison was uncanny. I related the story, commenting that when people undergoing similar situations to themselves, recognise the need to help one another.

Clive nodded, 'Yes, it's true. Brothers know they must support each other whenever they can in this world.'

'And what was your first job?'

He stood up and called out something that sounded like one long word: 'mynadoors!' It turned out to mean 'mind the doors', which he had to call out at every stop when working as a guard on the Underground, his very first job in London.

Sonya started to collect up the plates and cutlery, 'Don't bother telling us about the some of the things you had to endure, Clive.'

'You mean about things that people said on the tube?' He grunted. Sonya rolled her eyes seeing that he was determined to continue.

'The evenings were worse, especially at weekends when the drunks were going home after a night at the pub. They came out with all kinda insults.'

There was no need to explain.

'Yep, one last thing, before we go and sit next door.' Johnny and Angela got up to help clear the table. 'Yep, I think one of the most painful comments was from a woman who shouted at her little boy because he was misbehaving: 'Behave yourself or that big black man will come and eat you all up.'

★

We settled down in the sitting room. Clive went straight over to the radiogram.

'OK, and now for a great musical offering from a talented Jamaican musician.'

He had his back to me so I couldn't see what record he chose. Then I realised that the quiet music I thought I'd heard the previous night had sounded familiar. The gentle piano introduction, followed by a tender flugel horn and then the alto sax of the man Dad had been raving about:

'Joe Harriott!'

Clive laughed, 'Wait – how did you know that?' I giggled, 'That's the music we listen to at home. We are a jazz family. I was named after an American jazz singer.'

'Well, blow me down, girl, who would have thought it? And what's the name of the song?'

'"You go to my head".' He sat down and slapped his thigh.

'OK, who's the bass player on this piece?'

'Erm, I don't know.' He grinned as he declared, 'That's the

great Coleridge Goode, another wonderful musician from back 'ome.'

He told me about the famous Alpha Boys' School which produced a number of wonderful musicians who went on to become internationally known.

He played several more tunes by Joe Harriott, as well as some British and American musicians, trying to find out who I knew about and the names of standard jazz songs. We carried on trying to out-do one other for the next hour or so, while the others sat by grinning.

★

I so enjoyed spending time with Angela's family; they always welcomed me to their home and sometimes took me along to gatherings with their friends. It was comforting to spend time with people who made me feel relaxed. I was able to throw off navigational tactics for a while. I also learned a lot about Jamaica. They were very interested to hear about my parents and what life was like living in the countryside. I don't think they had ever come across someone like me; the fascination was mutual. I promised to introduce them to my parents when they came to London on a visit.

Me and Angela worked hard at our studies. Mum's words about doing well often rang in my ears. One evening her dad was waxing in sombre mood as he talked about the importance of study and hard work.

'You have to wield a two-edged sword if you want to reach anywhere in this country.' He looked hard at Johnny, 'And especially for you son, jes remember that. Life is going to be hard for you as you grow into a big man.'

'I know, Dad, you always tell me that.' He stood up and went to get his coat from the hallway.

'I'm going out for a while to meet my mates. I'll be careful Dad, not to worry.'

Clive nodded, hugged his son and sat down.

Chapter Forty-Three

It was the end of my first term. I stood up and looked out of the window for about the last hour of the journey, suitcase to the ready. I pulled up the hood on my duffel coat as we drew into the station and scanned wildly around for Mum and Dad as we slowed down. I was probably the first one to alight from the train and couldn't help but weep as they rushed towards me and held me tight, really tight.

I ran up the path as soon as we reached the house and spent some time walking slowly from one room to the next to check that nothing had changed. Thankfully it hadn't, apart from the addition of one of Mum's most recent art works which hung proudly above the fireplace. It was clearly a homage to music. She had used clumps of bright paint for the background and stuck on top was a figure made of twigs bearing a vague resemblance to a man blowing into an instrument held high above his head. I wasn't sure if it was a saxophone, a trumpet or perhaps some other musical instrument that I wasn't familiar with.

When Terry and Maureen came over on Christmas Eve, it was duly praised by us all. We all thought it was beautiful, although Terry did point out that he hoped the glue used to stick the twigs on would be strong enough to prevent them from falling into the fire.

My new hairstyle was the subject of much discussion over the holiday. Maureen was keen to find out the name of the product that could make such a dramatic transformation until she was reminded that she wouldn't have a need for it among her clients. Dad stared at my hair and tried to ruffle it back into its previous state as Mum mourned the loss of my 'curly flowers', while dabbing her eyes.

I went on at length about the lectures and the copious reading list and the other students. I didn't mention that my social life was quite sparse until Angela and I began to do things together. I told them about her family and brought out the treasures I had bought in the market a few days previously. I'm not sure that we cooked them properly as we weren't sure which of the spices to use. The plantains I brought had gone soft and soggy, so Mum decided to try fry normal bananas instead, We all had a good laugh as the pan ended up being full of mushy yellow stuff; the dire consequences hardly lending themselves to an appealing meal. I suggested that hopefully Mum and dad would meet Angela and her family one day and sit down to a real Jamaican meal.

Christmas came and went too quickly, it was soon time to set off again for London. It didn't feel quite as painful as the first time as we looked forward to visiting our beach sanctuary next time I was home, depending on the weather.

Chapter Forty-Four

We had just reached the station when a glossy black car drew up right beside us. I looked across as the occupants all climbed out. Julie Penrose and her parents. Julie and I both paused for a moment before approaching one another, embracing as if we'd just completed a fifty-mile race on one leg. We both burst into tears, linked arms and started gabbling away. Both sets of parents stood by, nodding politely at one another and looking as if they were not sure what to do next. Mrs Penrose managed to squeeze out a painful smile and began searching around in her handbag as if she were looking for the crown jewels.

Julie and I marched ahead across to the opposite platform. Behind us the parents tried to make small talk and declared without much conviction how pleased they were to have met up 'at last'. Although Mum managed to make sure to announce that I was going back to London to study; 'I expect you already know that Sarah is training to be a teacher?' The questioning tone at the end of her words were met with a gritted-teeth kind of, 'Oh, lovely', from Mrs P.

The train was due within minutes. After a few hasty hugs and goodbyes Julie and I climbed aboard. Mr Penrose began pointing towards the front of the train and mumbling about Julie's reserved seat in First Class. She dismissed him with a flick of her hand. I couldn't resist a smirk as I noticed Dad rolling his eyes.

★

I noticed a sparkling ring on Julie's left hand as she hoisted up her suitcase. She took off her coat; she was done up like a dog's dinner, tight red skirt, high heels, thin chiffon scarf tied to one side. She looked somehow more grown up than I expected. Perhaps this was the accepted first-class traveller look. I felt quite casual in my flares and baggy top in comparison. Or maybe I was too cool …

We settled into our seats and for a moment or two neither of us knew where to start.

'So, Jules, I can't help but notice the ring on your finger. Tell me all your news.'

And so she began. Galloping off like an excited racehorse she told me about her beau, who had been employed by her father's company. I didn't get to find out what his job was. She poured a cascade of information around my head. She was not the girl I remembered from our time together:

She and Jeremy hit it off straight away – smoothing aforementioned ring as she talked,

Jeremy's father was the son of one of her dad's management team,

Jeremy drove a something car – (Can't remember what make she said),

His parents owned a swanky house overlooking the river, with its own private beach and a causeway for their yacht,

The yacht was named …? (I missed that bit too),

Jeremy's parents also had an apartment in London; an aunt from Scotland was living there for a while and Julie was going to stay with her for a few weeks,

The aunt was going to help her choose a wedding dress and …

I interrupted her, 'Why don't we go down to the buffet for a drink, Jules?'

We sat at one of the small tables near the windows and ordered vodka and coke. Julie began to slow down by the time we'd had a couple more. She got rather spikey and non-committal

171

when asked about 'barbecue boyfriend' and didn't want to recall whether or not he had fathered her baby. It was made clear that Brightview baby talk was not a subject she wanted to discuss. Being at a loss, I wasn't sure how to respond. I had hoped that we would be able to reflect on our time together and perhaps comfort one another at the terrible pain and loss we had both shared. And I wanted to tell her how much I had appreciated her company and her friendship.

She got up for more drinks as I began to tell her about my teacher training experience and tried to relate a few anecdotes. I didn't tell her about Angela and her family because I realised I may as well have been talking about aliens from another planet.

The train was due to reach Paddington within a few minutes. We were both drunk by then, having hastily exchanged addresses on a couple of serviettes given us by the bartender. We charged along the gangway, grabbing hold wherever we could as the train swayed from side to side, panicking as we tried to remember in which carriage we'd left our things, glancing up to find our suitcases as we lumbered along.

We finally alighted and paused for a moment before hugging one another with promises to keep in touch before we went our separate ways. I looked behind me a couple of times as I walked away but Julie didn't once turn around. I watched her teeter off on her high heels towards the taxi rank before I took the steps down to the underground. Whatever we had once shared was relegated to the past.

Chapter Forty-Five

I was keen to get to know more students and joined a couple of extra-curricular activities, namely, the drama club and the music club, run by two students in the year above: Rosie and Carole. They were both so enthusiastic and self-assured. I wanted some of that confidence to rub off on me. It had taken me a while to realise that if I was to make the most of my new life, the only way was to get out there and do it.

Drama club members met every Wednesday evening in the common room. It soon became clear that many of the others were familiar with plays and playscripts, particularly those who led city lives. Everyone was asked to bring an excerpt from one of their favourite plays and give an introduction to the story before reading their favourite speech aloud to the room.

I'd never been to a real theatre in my life apart from going to a pantomime in a church hall one year. The fourth and fifth form girls at school performed a play every year but I'd never had the courage to audition, and I missed my years in the sixth form due to my 'mistake'. During the miserable time I spent catching up with my A-Levels I didn't have the motivation to join anything, nor yet to be socially visible.

I watched the other students strutting their stuff for the first couple of Wednesdays and spent several evenings in the library trying to find something suitable, until it struck me of course:

who better than Shakespeare? I remember reading a few of his plays in my third and fourth years at school. I didn't much enjoy the histories and the comedies were fun, but my favourite of all was a speech from *The Tempest*.

It was my turn to make a presentation. I was quite nervous to start with but began to warm up. I talked about the background, the characters in the play, especially Prospero and his magical ways, even though everyone was no doubt familiar with the story. I had practised the reading over and over again in front of the mirror and was pleased to render Caliban's words with sincerity and strong feeling.

> *'Be not afeard. The isle is full of noises,*
> *Sounds, and sweet airs, that give delight and hurt not.*
> *Sometimes a thousand twangling instruments*
> *Will hum about mine ears, and sometime voices*
> *That, if I then had waked after long sleep*
> *Will make me sleep again; and then in dreaming*
> *The clouds methought would open and show riches*
> *Ready to drop upon me, that when I waked*
> *I cried to dream again.'*

After the reading, I felt my body swell with pride and emotion. I looked out at the gathering before me: these were people who would go on to spend their careers in helping children and young people to enjoy and achieve the best they could from life.

I put my notes aside and instead spent a few more minutes talking about the power and beauty of Caliban's words: he who was merely a slave and the son of 'the damned witch Sycorax' who had been banned from the island.

The room fell quiet for a moment or two, until someone piped up that maybe it was time for us to go to the pub.

★

I thought I might as well join the music club too. Those who were lucky enough to have a small record player would invite others into the common room on Saturday nights. If not, a group of us would go out to listen to live music. I was keen to make more of a contribution and enjoyed our trips to various venues to watch and listen to a variety of all that was available to us in London.

Someone suggested that we go and listen to some classical music, so the following week we went to a damp little church in east London to hear an astounding choral piece: Verdi's *Requiem*. It reminded me so much about Dad's love of choral music. It was so beautifully sad and powerful that a couple of us shed a few tears by the time it reached 'Lacrymosa dies illa;' the soaring soprano being met by the chorus, a blanket of comfort, rising then diminishing into sadness. However, that might have been because we spent a couple of hours in the pub beforehand.

The following week, Charles, a student affectionately known as Charlie, persuaded us to go to Bunjie's Folk Cellar. It was right in the centre of town, and I was quite excited at the prospect of going somewhere fancy. I was disappointed that it really was in a cellar, far below ground, hence the name …

We went downstairs to a shabby-looking place, with posters stuck over the walls and a bloke with big hair, playing a guitar and singing. The others were raving about how cool he was, how musical and how talented. I hesitated to comment, because I thought I must have been missing something important and didn't want to look like an uninformed idiot. Unfortunately, his music simply reminded me of an image you might see on TV of a group of people sitting around a campfire singing old songs, reminiscent of an historical idyllic past. I couldn't relate to what was seemed to be nostalgic memories of a yesteryear entrenched within a heritage that eluded me.

Chapter Forty-Six

Charlie and I first got chatting at the music club and found that we had a lot to share. He always made a point of coming up to sit beside me at the end of the evening, his long legs spread apart as he pushed his floppy brown hair to one side and adjusted his glasses. I couldn't be sure if that was because he was shy. He was very interested in my broad experience of jazz and my appreciation of choral music.

He and I became good friends; I particularly liked the fact that he seemed more open minded than many other people I'd met, and took everyone at their face value. He didn't immediately ask where I came from or how I had ended up in London. I didn't feel as if I needed to behave in any particular way in order to feel accepted. His outlook taught me to reflect on things which I'd previously considered as alien to my understanding of the variety of cultural experiences available.

He invited me to an event on a riverboat after three or four weeks. It didn't occur to me at the time that our first trip out together was probably intended as a proper date. I liked him a lot and was flattered that he asked me, although I wasn't sure how I felt about the other stuff. After all that had happened in my past, I was confused. Would it be a terrible thing if he knew? Would he be able to tell if ...? How truthful would I have to be? Would it prevent him from liking me?

★

It had been chilly with a sight drizzle on and off for most of the day for our so-called date, so the hair problem was a cause for concern during the afternoon. Angela was curious as to why I'd accepted his invitation in the first place. I didn't know why either; I suppose I was pleased to have been asked. She made no comment, but very kindly helped me to run her heated hair straightener through my curls before I went to meet him.

We climbed aboard the boat on the embankment at Charing Cross at seven o'clock on Saturday and chugged up and down the Thames accompanied by a live band and a bar. It was quite windy on the river as the evening progressed and we agreed it would be an idea to have a couple of drinks to warm ourselves up. The week before, I had become emotional and silly after two vodkas and lemonade in the pub, so I resolved to be careful. Apart from the occasional glass of wine with Mum and Dad, I was not used to drinking alcohol, since it clearly disagreed with me, but I did have quite a few wines that evening and ended up trying to teach him how to jive. When the band started up with Chubby Checker exhorting us all to do The Twist, a girl climbed onto the bandstand to demonstrate and we all joined in. I tried to twist down low and almost lost my balance, resulting in Charlie grabbing hold of my arms. He still held on to me after the song came to an end.

The evening was almost over, and the boat was returning to Charing Cross. I looked across at the huge, recently built additions to the centre for the creative arts: a design known as Brutalist. It wasn't exactly beautiful but lit by the lights everything looked wonderful to me: the cathedral of St Paul's, the dark chimney of the power station along the bank, the red buses crawling across Westminster Bridge … I had dreamed for so long about what London would be like and I vowed never to leave it.

The band played a slow tune as we approached the pier, and couples began hugging and swaying together. Things suddenly felt rather awkward between us. I was beginning to sober up and decided to look around for my scarf.

★

We sometimes spent Saturday afternoons at art galleries and museums. We enjoyed going to see the latest art exhibitions. Studying the other visitors was just as interesting as they carefully read the informative notes on the wall, before standing in front of each painting, their heads on one side and a gentle nod of understanding to one another. Maybe they pretended to understand the artists' work; we often did much the same ...

We discussed how much we had both loved Verdi's *Requiem* and decided to check out another choral piece. Charlie was very interested when I told him that my dad's choir had sung Elgar's *Dream of Gerontius* and found that it was to be performed at The Royal Albert Hall a couple of weeks later. It was my first visit to that venue and as we came out of the South Kensington tube station and walked towards the building I was overwhelmed by its beauty: the huge round shape, the rust-coloured bricks and the dome above, standing proud in the early evening dusk.

I sat in awe as the tale of Gerontius and his dying moments resounded around the splendour of our surroundings. The power and beauty of all those voices blending together as they plead to the Lord for his rescue him, and his own dying words overwhelmed us both. By the time the voices sang high, 'Go forth upon thy journey, Christian soul', I was in pieces. There was so much that we shared and enjoyed together.

★

Charlie persuaded me to go back to Bunjie's a couple of times. I enjoyed it more than I had done previously because I took the time to listen more carefully to the melodies. The music made me think of the old English folk songs we'd learned at primary school, such as 'Scarborough Fair' and 'The Oak and the Ash', I

178

could sense the connection to the music of that bygone era as we sat in that cosy basement room.

One evening when we were making our way back to the tube, I was trying to describe how I sensed the history of popular English folk song: the plaintive melodies and poignant memories reminiscent of a bucolic past. People came streaming out of the club afterwards, chattering excitedly. One man who had been sitting alone all evening, crossed the road and began whistling one of the songs which had been sung by a woman accompanied on acoustic guitar: 'Where Have all the Flowers Gone?' Charlie started humming the tune along with him as we walked, glancing sideways and raising his eyebrows at me as I put my arm through his.

'I was just thinking about another song we learned at school. Do you know "Greensleeves"?'

He nodded, 'Oh, yes, of course! I remember running outside with the other kids when we heard the ice-cream van. There was always a race to see who could get first to the front of the queue.'

I giggled as I remembered something about 'Greensleeves': 'A girl at school once told me that Henry VII wrote it. Apparently, he was very musical.' I paused for a moment, grinning, 'Don't know how true that is ... because come to think of it, I can't imagine how he found the time; he was too busy marrying all those wives and beheading them one by one.'

He stopped walking and turned towards me, smiling.

'Yes, and that song: hundreds of years old, with a dubious past, is still being played to attract the excitement of innocent children. Oh dear, oh dear.'

He was openly smirking. 'However, my girl, your friend was wrong; I heard a different tale. The song came about sometime in the sixteenth century, probably Elizabethan, and more likely the words are a reference to – erm – how can I say – a lady of ill repute.'

I frowned, 'How come?'

'A lady with grass stains on her clothes, suggesting that she'd been rolling about in ...'

I quickly interrupted, 'Oh ... maybe none of the interpretations are true. It's all rubbish anyway.'

Somehow, the spell had been broken and we continued in silence until we reached the tube station.

★

We made a pact that I would introduce Charlie to jazz. Before I joined the music club, I had been out searching for jazz, and came across a famous pub in Chelsea which was well known for promoting some of the best musicians in London. I went a few times by myself for a weekend gig, looking like some sad wench who had been stood up by her reluctant date. But nothing else mattered as soon as the band began setting up their instruments and launching into some kicking music, together with a pint of Red Barrel to give me confidence.

I sat upstairs in what was known as 'The Birds' Nest'. I would sit down with my beer and try to look cool. Sometimes, there was a band including a hefty brass section, and a girl on vocals. Of course, I had to do the 'jazz head' thing, which involves serious nodding accompanied by a straight face, denoting someone who really digs what the musicians are up to, obviously having an informed knowledge of the sophisticated art form. I didn't like smoking, but occasionally tried juggling a cigarette at the same time, not an easy task: beer, cigarette, jazz heading ...

★

Charlie and I were at The Birds Nest one evening and we were lucky enough to see a very popular band: The Sandy Brown-Al Fairweather Band. Sandy Brown launched into 'Lady Be Good' on his clarinet, accompanied by the rest of the musicians on bass, tenor sax, piano and drums, all of them shooting straight into joyful bebop backing. Charlie quietly hummed along to the tune and got stuck into serious head nodding during Sandy's improvisation. I leaned across and whispered 'ten out of ten' to his response.

We decided to go to Ronnies one evening. Being aware that the tickets might be expensive, we decided to take it easy on buying alcohol and would stick to soft drinks only. Charlie insisted that cost would not be a problem and that 'all would be revealed'. We strolled through Soho, looking around at people that I assumed to be 'cool'.

Once inside the club we were pleased to find ourselves sitting quite near the front of the stage. Charlie ordered two lemonades when the waiter came to take our order: I stared at him and frowned. He quietly raised his hand at me and set both glasses in front of him before reaching into his jacket pocket under the table and taking out a small bottle of whisky. He surreptitiously topped up our glasses throughout the evening. Is that what's known as sleight of hand? Dunno. I just know that I was terrified that we might get thrown out, but somehow, as time wore on, my fears grew less and less. Funny that.

For the first few minutes of the song, 'Sometimes I'm Happy' the pianist reminded me of one of Dad's Thelonius Monk records, but after a while it was clear that he was cleverly devising his own sound. By the time he and the other musicians got seriously stuck in, Charlie was duly doing the head nodding thing. I raised my eyebrows at him and smiled at the bass player who caught my eye and smiled back in return.

Chapter Forty-Seven

A group of us decided to go to the pub to celebrate the end of the summer term. I suggested that we go to The Six Bells: I knew a few people there because I sometimes helped out behind the bar on Saturday afternoons and wanted to show off in front of the others. Charlie joined us, trying to make out that he was my boyfriend. I wasn't sure if he was, but we both went along with it anyway. I always knew he was quite keen, but didn't know if I felt the same.

Apart from Angela, Charlie had been my treasured companion for quite a while, and we had a great time going to music gigs. The occasional difficulty was getting back by midnight when the college security guard locked the main gate. If we were out past midnight, we would climb over the gate, and then creep off to our separate ways in different parts of the building, trying to keep quiet. I once tore the hem of my Biba trousers on the sharp spikes; I had bought them with my bartending money the previous week; that put a bit of a damper on the evening, but not for long.

After the others left to go home, we decided to carry on having fun. We were lucky enough to get into The Flamingo to see Georgie Fame and the Blue Flames. When the band kicked into the tune 'Yeh Yeh', everyone took to the floor. Neither of us were very good dancers; Charlie insisted on jigging about directly behind people and pretending to mimic their cool moves until someone turned around and threw a beer over him. The Blue Flames set started at midnight on Fridays and Saturdays and went on until six in the morning.

We stayed until the very end, crept out into the chilly mist, teetered drunkenly over to Hyde Park, and tried to get some sleep under the bushes until a policeman came along and suggested that we move on.

★

Later that morning I got my things together because I was staying over at Angela's house. We had to sleep head to toe on a little bed in the attic room because hers was being prepared for my parents, who were arriving later. They were coming up to London to have a short break and meet the Williams family; Clive and Sonya insisted that they stay at their house. It was to be the very first time we had all got together and we looked forward to a pleasant couple of days.

Angela had snored for most of the night; we were both seriously under the weather. We had a great time though, everyone enjoyed themselves and we all promised to keep in touch with one another over the summer. Carol and Rosie drew me aside during the evening, suggesting that I might like to flat share with them both once I'd finished my training. They were a year above us and well established their careers. I was delighted to be asked and we duly swapped details. My plan was to stay on in London for a couple of weeks longer, now studies were over for a short while. It was ostensibly to earn some money at The Six Bells and start a savings account. In fact, it was so that I could go out and enjoy myself before going back to the quiet beauty that was home.

And of course there was Charlie …

★

Sonya knocked heavily on the little attic door calling out that she had prepared our coffee and toast. We spent the next few hours helping with housework and cooking before my parents arrived. Mum and Dad seemed to get on well with the Williams family. Clive and Sonya cooked up a big Jamaican meal that evening, complete with jerk chicken, rice and peas, and fried plantain, accompanied by a big bowl of salad. I helped Angela to make a jug of carrot juice, being pleased to show Mum and Dad what I had learned from my friends.

★

After dinner, Johnny made his apologies and went out to meet his friend and get his hair cut. There was a lot of discussion between Clive and Dad about their lives, neither of them of them affording much opportunity for the rest of us to make our contribution, but it didn't much matter. Their growing-up stories portrayed such a difference in the way that the legacy of slavery affected the different countries of their birth.

It was interesting to compare the differing cultural background of life in Jamaica to that of black people in America. The island of Jamaica is known as home for mainly black people; the majority of them descendants of slavery who developed their own culture over the years. Clive was on full form once he began to talk about events, words and phrases which had evolved over time in their connection to African languages and cultures.

America is a large country, where black people are a minority, subject to Jim Crow laws and still suffering from the legacy of slavery in so many ways. Dad's conversation with me that day on the beach when he told me about W.E.B. Du Bois' theory regarding Afro-Americans and 'double consciousness' also came up in conversation. Dad very diplomatically related how that back in the 1930s, people arriving from the Caribbean, known then as West Indians clearly differed from black Americans.

★

'Tell us about when we went to Jamaica for Papa's funeral.' Angela looked around at my parents and me, 'It's about the rituals we always follow when someone dies, isn't it, Dad?'

'Yes, it certainly is, baby.' He looked around, 'You ever hear of nine-night?'

Mum, Dad and me duly shook our heads.

Sonya nodded, 'I'm sure Clive will be pleased to tell you all about it. As you can guess, my husband is never shy about taking the stand when he gets the chance.'

We chuckled as she continued, 'It was three years ago. Of course, every country has their different ways of giving their loved one what is known as a "good send-off". Ours is called a nine-night.' Clive held his glass heavenwards, 'This one's for you, Papa.'

He went on to tell us about the event which lasts for nine nights and days in the home of the deceased, because it is thought that it takes that number of days for the person to make their last journey. It is often considered to be the time when they will return to their African descendants.

'People gather together to spend time talking about the person, to share anecdotes, socialize, eat, drink and make music to celebrate the person's life. Nobody needs to be invited.'

Sonya piped up, 'Yes, it takes a lot of food and drink to entertain the visitors, but most people bring offerings too.'

Nodding and smiling, Clive joined in, 'It certainly does!' He looked at his wife, 'And my fine lady spent most of her time stirring the cooking pot.'

'The music was great, there was jazz, ska … oh yeah and that slow, rhythmic music, which the old lady was singing, with her husband on that little drum …' Angela rubbed her chin as she tried to remember what the music was called.

'You mean mento?' responded Sonya. 'Mento is traditional Jamaican folk music, it's very important as part of our culture and our identity. Especially after we gained independence a few years ago. The music is a kind of mixture of Africa and Europe, which I suppose is connected to the history of that time.'

Clive grunted for a moment, then clapped his hands together, 'Yes 1962; now that was a year for real celebration. Really popular, in fact that's where ska music came from.'

He paused, 'And you must remember when the old couple got up and danced the quadrille as they quietly sang.'

Sonya told us all about the quadrille, a dance which apparently developed in the privacy of their slave quarters, as a quaint mimicry of the minuet enjoyed by their plantation owners while they looked on: quiet, servile, timid, their heads bowed. Sonya's rich tones grew softer and slower as she spoke. The room fell quiet.

★

Dad's telling of the occasion when he went back to Harlem to bury his mother was much more muted than Clive's colourful display. He was concerned about how to plan the arrangements for the funeral, being unfamiliar with her friends since he'd left home to join the Allied Forces years before. Gramma died when I was quite young. I loved listening to Dad's stories about her as a brave, compassionate woman who, despite much hardship in life, had made a positive impact on those around her. Mum and I were unable to accompany him because we couldn't afford the 'plane fare.

'Florence sent me a telegram to notify me of Mom's homegoing. That's the word we use in the States. I knew her as Aunty Flo when I was a kid. She was part of life, she and my mom were lifelong friends, having been through so much together.'

He put his head in his hands for a moment, 'But that's another story.'

Mum cuddled up to him. She had been quiet during most of their stay as she absorbed so much about the lives of people she had never been familiar with, although she and Sonia quickly developed a warm friendship, as they chatted and giggled together. 'It's OK darling, you are among friends.'

Dad continued, 'Dear Aunty Flo had planned everything. Back home, the wake usually lasts two or three days, and just like other black folk across the world the homegoing is celebrated with music and dancing, talking and sharing warm memories as well as being unafraid to show their sorrow as they send them on their journey to their African descendants.'

As he talked, he grew increasingly sombre. He spoke a lot about his mother and her hardships, from the time she fled from the South up until she met the man who was his biological father.

Aunty Flo had arranged everything, right from the jazz band which led the service, the musicians all dressed in white with gold trimmings, the food, drink and singing of African-inspired spirituals, which had been learned over decades of oppression.

Just as Clive had done, he held his glass aloft, and said the word, 'Ase', pronouncing it: 'Ashay.' Being unsure of its meaning, he thought it might have been derived from the Yoruba language: going home to peace, God and freedom, but he wasn't quite sure, thinking it may mean the same as saying 'Amen'. We all joined him in repeating the word anyway.

Clive soothed the moment as he asked, 'Looks like your Aunty Flo is a wealthy woman. How come?' Dad glanced over at Mum; she nodded with a grin on her face and gave a small laugh.

Dad went on, 'Well, what I omitted to say was that me and Mom were never quite sure as to how she made such a comfortable living, but hey, that's a tale for another day... Aunty Flo's life was completely different to Mom's, and was never discussed, but they had always been there for one another, so I guess that was all that mattered in the end. We both loved her. Of course, I paid her back for all the money she had spent to ensure that Mom had a good send-off.'

Mum chipped in, 'Yes, it took us a few months though, but worth it. I'm only sorry that I never got to meet her.

'OK, let's cheer ourselves up!' Clive topped up everyone's drink and sat down, holding his chin in thought. I refused any more, the activities of the previous night and lack of sleep having caught up with me. Angela winked and nudged me on the arm.

'You are serious music man, eh George? Your daughter has certainly been brought up to appreciate jazz.' Dad nodded, 'Oh yes, It's the best American music.'

'That's true my man, but we have our own jazzers in Jamaica too you know. You ever hear of Joe Harriott or Coleridge Goode?'

Dad slapped his thigh and the two men continued to discuss the merits of Joe Harriott and what he brought to British jazz back in the 50s.

'The thing is, we don't have the chance to listen to any live jazz down where we live.'

Clive clapped Dad on the back. 'Well, we can soon rectify that. Let's go and listen to some good stuff tomorrow night. Hope you two are not in any hurry to go back?'

Sonia got up to make some tea and brought it in on a tray accompanied by hefty slices of cake, 'I know it's not Easter, but I thought you might like some Jamaican bun. We eat this on Good Friday with cheese. And we don't eat meat on that day, only fish.'

Mum smiled, 'It looks very much like the saffron cake we make in Cornwall.'

Sonya held out the plate, 'It's like hot cross bun, but more spicy. Who wants to try some?'

I sat back, looked around the room and treasured all that I had learned.

Chapter Forty-Eight

We loaded up into Clive's car. Angela, me, Mum and Sonya all squeezed together on the back seat, Clive and Dad in front.

Johnny dropped in during the evening to let his parents know that he would be spending the night at his friend's house; Clive insisted that he come back early enough the following morning to see us off.

Mum was all dolled up in one of her own creations, a dress made of several different patterned fabric pieces sewn together. I think she may have misjudged the length and spent some time pulling it down around her knees for the first few minutes.

I had no idea where we were going, but we clearly weren't going into central London as I chattered on about some of the places I had visited with Charlie.

Mum gave me 'the look': 'You seem to be seeing a lot of this Charlie. Didn't realise you were so close.'

I felt my neck grow hot, 'No, it's not like that, Mum, we're only friends; we both like music and I was thinking of joining a choir which he belongs to and ... well, you know, could be nice to sing and ...'

I tailed off at that point when I noticed Dad and Clive smirking at one another.

★

We drew up outside a big pub in Old Jamaica Road, called The Lilliput Arms. Clive pointed to the road name: 'Yeah, we all know what that name of the road means, don't we?' He grunted.

'Anyway, forget that. I just thought you might like to see a little more of South London before we head into town. This is a lively pub; me and Sonya used to come here every Tuesday night when they have some really good jazz on.'

'That's really kind of you, brother.' Dad was in his element. It had been many years since he had enjoyed live music.

'My pleasure. We came across one of the best jazz singers in the UK. She's usually accompanied by a brilliant band. She's very friendly and always open to requests, usually sings one of my favourite songs. When I told her, she responded by saying it was one of her favourites too. She always included it when she noticed us coming through the door.'

I piped up, 'What's the song?'

Clive touched the side of his nose, 'Maybe you'll find out sometime. It's a secret.'

'She's lovely, quite petite, lively, and talkative. As a matter of fact, I think she and the guy on piano might be quite close, judging by the way they swing so well together.'

Clive intervened, 'Yep, she's not been here for a while though. The bartender told me she's moved on somewhere else. But don't worry, I have a surprise for you all tonight.'

Mum was in holiday mood, 'Wow, sounds good!'

Dad was looking out of the window at the surroundings, 'This is the docklands, isn't it?'

'Yes, the pub's usually busy, full of men coming off the big boats in the docks we passed back there.'

★

We managed to find somewhere to sit while Dad and Clive went up to the bar to get the drinks. Angela leaned across to speak right into my ear, 'See what my dad means about plenty of men

190

in here …' she raised her eyebrows, 'I think we should come here by ourselves one night, don't you?'

'Mmmm', I giggled and looked around. 'Although most of them look too old for us.'

She agreed, 'Oh yeah, maybe you're right. Looking forward to hearing some live music though.'

I noticed Clive talking to a man at the bar. He was the same shade of brown as me, tall and distinguished, wearing a moustache. He looked about the same age as Dad and it appeared that he and Clive knew one another. He held Dad's shoulder for a moment after they shook hands, but after a short conversation the man quickly downed his drink and waved goodbye to us all as he passed by.

They came back with our drinks; Sonya passed them around. 'Isn't that the same man we spoke to a couple of months ago, Clive?'

'Yes, it is. Nice fella. He's rushing off to catch the overnight train back to his family. Think he lives somewhere down your way,' looking across to me and my parents. Dad responded, 'You don't say, well, well, how about that …'

'Can't remember exactly where it is. He's an engineer on one of the big ships that docked earlier – came in from Paris a couple of hours ago.'

Mum and I smiled and nodded, delighted to think that there were other people like us who lived in our part of the country.

★

Clive was looking at his watch, 'OK folks, let's make our way up to Soho. Our trip's not over yet.' We finished our drinks and got back in the car. I glanced at Angela and squeezed her knee, I was that excited. Central London was buzzing with activity as always, but Clive was able to find a tight spot to park in a side street and we walked over the Ronnie Scott's Jazz Club. There was a queue at the door, but we managed to get in and sat within good view of the stage.

It was a wonderful evening, sitting in that world famous club, the red lamps on every table casting arcs of brightness into the alluring jazzy atmosphere. Norma Winstone, the singer gave a superb rendition of 'Joyspring', during the evening. Her ear for rhythm and dynamics of each song cleverly matched by the technical expertise of the pianist, the bassist and the drummer. She introduced them all: Gordon Beck the pianist, Kenny Baldock the bass player and Alan Ganley the drummer. The audience whistled and applauded as she named each one. She gave a little wave in our direction when she finished singing 'Joyspring,' much to Clive's delight, who insisted that she must have spotted him in the audience.

Chapter Forty-Nine

Carol and Rosie had gone shopping along the Kings Road and Carole was convinced that she saw Mick Jagger going into the Chelsea Potter pub. They also spent a couple of hours wandering around Kensington Market. It was Rosie's first visit to Biba and she came back with a dress, a waistcoat and some strange looking make up. Somehow, they had both managed to get the day off from school. I didn't ask how, what or why.

★

'There you are. We were wondering where you'd got to. How was it then?' Carole gave me a hug as I walked through the door.

Rosie helped me off with my coat, 'Come on tell us all about it, love. You're late.'

They were both bedecked in their pyjamas with cigarettes on the go after their busy time in Chelsea. The place looked as if they'd had a tidy up; there was even a bunch of flowers leaning sadly to one side in the toothbrush cup from the bathroom, temporarily gracing the centre of the dining table.

Carole gestured towards the food, 'Ta-da! We thought we'd cook your favourite for supper.' They both referred to the evening meal as supper, whereas at home the evening meal was known as our tea. I soon got used to it: two posh girls with lives as different to mine as salt is to sugar.

'I stayed late to straighten out the classroom for tomorrow. My feeble requests in asking the kids to tidy up didn't quite work.' I threw my bag on the sofa and flopped down. 'Most of them mooched about and one little girl smugly announced that "Mummy always does the tidying up."'

Rosie laughed, 'Don't worry love, you need to trick them somehow. I stand near the blackboard and write down the names of those I see who are trying to be helpful as they've been asked. Works a treat.'

I sat up, 'Yeah, I'll try that … then a couple of the older teachers waylaid me as I was on my way out. They wittered on as if they've both been at St James' since it was built in the last century. Sounded like it anyway … crikey.'

Carole was fiddling with the plates and crockery. 'OK, girlies, let's sit down and eat. I even bought a bottle of wine to celebrate Sarah's entry into the rigorous world of teaching.'

We devoured our spaghetti bolognaise washed down with shiraz in less than an hour.

The difference between my childhood as compared to those of Carol and Rosie was glaringly obvious. It took me a while to realise that their confidence was engendered by the unspoken knowledge and calm assumption that the world belonged to them. Over the years, I learned a lot about how diverse groups of people living in a big city like London make their way through life, and the issues and attitudes that arise.

I was disappointed and perplexed when Angela wasn't keen on joining the music and drama clubs with me. When asked why, she simply mumbled that they were different from the people she felt comfortable with. I didn't persist, but often pondered on how she saw her own place in the world. Could it be because my family was different from hers? Is it because she could only feel at ease within the confines of her home and close family friends?

I was diffident on the first few occasions. Carol and Rosie immediately befriended me, but their open demeanour and cordial welcome left me feeling frustrated and embarrassed. At first, I considered them to be patronising but after a while I felt able to trust their genuine intentions. The three of us often went out together, wandering around the city and taking delight in the wealth of cultural activities on offer.

They both started their teaching careers in the same school. I thought it seemed rather coincidental but decided not to ask too many questions. I only knew that Carole's dad had some connections with the establishment. It was an expensive independent school, set in a leafy area beyond the tube map. Rosie's dad had bought her a small car and they set off together every morning to the place where trees grew freely, and all the pupils had homes with gardens. Rosie showed me a few photographs of her class; the little boys wearing long shorts, smart blazers and side partings, the girls in starched gingham dresses, their hair tied in neat plaits.

They often regaled me with tales of their teaching days, warning me of how tough it would be, and relating anecdotes about the children and a few overbearing parents. They were good fun though. We vowed that we would always be friends, no matter what the future held for us all, and lived quite happily together. We looked out for one another, sharing domestic chores, cooking; advising and listening when things were particularly stressful at the chalk face.

Chapter Fifty

I was attempting to get my class of seven-year-olds into a quiet line at the door ready to go into the school hall when Batman came running down the corridor. Myself and the teacher in the room opposite rolled our eyes at one another as we calmly maintained order.

St James was a Church of England school, and Jeremy the local Curate visited every Friday morning to conduct assembly. He was quite a young man and clearly thought turning up with some fun idea on each occasion would get the kids on his side. His black cape fluttered behind him as he ran, calling out if Batman really could save us all from disaster; his longish dark hair, which one might consider to be less than appropriate for a man of the cloth, fluttered about his neck. I wondered how he would make the connection with Jesus as our Saviour once we were all sitting down to hear his words of wisdom.

Elizabeth happened to be nearest the door; she immediately burst into tears as he galloped past, while most of the children whooped and shouted. She was a shy, nervous child, and sometimes missed Jeremy's performances, preferring instead to sit in the secretary's office looking at a book. I should have remembered to send her on an errand beforehand. When I mentioned my concerns to the headteacher, I was told in no uncertain terms that it was not my place to criticize a man of God.

The children were finally settled, sitting quietly and cross-legged on the wooden floor, with the staff sitting in chairs along the walls. Jeremy had calmed down somewhat and tried to be more serious and curate-like as he talked. I looked up at a cloud drifting past the window. Apparently during Victorian times, school windows were inserted high up on the walls so as not to distract the pupils, which is a pity.

I once came across a German book for children in a charity shop entitled: *Struwwelpeter*, written in 1845 by Heinrich Hoffmann. It was full of stories written to frighten children into behaving appropriately, each tale relating what happens to the characters if they don't. The one I remember most is the horrific story of a little boy who wouldn't stop sucking his thumb: Little Suck-a-Thumb. Since he wouldn't or couldn't stop; *'The door flew open, in he ran, the great long red-legged scissor man ... And caught out little Suck-a-Thumb. Snip snap, snip, the scissors go and Conrad cries out oh, oh, oh!'* Horrific stuff! I vowed that I would always treat the children in my care with compassion, consideration and patience.

I thought about the previous three years: sitting in lectures, scribbling notes which I found difficult to read afterwards, attending seminars, discussing the variety of ways that children learn, writing essays about child development, doing the research for my final project, and so much more.

I was nearing the end of my first term as a newly qualified teacher. The studies had been demanding but stimulating, and I loved every minute.

The reality of being presented with thirty small people whose daily lives and learning depended on me, my skills and effectiveness was a privilege and a huge responsibility. It meant making allowances for the varied personalities, concerns, and levels of learning abilities. I soon realised just how much I learned from the children themselves.

★

I looked across at Derek as he rolled his grey socks over down to his ankles, first one, then the other … one – then the other. After a moment or two he carefully rolled them back up again. And he had a habit of tilting his National Health spectacles back up onto the bridge of his nose. Clearly Batman had not made much of an impression on him that morning. He caught my eye and gave me a lopsided smile.

As well as whole class teaching, I tried to ensure that every child had the opportunity to take the lead in small group activities. I saw it as a tool in helping to build their self-esteem. Derek struggled with learning, had problems with his reading, and was seemingly terrified of mathematical problems involving more than two digits. But the dear boy had other beautiful qualities. He was the child who was always the first person to comfort anyone else who was upset in the playground. At lunchtime, even though his packed lunch looked less filling and healthy than it should be, he had clearly been taught at home to share with others.

We spent the afternoon enjoying a variety of activities as decorations for our room at Christmas, and also to make a contribution to the main hall, which would have the group leader's name displayed in the corner. It was customary for each class to be walked around the school in the morning on the day of the nativity play to admire everyone's work.

There was a lot going on in the classroom: a collage of a star shining above the stable in one corner, a group making paper chains, others painting pictures of the various characters in the story, including the sheep of course, and a few sewing cross-stitch messages related to the season. The letters were sometimes difficult to read afterwards and the phrases not quite in keeping with the expected tone of Christmas messages:

'Jesus was special.'

'Mary was really, really tired.'

'Baby Jesus didn't have any clothes on.'

'The kings walked an awful long way to see the baby.'

It was unanimously agreed that our piece for the hall display would be the big wall collage. I chose Derek to be the group leader: a role he would maintain during art and craft afternoons until the project was finished. He rose to the occasion with pride and compassion.

★

Dominic was late again. I was in the middle of calling the register when I heard his plaintive tears outside. I asked the others to be quiet as I stopped ticking off their names and went instead to the door.

His mother shook her head in despair as she edged her son through the doorway before rushing off down the corridor, dabbing her eyes with her sleeve. I sat him down in the book corner with the other children. We always started our day sitting together on the rug: a warm and friendly way of connecting before we went about the business of the day.

'Why is Dominic crying?'

I duly dispensed 'the look' at the speaker and paused for a brief moment before I continued to check off the register. Said speaker, Fadeke lowered her head, looking suitably humbled, while Derek gently shifted across to hold Dominic's hand.

I closed the register and brought out my shopping bag from behind a cushion and held it up. 'I'm sure most of you did your homework last night in practising your reading.'

Dominic sighed quietly to himself.

'Well, I did my homework too.' I tipped out the contents of the bag.

'Zig-zag books. I made these while I was watching TV last night.'

'What did you watch? What are they for, Miss? Are they for us?'

'Yes, they are, Fadeke.' I held one of the books up, 'As you can see, each zig-zag book has six pages which you are going to share with a partner. There are thirty children in our class, so how many books did I have to make last night?'

Dominic's hand shot up, 'Fifteen.'

'Yes, well done Dominic.' Derek patted his friend's back.

'But what did you watch, Miss?' That was Fadeke.

★

Dominic's mother was at her wit's end regarding her son's progress. She had dropped in to see me a few days before while he was outside kicking a ball around. She was very anxious about his learning, telling me that every evening when she asked him to read to her, he insisted on standing outside on the balcony of their flat, shouting out every word as he turned the pages of his reading book, hating every letter and shape of the words. I tried to reassure her how well he was doing in mathematics, art, music and so on and promised that I had planned activities to encourage Dominic and other children with their reading.

She was horrified when I said that he didn't need to bring his reading book home for a few weeks until he felt more confident. I suggested instead that perhaps he would develop his love of books if she were to read to him every night instead. I picked up a couple of books from the shelf that Dominic might enjoy. She flushed and hesitated for a moment before shyly admitting that she had been a slow learner at school and had spent many years trying to hide her shortcomings. We decided instead that telling him a story would be comforting for them both at bedtime.

While I was busy making the booklets the previous evening, I had thought carefully about which children I would partner together. I thought that they could all benefit by working alongside others sometimes. Shy Elizabeth would surely appreciate Derek's kindness and Fadeke would make a good partner for Dominic. Within half an hour, the class was divided up into pairs.

★

Dominic's mum's confession reminded me of my first opportunity at teaching, before finding a permanent job at a primary school.

I had only just graduated and was wondering where and how to start applying. A friend of Carole's told me that the local community centre was looking for someone to support adults in improving their reading skills for two evenings a week. It was only a temporary position until such time as they could appoint a permanent teacher.

I felt rather nervous at first, being in the position of teaching people years older than myself, those who had to constantly negotiate their daily lives. It was quite a small class of about a dozen brave people, led by myself and Sylvia, a wise and experienced woman. It took courage to turn up every week, but we did all we could to be encouraging and tried make everyone comfortable, the lessons usually ending with cups of tea and cake.

We all decided to have a small party at the end of the course where everyone would contribute to a buffet and take turns to read aloud to the class. When the evening arrived, we were all quite nervous since this would be the first time that the students would have ever been asked to read aloud. Each person began with a couple of sentences, talking about how their lives had been blighted. There were some sad tales of those who would have to pretend that they had mislaid their glasses or were too busy to help their children, when they came home with a letter from school or asked for help with their homework. A couple of people made silly jokes which helped to lighten the mood before reading their chosen piece. By the end of the evening there was a lot of hugging and back slapping as we all made our congratulations. Sylvia and I dabbed away our tears as we cleared up the dishes after the students had all gone home.

Chapter Fifty-One

Rosie, Carole and I enjoyed entertaining friends at home, evenings which usually included sharing a big pot of clumsily cooked food, accompanied by an abundance of wine and beer. Some of our guests were teachers and a couple of Rosie's friends who worked in the financial sector, those being the ones who provided the most expensive wine. Charlie began to take an interest in the world of big finance. That's when things began to subtly change between us. Up until then he was quite content with our lives, sharing our musical interests, sitting in the dark caves of stimulating jazz or clutching hands when a beautiful mix of human voices reached the rafters, bringing tears of pleasure and sadness, or some other heartrending music piercing our bodies with joyful pain.

★

The advent of a different kind of jazz, formed by some South African musicians, had come to Britain during apartheid. I was chatting to one of the musicians at The Six Bells, who had been very impressed when he went to see an ensemble called Jabula at The 100 Club. Me and Charlie didn't want to miss out on anything and decided to go and see them as soon as we could. We strolled along Oxford Street, found the building and walked down the dark stairs into the club.

The audience went wild once the band began playing; the lively, complex rhythm and stimulating melodies were astounding. Some people couldn't resist getting up and having a little dance on the spot as they revelled in music probably unfamiliar to most of us. I couldn't resist approaching one of the band members during the interval, a saxophonist by the name of Michael Bami Rose, known to his friends as Bami. It was obvious how much he was enjoying the gig; his body was on the move throughout and his solo spots full of joy and fun. I discovered later that he was one of the few UK jazz musicians who had experienced working with Jabula. I told him how much I looked forward to seeing him perform again one day.

★

We were halfway through dinner when Rosie made her announcement. She and Carole glanced across at one another; it was clear that Carole already knew what was to come. The two of them were very close and often went out together or spent the occasional weekend at a cottage in the Cotswolds belonging to Rosie's dad. I usually spent my free time with Charlie, or sometimes went off somewhere with Angela and her family.

On one occasion my flatmates took me with them for a long weekend during the summer break. There were seven of us altogether, including both sets of parents. We went for long walks and savoured the beauty of the countryside. As we strolled along, I learned a lot about their childhood experiences. The evenings were somewhat less enjoyable. Rosie's dad was very interested in me and my background. It was like being cross examined, his patronizing attitude making me feel uncomfortable. My friends could see that I was squirming, trying hard to lighten the conversation.

The lives of those whose place in the default position is acceptable and unquestionable uncovered a gaping pit. But whatever our futures held for us we were a team, confident that we would always remain friends.

Carole stood up, waving her glass around, urging Rosie to 'spill the beans' about her news. Her announcement engendered a ripple of amused shock-horror at the very thought of moving out of the city we all considered to be the hub of the universe: she had been offered a management position at an independent school outside London. It also meant that we would have a spare room to let to anyone who may be interested. Donald raised his eyebrows at Charlie giving him a slight nod at the same time. There were yet more beans to spill as he urged Charlie to disclose his own news.

Apparently, Donald had introduced him into the exciting world of high finance. Charlie had already handed in his resignation as a maths teacher to join the band of high fliers in the traders' world, which he had wangled with his friend's glowing reference and so-called 'insider information'. He hadn't discussed it with me; I had no idea of his plans, even though I knew he was unhappy with his teaching post. He grasped my hand under the table and turned to look straight into my eyes.

Chapter Fifty-Two

Mark had a flashy job in the City, and his wife Becky owned and managed a trendy local bookshop. They were out having lunch with a couple of friends from the golf club and asked their son to come along too but he wasn't keen. Their friends were nice enough, but for Kenneth the thought of Sheila stroking and rubbing his hair made him cringe with embarrassment every time they met.

His skin dark and gleaming, the handsome, gangly thirteen-year-old lay on his bed, arms linked above his head as he thought about how he might spend the afternoon. His plans to meet up for a kickabout with a couple of school friends hadn't worked out. His friend, Rob was supposed to have 'phoned that morning to arrange when and where they would meet, but in the end, he couldn't make it.

He looked around his room, cluttered with games, books, posters on the wall of musicians, sports stars, and film actors. Life was comfortable; he had all that anyone could need. Their house was warm, wealthy and spacious, although he was often reminded how lucky he was. He remembered asking for a new bike for his eighth birthday; having noticed other kids his age riding them in the park. His parents agreed to buy it on the proviso that he took responsibility for feeding Ruby the cat every day and watering the vegetable patch regularly. His efforts were noted on the wall calendar and ticked off as appropriate for about six weeks. The bike duly appeared on the day as requested. That's when he learned that nothing could be taken for granted and he had his part to play in the running of the home.

He'd been sent to a highly rated prep school, and recalled setting off in a starchy uniform and lurking shyly in a corner for most of the first couple of weeks. He went on to St Benedict's Boys' grammar school after that and was in his third year. An impressive Victorian building set well back from the road, St Benedict's was a proud statement of grandeur for passing drivers as their engines idled during rush hour.

He was about three or four years old when he asked his parents why his skin was a darker colour than theirs; his questions usually passed off with some awkward, silly joke about playing out in the sunshine for too long or other such nonsense. He was told about his adoption a year or two later. They told him that his birth mother was either unable to keep him or perhaps she just didn't like babies very much. Both explanations left him feeling as if he hadn't been worth keeping, but he always knew that his parents loved him dearly and that was enough.

Until now. If he came home and related some of the comments or names from other pupils, he was told to 'ignore it' and they both made a point of demonstrating how much they cherished him. He worked hard at school and was well behaved, very conscious that if there was any trouble it was often likely to be thought that he had been involved, since that had happened a few times since he'd been there.

One incident involved a boy being deliberately shoved against a wall in the yard, resulting in a large bruise on his forehead. The teacher who first arrived on the scene went straight up to Kenneth on the assumption that he was responsible. If he was anywhere nearby, he was always the first one to be intensely questioned, as if his very presence was enough to be considered unworthy of decency.

On another occasion a pupil's locker had been tampered with, his PE kit only to be found later dangling on Kenneth's peg in the cloakroom. It had obviously been planted there, no doubt as a result of him having responded to a bully who'd pulled his kinky hair and called him 'coconut head' a couple of days previously. Several other boys enjoyed using the offensive nickname as they waited behind him in the lunch queue. The key perpetrator was apparently dealt with in a mild discussion about name calling. It had been difficult to explain at home and at school and it was eventually agreed between his parents and the school Principal that Kenneth should have his hair cut very short in order to avoid similar comments.

After a while, Kenneth realized that he would have to choose his friends more carefully and began walking away if he ever found himself anywhere within the vicinity of unacceptable behaviour, deciding instead to spend his leisure time with others considered as 'nerdy' as himself. His parents were pleased; they had high aspirations for him and were pleased to befriend the parents of other well-behaved pupils.

★

They were eating dinner one evening a couple of days later. 'I've been chatting to one of the security guards at work today. Nice chap he is, always polite, with a smile for everyone.' Mark got up from the table and ruffled his son's hair as he spoke; the boy moved his head aside with a groan while Becky shrugged and rolled her eyes.

Dad continued, 'I was asking my mate if he knew any decent barbers where we could get your hair cut … erm … well … properly. Don't think the chap who cuts mine would even know where to start.' He grinned widely while the other two stared back at him. His mum usually cut Kenneth's hair, her skills with the scissors leaving a lot to be desired.

There was a brief silence. 'Well, I just thought that we should get it done after our little chat with the school principal.'

Kenneth pushed his plate aside and went off mumbling about something he had to read for homework.

It was arranged for the following Saturday morning. He recalled how uncomfortable he felt when he and Dad went to pick up his 'mate' at his house and they went off to the barbers' shop. Dad kept up a forced lively chatter as they drove, while the man sat in the front passenger seat, catching Kenneth's eye in the mirror every so often, slowly shaking his head and wearing a patient grin.

The shop was on a quiet street in a different area of south London. The barber's shop was one of a row of small shops, huddled together under old buildings, which looked like apartments. Kenneth noticed how different the area looked when compared with the quiet roads near his home, where every house had the mandatory smart car on the drive and well trimmed bushes on either side leading up to gleaming front doors featuring stained glass windows.

There was an awkward few moments when Dad tried to push an extra five pound note into his mate's hand saying how pleased he was to have his help and advice, blah, blah, blah. The man frowned, said he would stay with Kenneth while he had his hair cut and see him onto the right bus home afterwards.

He and Kenneth smirked at one another as they watched his dad drive away. He enjoyed being able to go on his own regularly every four or five weeks after that. He soon became friendly with the man's family, and met his son who suggested that they get together sometime, but they hadn't got around to arranging anything so far.

★

Kenneth got up off his bed, went over to the wardrobe and began searching around on the top shelf. He scrabbled around behind a load of his outgrown clothes that had been shoved to the back until he found it: the box Mum and Dad had presented when they told him about his adoption.

He could still picture that day. He was about five or six years old, staying in his room as instructed while he waited for them to bring him 'something very special'. He sat on the bed, squinting at the sun slanting through the window. Mum came first and sat beside him holding him tight, her hair dangling across his shoulders. Those hugs always made him feel safe. Dad came in behind her carrying what looked like a brightly coloured shoe box. He sat on Kenneth's other side and slowly opened it.

The lid was covered with bright geometric paper shapes. Inside were tiny baby jackets, covered in fancy stitching, one of the items decorated with what looked like small shells sewn around the edges. Mum picked up the baby clothes, held each one up against his chest, remarking that he was now big enough to be told about the wonderful moment when they became his parents.

He was confused, not understanding how anyone could have two mothers; his piping voice and childish questions met with hugs and assurances as Mum tickled his face with the fluffy things which had been placed carefully around the clothes. The whole ceremony meant very little to him at that age, but he remembered clutching his teddy bear even closer than usual that night, trying to imagine how it might feel to be held by another mum.

The box was put away at the back of the clutter.

★

He lifted the lid off and examined the tiny garments again which looked as though they had never been worn. He put everything aside and found a slip of paper with the written message:

Good luck, little one. I will always remember you.

He read it several times; surely this was not written by a mother who didn't want her baby? He picked up each item, his eyes damp as he studied them one by one. He slowly turned the box around, looking at the patterns made from sticky coloured paper on each side, some bits crumpled and falling off. He turned it upside down and looked underneath, trying to recall what he had noticed when he first saw it as a small boy.

A piece of floral fabric had been stuck over the base. When he looked more carefully, he noticed that four alphabet letters were sewn into each corner. They were almost hidden among the foliage, each one coiled into a design making it difficult to decipher. One of the corners of fabric had been slightly peeled off and underneath was a tightly rolled piece of paper, shoved inside. On opening it, he found a second message, this time written in very shaky letters: *Maybe we will meet again one day.*

Chapter Fifty-Three

Kenneth could always tell when Mum and Dad had probably enjoyed a glass of wine over lunch. Mum usually got all silly and touchy-feely and Dad insisted on telling jokes which were slightly rude and embarrassing.

He had spent a busy afternoon, and wasn't sure what to do next. 'I'm just going to make myself a coffee, shall I make some for you two as well?'

'Sounds like a plan, son, thanks,' Dad called over his shoulder before plonking himself down on the sun lounger. Mum was already spread out on the lawn, with her eyes closed.

He busied himself in the kitchen and went to join them in the garden. Dad sat up to drink his coffee, Mum seemingly drifting off to sleep as she mumbled her thanks.

'So, what have you been up to then? Did you hear from Rob afterwards?'

'No, he was too busy, had to go and visit his cousin or something. I've been doing this and that, just messing about ... I was searching around for a book I read years ago, and found this instead.' He took the small roll of paper from his pocket and handed it to his dad.

His father squinted at the small writing; he glanced up at his son. 'Who sent you this? Where did you find it?' Dad carefully balanced his cup on the grass and waited.

'In the box … the special box you showed me when I was little. That was when you told me about …'

Dad held up a hand to stop him. Ruby, the cat wandered across from her hiding place in the long grass at the bottom of the garden and began nuzzling at Kenneth's feet, looking up, her grey eyes soft as she waited to be stroked. Kenneth picked her up and held her on his shoulder as he gently tweaked her furry neck. The quiet buzzing from the lavender bush seemed to fade away as he watched his father lean forward, with an almost inaudible sigh.

'Look son, there are a couple of things I should tell you', his voice quiet as he glanced across at his wife. 'Let's go inside, I don't want to disturb your mum.'

They went indoors. His father had told him to wait in his room while he went to get something, just like that day years ago. He had been so excited then wondering what amazing surprise his parents had in store as he sat swinging his short legs as the minutes passed. The sun had been shining on that afternoon too.

So much had happened since then: good things, bad things and confusing things. He wanted so much to find out more about who he really was, his questions usually met with reassurances that he would always be their 'precious boy'. Mum came out with the same words every time, taken from a quote she'd read somewhere: 'Yesterday is the past, tomorrow is the future and today is a gift.'

He had to be content with that.

He heard Dad open the door of his study, followed by the sound of a key turning in the lock of his office drawer. Some nights Kenneth was woken up by the sharp squeak of the study door as his father went to make long-distance calls to overseas clients in the middle of the night. He often found it difficult to get back to sleep, especially if heard his parents talking in whispers or quietly laughing afterwards.

Dad came in, handed him an envelope and sat down, saying nothing. After a moment he stood up and went to the window pretending to look out, but slowly turning around to see

Kenneth's response. The boy looked at the envelope, which had obviously been opened before. There were there letters inside. On the front, in very curly handwriting was one word: Confidential. He read the first one in bed that night.

★

Hello little man,

Welcome to this beautiful, yet confusing world. Today is a very special day for you as you leave to live with your new parents. They will love and cherish you, keep you safe and do their very best to ensure that you enjoy a happy and loving home. As you grow up into a man you will realise that things can sometimes be complicated and disappointing, but I'm sure you will find ways of steering a path towards whatever your aspirations might be. Believe in yourself, value yourself and others, and work hard to achieve your dreams. Appreciate the advantages that life can bring and stay brave and confident when they go wrong.

Your biological mother is heartbroken that you must leave her but understands how important it is that you have the opportunities she is unable to give at this stage of her own young life. It's my responsibility, along with her mum, to comfort her and try to help her to meet this next chapter with courage, positivity, and energy.

All three of us will always remember you and keep a place for you in our hearts. We might never have the opportunity to talk to you as you grow up, but we wish you every happiness. But nil desperandum – who knows what the future might bring?

Sending you love xxx

Chapter Fifty-Four

Ever since Kenneth found the second message stuffed underneath the box, weeks previously, he had thought hard about how he could find out more. He lay awake in the darkness, night after night, trying to imagine what his birth mother looked like, and what they might say to one another if they ever met. After a while he began to whisper a mantra into his pillow before settling down to sleep: 'not if – but when, not if – but when, not if – but when'. He was convinced that saying it three times over meant that one day it would really happen, he would meet this elusive woman face to face. Would she recognize him as her son? Would she hug him like Mum? Would she stand back and look proudly at him? Would she be as brown as him? And most of all, would she still love him?

When his mother came in from her nap on the lawn that evening, it had been difficult for all of them. He and Dad had a short conversation before she came in after dozing off in the late afternoon sun. Dad had warned him to take it easy on her. She breezed in, heading for the cold tap.

'My head is pounding, that will teach me – that's what happens when I drink wine at lunchtime and ...' She hesitated as she looked at their faces, sensing something in the air as she looked at her husband and her son.

★

The boy – taut – tense – hands clenched at his sides. Perplexed and in pain, the man looking from one to another – frozen – watching as a schism appears beneath – above – all around, the solid base of love, compassion and care seemingly collapsing before them.

'Why did you both choose me anyway?' In response the woman's confident voice reduced to a murmur as she moved slowly towards the stairs – enfeebled – broken.

★

Since then, the family atmosphere had subtly changed, especially when they sat down to eat together in the evening. The usual discussion regarding *how was your day, blah, blah, blah* took on an awkward tone: three amateur performers working hard to sound real. Dad either gabbled away about his day at the office or made a feeble attempt to praise the food on the table.

An underlying tension as delicate as a spider's web hung about their shoulders; things gradually appeared to level out over the following weeks.

Chapter Fifty-Five

'Now – be careful, you two. Keep an eye on the notice boards and if you get lost just ask any of the station guards, or the bus driver. That's what they're there for.' Kenneth made a rude gesture behind her back, as he zipped up his jacket.

'This is where we live, Mum, we should be able to travel around on our own city. We're old enough now, don't you think so, Rob?' His friend nodded politely.

'Anyway, just be careful up in town, there are all sorts of people wandering about these days. I'm sure Robert's parents would agree.' The boy gave another tired nod.

Becky followed them to the front door. She held her son's hands, looking intensely at him, 'I love you, son, you know that, don't you?' He squirmed, as Rob stood by grinning.

'Yeah, Mum, love you too,' mumbling as he moved away. She stood and watched as the two boys strolled off down the drive.

'Crikey, what's got into your mum, Ken? Anyone would think we're going off to climb Mount Everest.'

Kenneth hesitated to respond, 'It's a long story. I'll tell you all about it. C'mon, I think there's a bus up to Elephant in a few minutes,' striding ahead, his face burning with embarrassment.

It was Tuesday morning during half-term break, he and Rob had decided to make a trip into central London. It was the first time either of them had been allowed to travel into town unaccompanied by adults. They hadn't decided where they might go, just wanted to mooch around and take in the buzz, the noise and the tourists with cameras slung around their necks.

Rob's parents were close family friends; over time Kenneth felt that he could trust him with his secret. It was obvious that he had been adopted, but oddly enough nobody ever mentioned it. They were all sharing a barbecue one afternoon and the two boys slid away upstairs with a couple of beers while the adults got slowly drunk and were gabbling away at one another about seemingly nothing. Kenneth had tried to talk to Rob about his adoption, but they both ended up play fighting instead.

★

'So, come on then Ken, where shall we start?' The boys got off the bus at Elephant and Castle and were making their way to the Bakerloo line.

They looked about deciding where to go first and ended up sitting in Trafalgar Square for a while, eating ice-creams, watching the pigeons wandering about looking for crumbs dropped by the tourists, and splashing one another as they dipped their hands in the fountain.

The next port of call was the cartoon cinema on the corner of Piccadilly and Shaftsbury Avenue, Rob declaring that he had always wanted to go there because you only had to pay once and you could sit and watch the repeats over and over again. The woman on ticket sales insisted that they must sit in the circle, because of their age. They sat for a couple of hours munching popcorn while their clothes dried off. Neither of them was quite sure as to why the downstairs seats were considered less suitable; a few years later, Kenneth understood why …

They took a bus back to the Elephant, tired and worn out as they sat quietly on the top deck, reflecting on their exciting day.

Chapter Fifty-Six

Kenneth and his dad decided to design a centrepiece for the back garden. When he was a small boy, he and his parents enjoyed collecting interesting stones and shells when they visited the seaside. Their findings weighted the car down on their journey home, only to end up piled high against the garden shed.

Mark was trying to follow the instructions on how to mix the cement properly as they discussed what the layout might look like. Kenneth was sorting through the stones, being more interested in the shells. He picked them up one by one as he tried to look up their names in his *Ladybird Book of The Seashore and Seashore Life*. After hunting around he'd finally found the book shoved under a pile of papers. He'd had it for as long as he could remember, the words faded and grey and some of the pages still stoically trying to hang on.

Mark stopped what he was doing for a moment and looked across at his son as he stooped over their precious collection. 'Your mum and me have booked somewhere different for our holiday.' He stopped what he was doing for a moment and looked across at him, as he stooped over their precious collection.

Kenneth sat back on his haunches as he sifted the smaller shells through his fingers. 'You've already booked? Fab – where are we going, Dad?'

'We thought we'd go to Cornwall. We've only been there

once or twice.' He paused for a moment. 'And that was ages ago. Thought you might like it.'

Mark put down his tools, wiped his sleeves across his face, and waited. He noted how his son was beginning to sprout up; his arms had begun to take shape and a very slight fuzz had appeared along his top lip over the last couple of months.

There was so much hanging in the air which neither of them wanted to acknowledge. Their family life had reached a place of relaxed peace and laughter again since that painful evening back in the spring. Even the dog seemed aware of the slight change in tone. He crawled out from under his favourite bush where he'd been dozing and shambled over to Kenneth, who bent down to stroke him before speaking, his brows tightening, his head on one side, it seemed like minutes before he answered.

★

The evening drew on and it was beginning to get dark by the time the project was finished. Tommy, a lively cocker spaniel, had to be shut indoors in case he trod in the cement, while all three of them worked together and created a circle with a hole in the middle. There was a lot of discussion about the shapes, colours and size of every stone before it was carefully put in place. The shells were used to fill small gaps and decorate the edges. Becky suggested that they might find something special to put in the middle one day. They sat around it in the dark, eating the remains of some warmed-up apple pie and drinking tea.

Mark stood up and raised his mug of tea to the dusk. He coughed a couple of times, as if preparing to make a grand proclamation: 'OK, let's raise our mugs. Here's to the "doughnut".' They all tittered before raising their mugs: 'To the doughnut.'

Kenneth went off to bed. He could hear his parents talking and laughing quietly until it grew too dark and chilly outside. He was thinking about all that he wanted to learn about his past.

And about Cornwall. He knew he would need to be patient, and was happy that Rob would always be there for him.

Chapter Fifty-Seven

The weather was benign, Cornwall was beautiful; what could be better?

Mark and Becky had booked a large caravan, so that the dog could come too, and Rob had been invited as well. The journey had occasionally been uncomfortable because Tommy only seemed happy when he could poke his head out of the window and feel the wind playing with his big, floppy ears.

They were into their third day; the first couple of days the two boys raced about throwing the ball for the dog, eating ice-cream or swimming. Mark and Becky were happy to relax and watch them enjoying themselves. The evenings were spent sitting outside and watching the stunning sunset until it was dark before going to bed, looking forward to another lovely day.

Mark suggested they go for a long walk. They didn't plan where they would go, but would drive about until they found somewhere quiet to park and see how many miles they would cover.

They drove across to the opposite coast until they came to a sandy beach huddled between large cliffs on either side. They stopped there for a while to eat lunch and went paddling before deciding to get back in the car to find a good place for walking. Rob got his binoculars out to take a look at the lighthouse. He got quite excited and began telling the others about a book he'd read as a child about a lonely lighthouse keeper.

An elderly lady was standing on the shore looking out at the horizon. Her white hair straggled about her face as she drew her skirts away from the foamy edges of the waves.

She shuffled nearer as they were talking. 'I spec you're on 'oliday. This beach is very popular, we get 'ordes of people from up country every summer. We call 'em "emmetts" – not being rude or anything.' She laughed.

Mark nodded and laughed too. 'Emmetts eh?'

He put his head on one side, wearing a fake frown …. 'Oh, right – I get it. I'm not surprised. After all, everyone knows about lovely Cornwall and how friendly Cornish people are.'

'S'pose so.' She looked at Kenneth and Rob: 'Two 'ansum boys you got there.'

Mark smiled, 'Yes, aren't they? It's their first trip to Cornwall. Do you live nearby?'

'Yeah, lived 'round 'ere all me life. My boys loved it. But they both went off to Australia a year ago … They'll be back though, you mark my words. Why would anyone want to leave all this?' She opened her arms wide, embracing the surroundings.

She paused. 'You know what? I been walkin' this beach every single day, come rain or shine, ever since my old man died a while ago.'

Mark began to offer his apologies when Rob chipped in as he pointed, 'Does the lighthouse keeper still live in there?'

The old lady gazed across at the building, 'No, we call it the Pepperpot 'round 'ere. Hasn't been a lighthouse for a long, long time. Was used as a Huer's hut afterwards. That's where a man would keep 'is eye open to look out for shoals of pilchards.'

'Was he a fisherman?' Until then, Kenneth had stayed quiet, fascinated by the old lady's strong Cornish accent. Perhaps his real mother spoke that way too. Becky stepped forward and squeezed his shoulder.

'No, no – 'is job was to shout out and let the fishermen know they should get out there double quick to get a good catch.'

She started to move away. 'Anyway, better get on and leave you folks to enjoy yerselves. 'ave a nice 'oliday.'

She slowly walked away along the beach towards the towering cliff.

Chapter Fifty-Eight

Beccy and Mark didn't talk much as they drove along. Tommy sat on the back seat, busily shaking off the wet sand stuck in his fur. That didn't go down too well with the boys as they shouted every time they got showered with it.

'What are those big chimneys? There's no smoke coming out.' Rob and his binoculars went everywhere together. 'Oh look, there's a big one up ahead.'

'Erm, to do with the old mine shafts. I think there are a few around this area.' Mark was looking out for a layby where they could park the car safely.

Becky pointed, 'There's a space up there, Mark. We need to stop and get this smelly dog out in the fresh air … Oh, no he just farted … yuk.'

Everyone fell about laughing as they climbed out and took in some deep breaths.

Kenneth gazed around. 'There's a little lane over there. Oh yeah, look Dad. There's the big chimney thing and some old ruins.'

Becky put Tommy on his lead: 'Don't want him running off here, we'd never find him.'

They crossed the road to the entry of what looked like a large area, with ivy climbing up the ancient walls. Ahead lay a vast green expanse all around an area gently sloping down to where a couple of teenage boys were kicking a football. It was quiet, calm, and reminiscent of past times.

They followed the lane, the dog sniffing here and there among the bushes, straining away ahead as far as he could. He stopped for a moment and started to bark, as a tall man came around the corner with a dog, a cocker spaniel like Tommy.

'Alright, alright, calm down, Jack.' He looked up as Becky was trying to restrain Tommy. Everyone stood about as the dogs sniffed about getting to know one another. Mark gestured at their surroundings. 'This is an interesting-looking place. Are you familiar with it?'

The stranger nodded sagely. 'Gosh, yes, this is one of my favourite walks. It brings back a lot of memories.'

He was an imposing looking man, tall and relaxed, emanating an air of confidence and wisdom. Kenneth was fascinated by his mystical aura, feeling shy as he ventured to ask questions.

'Dad said this place is something to do with mining? What's it called?'

'Oh yes, certainly.' He paused and looked around him, spreading his arms to indicate the sombre relics of a past age. 'This area, and much of the land around in parts of Cornwall, once represented one of the most successful businesses in the world – tin mining,' his benign smile gazing down as Rob blew a quiet whistle.

'If you look down there, where those lads are kicking a ball about, there used to be rail tracks, right beneath the soil. There were tracks all over so that the tin could be moved about. Just think, there's tracks zig zagged about in many parts of the county. Folk out admiring the view are probably walking over them as we speak.'

He hesitated for a few moments. 'This place is called the Great Flat Lode. Years ago, in working mines, metallic volcanic minerals were pushed up by fierce underground pressure, the findings appearing at 85% horizontal. In this mine the findings were 35% underground; the rock structure is huge.'

Mark wondered how he knew so much. Perhaps he'd been a miner himself as a young man. But he didn't like to ask him outright. Despite the grey hair and looking so healthy and fit, it was difficult to guess his age.

Rob stared up at the chimney, looking puzzled, 'Why did they need to build that huge chimney? What was it used for?'

The stranger sat on a rock and untied his dog's lead. He was clearly in no hurry, ready to enjoy sharing his knowledge and thoughtfully watching as the two dogs sniffed about in the bushes, sizing one another up with the occasional glance.

'Well, you see they had a steam engine, built beside the boiler house to vent the boiler. They had to pump out the steam. Also, there was a separate stack built to release arsenic into the air …'

Rob intervened, 'Arsenic? Crikey – that's poison!'

The man nodded, 'Yes. They were digging for tin, and the arsenic had to be separated from the tin, before being released. It was even used in cow feed until not that long ago, resulting in cows dying in the fields. Then it had to stop after that. They also dug for copper for about a hundred and fifty years, before it was all gone.'

Mark and Becky stooped down onto the grass, noting how the boys seemed very interested everything the man had to say. Rob was lively and curious and every time he showed his response, they raised their eyebrows at one another with a winsome smile. Kenneth lounged against a tall bush, quiet and reflective.

★

His face serious, he asked, 'Is it true that people came from other countries to learn about mining in Cornwall?' Mark and Becky exchanged a quick glance.

'Oh yes, they certainly did,' said the man. 'They attended the School of Mines, wanting to improve their knowledge. You will recall me saying that it was a very important and successful Cornish industry. They would have learned about what were known as top skills and the management of mining engineering. After they completed their studies most of them returned home to utilize that knowledge. Lots of them came from other countries rich in minerals. I think a few of them stayed behind or went to other places, like Australia for example.'

Kenneth, being particularly curious, 'Which countries were they?'

'Oh, my goodness, they came from all over, parts of West and South Africa, a few from the Caribbean and other places too. The students from Ghana, a country once known as the Gold Coast, would have learned how to mine for gold when they returned home.'

The boy went quiet before speaking again: 'Do you think any of them decided to stay in Cornwall?' He paused: 'It must have been a very dangerous job, especially all those years ago. Did people sometimes get hurt ... or die?'

Becky nodded at her son, reaching over to touch his hand. Only he would consider the dangers to the men below ground. She was proud of his tender concern for others. He was often the first to notice if she or Mark seemed unwell or unhappy. That was why they had both discussed the reason for bringing him to Cornwall for their holiday. After all that had happened some weeks previously, it was only fair that he should be given the opportunity to think about his background. They both agreed that they would try to answer honestly if he began to ask more awkward questions.

The man leaned forward, his hands on his knees. 'Yes, son. It certainly was dangerous. Lots of the miners contracted a serous lung disease, called Phthisis.' When he said it, it sounded like 'tissuss', but then he said. 'It's a difficult word to spell – p-h-t-h-i-s-i-s.'

'And it must have been dangerous going underground and climbing back out again ...'

'Yes. One man had to do what they called "barring down".

His job was to walk along and check if any lumps of rock were dangerous by testing them with a bar, which meant it would be too risky to mine … but that was often no guarantee that they would be safe.'

He gazed over at the expanse of grass ahead of them. 'When you look across this tender green landscape, just think about the young men who would have walked miles to work every morning, knowing that some of them might not get home at the end of the day.'

A quiet melancholy drifted across them as each one pondered on his words.

Rob had been rubbing the fur of the two dogs, he looked up, 'How did they get out again?'

'They used something called a winze in the old days, but part of the shaft would only come part of the way up the mine, so the men had to depend on using ladders. That was risky too.'

Kenneth went over to his father: 'Dad can I go and get that special stone I found yesterday? I left it on the back seat of the car.'

Mark nodded as the boy dashed off and returned with a lumpy stone which he placed in the palm of the stranger's hand, 'This is granite, isn't it? Do you think there's any tin inside it?'

The man turned it over, 'Oh, maybe not. It's well-nigh impossible to tell if there's any tin there just by looking. There would only be about two percent tin in there anyway.'

He held it up: 'Suppose you could possibly see a little bit by the spotting effect on the stone. Granite is a volcanic rock, made up of many minerals and there's lots of different kinds. Locals used to toss a piece up in the air for a few inches, if there was tin inside the weight would be higher. The weight of tin is heavier than water.'

He duly tossed it in the air before handing it back, splayed his hands wide and shrugged his shoulders. 'I'm afraid I can't answer that one, son.'

He stood up and the others followed suit.

Mark was still curious to know about this interesting man, 'Thank you so much for talking to us. How come you know so much about mining? Were you once a miner?'

'No, but I've always been interested in the industry. Since I was about nineteen, I loved steam trains, liked engineering, and took to studying the steam engine houses in St Austell. Then I gradually took an interest in mining history. Been studying it for years.'

The dogs were getting restless, so it was decided to put their leads back on. The man reached down and stroked his dog who clearly wasn't keen to be restricted again. 'Come on Jack, there's my boy, good lad.' The dog stood still as he was told.

Rob piped up, 'Why have you named him Jack? Is that your name?'

The man smiled, 'Now that's a good question. It's because a miner's greeting to other miners was always Cousin Jack.' He smiled at them, 'I'd better get home and give this greedy lad his dinner. Lovely to meet you all.'

As he began to turn away, the man noticed that Kenneth was lingering behind the others, turning the granite stone over and over in his hands before putting in his pocket. He went up to the boy and patted his back, 'You're a good lad and I can see that you want to learn about many things in your life. And believe me, son, I think you will.'

Mark stepped forward and shook his hand warmly as did the boys. Becky gave him a big hug, her eyes damp as she stood back.

He responded: 'Oll an Gwella.'

The others stood silently for some minutes as they watched the stranger and his dog wander away into the distance.

Chapter Fifty-Nine

I had been living quite happily with Carole and Rosie. We looked out for one another, sharing domestic chores, cooking, advising and listening when things were particularly stressful at the chalk face. We entertained mutual friends at home, evenings which usually included sharing a big pot of clumsily cooked food, washed down with an abundance of wine and beer.

Some of them were teachers and a couple of Rosie's friends who worked in the financial sector, those being the guests who provided the most expensive alcohol. Charlie began to take an interest in the world of big finance. That's when things subtly began to change between us. Until then he was quite content with our lives. We enjoyed going to the theatre and art galleries. We shared our musical interests as we sat in the dark caves of stimulating jazz or clutched hands together when a beautiful mix of human voices reached the rafters of the Royal Albert Hall bringing tears of joy and sadness.

We heard on the grapevine that there was some good music playing in and around Brixton and drove down to check out The Plough in Stockwell one evening. The pub had a reputation for stimulating jazz gigs. We got inside and fought our way to the bar; it was obvious why it was so popular. The place was crowded, the atmosphere exciting and lively as the band, 'Evidence' knocked out an array of music reflecting Salsa and African sounds. The pianist was clearly enjoying himself as he expertly broke into the rhythms and spirit of Africa. Charlie got into conversation with the barman who agreed that 'Roland, the guy on the piano' was a brilliant musician and well known for his interest in that particular music.

The following week we came across another pub in the same area. I recognized the tenor sax player: Michael Bami Rose, known as Bami. That evening he and the other musicians played a wide selection of familiar up-tempo jazz pieces.

As someone who can't play one note of music, I'm always fascinated by the way that jazz musicians can share the stage, exchange a few words, for example: 'How about "Night in Tunisia" in F?' and before you know it, they're firing away together. They will glance across at one other, a slight nod indicating that it's his or her turn to take a solo; that musician might launch into eight bars, sixteen bars or even thirty-two bars if they are well away into heady improvisation. The other musicians will support them until it's their turn to shine.

Charlie stood aside smirking as I offered to buy Bami a drink during the interval and asked him to play 'Cherokee' since it was one of my favourites. He raised his eyebrows and grinned at me before picking up his glass and going back onstage. When it was his turn to solo, he really went for it, lifting his instrument up high, his solo riding right along into the thirty-two bars realm. He played with the notes in a variety of ways, in tandem with the basic tune. The other musicians smiled in pleasure and Bami nodded his thanks as the customers called out and whistled in acknowledgement of his talent.

★

Charlie and me.

I'm not sure how it all came about between us. How did our lives blend together so seemingly easily? Did he also feel that something was not quite right, that our partnership was intrinsically wrong? Was it because neither of us noticed, or were we afraid to look?

Maybe it was because neither of us made any effort to look elsewhere.

Maybe it just happened because there was nobody else on the horizon or was it me: the naïve black girl from the countryside with little knowledge or experience of men. Apart from my big secret....

Maybe I was pathetically grateful for his attention. I don't like to think so.

My life had changed; Angela and I did not see as much of one another as before. She had met the man of her dreams quite early on in her teaching career, and moved away to live with him in Birmingham. We continued to exchange Christmas cards for a while, but it fizzled out after a few years.

★

A few months later, Carole had also moved out to live with her boyfriend, and we took the flat over. Charlie was earning good money by then; together with my salary we had no need to let the other two rooms out.

Chapter Sixty

And so it began. I still caught up with Rosie and Carole sometimes, but it was less easy now that they were both living elsewhere and starting new lives. Carole and her husband were ensconced in country living and sometimes popped into London to meet up for dinner or trips to the theatre for the occasional weekend, when they weren't out hiking or discovering stunning countryside haunts unknown to many.

Rosie and her boyfriend got married, became parents the following year and proudly sent us photographs of their son on his birthday. I had long stopped hinting about having a family; somehow Charlie managed to divert the conversation or argued that a baby would have been a huge inconvenience to the life we had built together. I was once on the brink of telling the story about my little boy but thought better of it. We drifted on as usual.

Our city colleagues were all blather, swagger and talk about the economy, money, and cars. The Charlie that I knew gradually became a changed man, as he enveloped himself in their lifestyle. Some days he came home high as a kite, having made successful trades during the day. On other occasions it was clear that things had not gone so well. From what I gathered, there was a lot of air punching and heavy drinking over pub lunches sometimes as they celebrated together. I also got the impression that Donald and some of the others were probably imbibing things other than alcohol, according to Charlie's casual comments.

★

We always made time to socialize with our friends. Charlie became as keen on jazz as me. I told him about the time when Clive and Sonya had taken me and my parents to see two of their favourite musicians at Ronnie Scott's. He was very interested, so we made plans to go, and invited them to come with us to The Phoenix in Cavendish Square which was renowned for its Wednesday night jazz sessions. We picked them up, drove into town and finally settled ourselves down in the basement bar. Clive, Sonya and I were particularly pleased to have the privilege of seeing Norma Winstone perform again, playing with The John Taylor Sextet.

The band played a selection of songs, some of them being John's own compositions, intermixed with a selection from a few of the forever lasting jazz standards. It was a beautiful evening. I was delighted when Norma announced that her next tune would be one of my most memorable songs: 'Round Midnight'. I had been collecting vinyl which included this song for years and have several renditions as sung or played by various musicians.

As Norma opened the first verse, the pianist John Taylor accompanied her warm, sweet voice with full tender chords, as each of the musicians took their turn to enter with similar feeling. I couldn't help but dab away at my eyes as the emotion rose inside me. Don't ask me why.

★

After a while Charlie and I were able to buy an impressive Georgian house in north London and spent a lot of time and money having it decorated and furnished to an elegant standard. I found his choice rather cloying but couldn't complain; we were lucky to be financially secure. I went along with it all anyway since Charlie had funded the whole project. I wondered what his thoughts would be regarding my mother's choice of décor.

We were living as a couple for over a year when Charlie met my parents for the first time. As soon as we arrived we were grandly invited to use their bedroom. The offer was met with some diffidence from us both as Charlie politely offered to sleep on the sitting room sofa, declaring that he often woke up in the middle of the night and might keep others awake, his words accompanied by an imperceptible wink in my direction.

Mum had certainly done her utmost to welcome us. She had prepared a variety of dishes she found in some of Mrs Spargo's weekly magazines, each offering having been honed to her own taste. I contributed a few of the more unusual vegetables from the street market in south London. The meal went down well. Charlie glanced around at the décor and was generous in his praise of Mum's artistic pieces around the house. He and Dad shared their love of choral music, and we played some jazz. Dad was suitably impressed when we told him about some of great musicians we had seen.

The following day was hot and balmy. We arranged to meet up with Terry and Maureen and spent a day at our very own sanctuary. We humped our picnic and swimming wear down the rugged steps. Charlie stopped for a moment, whistling softly as he gazed upon the view. Terry and Maureen were already there, towels spread out on a smooth rock and a couple of beer bottles gently rocking in a small pool beside them. Terry sauntered towards us, smiled at Charlie and nodded as he made a point of telling him that 'only special people' could be allowed to share our secret beach.

I put my head on Charlie's shoulder; here was the man I first met: charming, friendly, relaxed – all those things that I loved about him. Did I just say the 'L' word? Maybe I did.

Chapter Sixty-One

I usually visited my parents at least twice a year, going on my own during the Easter holidays and enjoyed having them all to myself for a couple of weeks. Charlie sometimes came with me during the summer holidays, but he often had important things going on at work and dashed off for two or three days. Dad was always pleased to see us together and occasionally made wry comments about looking forward to 'extending the family'. Charlie's usual response was to make a silly joke while I tried to change the subject.

I had planned to stay longer than usual one summer. Charlie came with me but left for London after a few days. Dad suggested that I give him a pleasant surprise by turning up unexpectedly, so that my 'dear man had someone to go home to' in the evening, the idea being that we would both return to Cornwall when Charlie's duties allowed.

★

I went out and bought a couple of new items which I knew Charlie would like and caught the train up to London early the next morning. I wanted to make sure that I would be in the house before he returned from the office. I put on one of my new dresses and hung about upstairs while I waited. The phone rang and I galloped downstairs to answer just as he put the key in the front door.

I had just picked it up as he stepped inside. He gave me a quick hug, glanced at the phone in my hand, said nothing as he gently took it and put it back on the stand before holding me more tightly. I wasn't quite sure why or what that meant. He admired my outfit, and we went out for a stylish dinner in town.

We spent the evening talking about my parents and making plans for how we might spend Christmas with them later in the year. They were both getting old, and we wanted to make it extra special. We chatted away happily, Charlie being much more relaxed once we sat down in beautiful surroundings. I reminded him of a special gig we'd been to during the previous December. We had followed the career of pianist Roland Perrin since we first saw him at the Phoenix a while ago and were very impressed by his interest and expertise in playing south African jazz.

I came across an article about a big band namely, The Brotherhood of Breath, which had first been put together by South African pianist and composer Chris McGregor in 1969 and performed all over Europe and elsewhere. The band continued to play, form and reform over the years, including several different musicians during over time. We were determined to go and see Roland Perrin when he joined the band at Blackheath Hall in south London.

I sighed, 'Crikey, that gig was such an exciting experience of rhythm, musical patterns and stunning talent on show.'

Charlie held his chin and smiled, 'Yes it was an amazing evening. What's the name of the tune which completely blew us away? Can't quite recall …'

'"Andromeda"! I remember how it went. Roland opened the tune, his hands dancing over the keys, being quickly joined by the heavy brass section. The drumming rhythm was so upbeat and different from the jazz gigs we usually go to.'

'Oh yes.' Charlie was animated. 'And what about the guy on the trumpet who played what sounded like err … can't describe what he did – like a kind of joyful game of music in the background at one point.'

I twirled my glass around and paused, 'He is another one of the British musicians who became part of the band.'

I paused, 'I'd love to see the band again one of these days.

★

As time progressed, the lively, erratic manner that defined my mother appeared to become rather more eccentric. Dad and I kept in touch, by phone and the occasional letter. He always made light of everything when he wrote, describing her as continuing to be the crazy wife that he loved.

There were a couple of domestic disasters as she spent more and more time out in the shed working on her artistic projects, while food was left burning on the stove. I hadn't been aware of the situation, but after a while it was clear that she wasn't too well and needed extra support. I didn't realise until I witnessed it myself. Dad was a proud man and clearly didn't want to ask for support. Apparently, Mrs Spargo had been kindly checking on her during the day while he was at work, but it became clear that Mum needed professional help as time progressed.

Within a few months, it was decided that we would make the appropriate arrangements. Dad gave up his job, but still worked alongside Terry with their second-hand car sales. Mum was very content in the residence we found for her, in stunning surroundings, where warm and efficient people cared for her every need. Dad visited her in the afternoons and kept us in touch, saying that as long as she had her art materials to hand, not much else seemed to matter to her.

Chapter Sixty-Two

Reflections

I had just returned from yet another trip to the charity shop, my chest heaving and my bunions burning. I heeled off my shoes and hung up my Gore-tex, the red one that Charlie bought me as a welcome-to-our-next-chapter gift, when we moved here. I paused for a moment in front of the hall mirror. My grey roots were grinning through the black hair dye, my previously proud curls looking weathered and tired, their tight strands withering with age.

My hair was finally allowed to do its own thing a few years previously, in accordance with what became the fashion for black women. There are some who still undergo what is now termed as having your hair 'relaxed', rather than 'straightened', being conscious that to use the 's' word might indicate a powerful desire to negate one of our most visible racial features, in the struggle to emulate some portrayal of what is considered acceptable beauty.

It saddens me that even my African women friends, their identity secure in the cradle of The Continent, want straight hair; dim memories of their pride and the significance of ornate and complex natural hair styles having been lost or simply rejected over many decades of colonisation.

Since moving down to Cornwall, I had stopped making much of an effort. I stepped back to look at my noticeably more rounded figure, swathed in a baggy blue fleece, my eyebrows having crawled together Frieda Kahlo style … I slid down onto the cold floor and leaned my head back against the wall as I gazed back into the past.

★

Moving back here seemed like the best idea. I went on ahead, so that I could support my parents. Meanwhile, Charlie stayed on in our house, driving up and down to London at weekends while he dealt with work as well as organizing the business of renting it out.

We spent months browsing through estate agent websites searching to find what we wanted. Charlie had always been an urbanite, but loved the trips we made to the south west, discovering and re-discovering favourite beaches, walks and pubs. Standing to gaze across the River Fal on a balmy summer evening was invigorating after the rigours of London stress, work stress, people stress, every damn stress.

We talked endlessly about patio extensions, conservatories, parking, shopping and all the rest. We anticipated doing a lot of entertaining and considered that we needed somewhere with extra bedrooms, and at least two more bathrooms, because our London friends would be sure to want to come and stay. I secretly looked forward to them bringing their grandchildren too, one day. I liked the idea of bashing about in the woods, or rowing on the river in some kind of Arthur Ransome utopia.

The house we found was in view of the river: the perfect home. Once we were settled, I spent my time in checking on Mum and Dad, as well as joining the local choral society. Charlie spent some time keeping in touch with the financial world, with a view to setting up his own business in the nearest town. Meanwhile he got stuck in with managing the house renovations. He created a stark modern interior within its old walls and spent hours in the garden: huge in contrast to the trendy paved courtyard we had back in north London, which was chock-a-block with pots of garish plants we bought at Columbia Road Market.

I switched on the coffee machine in the kitchen and tried to get comfortable on one of the damned hard stools that Charlie had insisted on when he redesigned the kitchen, complete with one of those ridiculous islands in the middle. They may look good on TV adverts, surrounded by slick young people of all shapes, ages and cultural backgrounds, but I found it annoying having to walk around the flipping thing all the time. Thankfully, the world may have changed since I was a young girl.

While we lived in the city it brought me great joy to see people jostling along with their lives when we went to south east London to visit Clive and Sonia; we always managed to make time for a browse around the fruit and vegetable market. Sometimes Charlie would stand still in the street and smile, blandly commenting that what we witnessed as not the whole truth. It usually resulted into lively discussion late into the evening over the Williams' dining table about what he described as 'the great monolith of race and class issues that bestrides the country'. All that talk sometimes made me feel uncomfortable, but he was right ... as per usual.

★

I'd often read that moving house after having lived in the same place for many years is not always successful, making new friends, altering your pace and everything else. Naturally our busy weekend trips, planning for our new future and sorting things out for my parents, took up a lot of time: a chunk of our social life had become seriously curtailed.

For reasons I could never comprehend, it seemed that Charlie and I were quite the favoured couple among our group of friends and work colleagues. Maybe it was because we were different: my background sometimes referred to in a 'sort of jokey' manner or

Charlie's working-class childhood. He didn't talk much about his past and made it clear that he wasn't amused. I often wondered why he always had an excuse for not taking me to meet his parents. When I asked him outright he became flustered and cross, mumbling that living on scanty means was one thing, but he couldn't handle their bitter resentment towards other 'people of the world': They sent us a Christmas card every year with the usual message of festive goodwill. On one occasion, I turned it over to read something scrawled on the back about meeting up one day.

Probably as an afterthought I suppose.

We had fun sharing trips out with friends, but on reflection we tried too hard to be clever; a lot of our conversations being unquestionably over-the-top. We enjoyed nothing more than analysing the latest play we'd seen. There's nothing wrong with that of course, I particularly love processing what I find to be particularly exciting and ingenuous after a stunning performance. Our Shakespeare discussions went even further, recent productions done in traditional style were certainly out, as far as we were concerned. What we considered as *de rigueur* was any play performed in a different language or modern dress, preferably with a bit of Rhythm and Blues or Soul music thrown in … surely The Bard himself would have loved these up-to-date interpretations. Come to think of it, dear old Shakey would probably approve. I think we often tried too hard to be super cool. We loved showing off.

Then there were the art exhibitions, often attending private views accompanied by nibbles and cheap champagne thanks to those arty types we met at house parties. The contemporary dance productions went down well too and the ballet … oh, it was wonderful, heady stuff, although as time went on I had the feeling that for Charlie those evenings were all about gorging his tired lust on those strong young bodies. Donald described the two of us as 'outgoing, lively, vital … I can't quite remember when that description began to fade, but we thought we would easily make new friends and keep up with old ones too.

I was very excited at the prospect of change. Home had become somewhere we came together briefly before rushing off again to play our parts in the whole charade in which we had invested so much of our lives. We whispered together into the early hours one night, after a wearisome attempt to recreate the coruscating sex we had once enjoyed. I told him that I'd had enough of soldiering on, and Charlie admitted to feeling jaded beyond belief. Before too long 'JBB' became a byword between us as we planned our new start. Some of our friends were surprised. Others were envious but said they needed to stay in London to be near their grown-up children and the possibility of becoming grandparents one day, but most of all they would never consider leaving the 'hub of the universe'.

Chapter Sixty-Three

Charlie rented a couple of smart offices in town and set up a business connected to various finance projects in London and beyond. He employed Frank, a man we met in the pub one evening. Frank was certainly switched on, had a lot to relate about his career, and could be depended on to keep the ship afloat, especially on those occasions when Charlie had to go back to London. Sometimes it meant going abroad to attend face-to-face business meetings.

He and Frank were firm friends, sometimes going for a drink together after work, their evenings mostly spent in discussing the current value of the pound and other such things. Charlie's trips away from home became more often than was previously predicted, he stayed in a hotel when necessary.

Meanwhile I applied for a part-time teaching job and was surprised when my application was unsuccessful. My CV was very comprehensive, including my role as member of the Senior Management Team in various schools, the Deputy Headteacher of another. Unfortunately, I had to decline the offer of a headship, when it became necessary to move back to the South West to support my parents. I had a very polite letter from the Chair of Governors of the school, stating that my application was refused, although I had interviewed very well. How jolly nice of him.

I didn't tell Charlie about my job application, surely he had enough to think about already, but I showed him the refusal letter. He related a conversation he had with Frank that same evening. Apparently, Frank had been friendly with the Chair of Governors at his daughter's school. Although such information should be confidential, the Chair told him about me and my interview, stating that despite my impressive CV, the parents 'might not be too happy' if I were to join the staff. I don't know what Frank said to the odious man, suffice to say he and his wife removed their daughter from the school and severed all links.

Charlie hit the roof when he found out and urged me to take out a formal complaint to the education department. We discussed it at some length, both of us considering the reasons why. I felt uncomfortable about doing so and he finally conceded that there was probably no point in taking the matter any further. After a while I landed an office job at the local branch of a large children's charity, which suited me very well.

Chapter Sixty-Four

Charlie had taken a rest for a couple of weeks while Frank and his secretary kept things going at the office. We were sitting outside a pub facing the river one evening, watching the yachts sailing restfully along in the water. There was just about enough wind to keep them going. Frank had taken us out in his boat on the occasional Sunday afternoon and encouraged us to join the sailing club. We made sure that we followed his instructions, pulling and steering as directed. We anchored up for an hour or two and even caught some pollock to take home for dinner on one occasion. We decided to go on some training as crew members, which was indeed a revelation; the whole process was not as straightforward as we thought.

Sailing gear is quite distinctive and expensive. We trolled around a couple of the more stylish shops to find the right clothes and Charlie also brought home some items he'd bought in London. We joined the sailing club suitably bedecked and ready to become one of the crowd. We met some friendly people, some appearing to be quite wealthy as they talked together about their boats. We were lucky to be taken out for some invigorating sailing trips. Charlie took the opportunity to try and engage them to take interest in his financial projects.

As seasoned sailors, they were all keen to get out on the water, whatever the weather. We were more circumspect; getting all that kit off when your bladder is just about to burst is a real drag, and banging through the wind and rain was not our idea of fun. I thought that Charlie's wry comment about 'these country types' not feeling the cold was rather harsh.

We were sitting over supper at the club one evening when I noticed a woman staring at me from across the room, her head slightly to one side: Julie Penrose. I recognized a slight resemblance to the young girl I once knew.

She strode across, took my hand: 'Is that really you deario?'

I held my hands wide, not knowing how to respond. My stomach throbbed with anxiety as I quickly glanced across at Charlie, who was at the bar chatting with Frank and his friends.

'It's Julie, you must remember me. Julie, or rather everyone calls me Jools now – Jools Mitchell.'

The way she threw her head back with that quick laugh towards anyone within earshot was all too familiar. She seemed to be alone, her eyes flat puddles despite the quick laughter. Her teeth and skin looked as if she had spent many years as a smoker, her hair now silver grey was drawn back into a teenage ponytail. I don't know why I had been so envious of her all those years ago.

'Of course, I remember you, Julie.' She immediately started in on telling me about her life in a few rapid sentences, her divorce, her house, her everything ... the words slightly slurring as she raced on. Heaven forbid that she might bring up our secrets. I didn't want to engage and had to think fast, putting my hand up to my forehead as I placed my other hand on her arm.

'So sorry to interrupt you, Julie, I can feel one of my headaches coming on. Charlie and I will be at the annual supper dance next week, perhaps we can get together then and catch up properly.'

'Oh, is that the charming man at the bar? I noticed him a couple of weeks ago and thought then that ...'

'Sorry Julia, I mean Jools, looking forward to seeing you soon.'

Charlie and Frank had moved to one corner of the bar, seemingly deep in a conversation which stopped abruptly as I approached complaining of my headache. We said our goodbyes and beat a hasty retreat.

We drifted away from the club soon after that, having agreed that maybe sailing was not for us after all. Charlie seemed as relieved as I was and set himself to getting rid of all the gear we'd purchased in our first fit of enthusiasm.

Chapter Sixty-Five

Things began to change. Charlie was often tired and miserable. He no longer wanted to get up early and go walking beside the river before work, which had become a habit when we first moved here.

I went walking on my own, but soon tired of it. We had pretended to one another that our lives were like a permanent holiday, although it didn't feel like that in the dark of a wet November night.

A few friends came to stay for long weekends, but not as often as we had anticipated. On those occasions Charlie would stir himself, working hard to resume his role as the dynamic host. We reciprocated by driving up to London for the occasional few days to catch up with friends, music and the theatre, but always returned somewhat irritated. After a couple of years, I began to feel that maybe the big move had all been one helluva mistake.

He began to get ready for the office earlier than usual while listening to the radio, an activity which was clearly preferable to chatting with me over breakfast. He sometimes began shoving a few clothes into a bag a few minutes before leaving the house, stating that he needed to spend a couple of days dealing with business in London, before clambering into the car and setting off without even a goodbye kiss.

I came across what looked like an important business folder left on the hall table. I presumed that he would drop into the office before driving up to London and called them to remind him that he'd left it behind. A chirpy young voice picked up straight away, 'Oh hi Suzanne, how are you? You've just missed Charlie. He didn't hang about in the office for long, think he must be in a hurry to see you!'

I put the phone down and decided not to answer when it rang a few minutes later.

★

I should have realized and tried to ignore the implications which crept in over time; I suppose I couldn't face the possibility of being betrayed. I tried to make light of his more frequent business trips to London, but he soon distracted me with one of his weak jokes. Couldn't he see that I had so much more to give? How much did he really care? Did he want to hear or was he afraid of what I might say? Why did he leave me? I had my story too, regardless of his oh-so-bloody-amusing-clever anecdotes. Did he ever stop to wonder why I wanted to leave the yacht club in such a hurry that night? Why didn't he ask me? Or was it all about how he felt – as was so often the case?

There was so much we had shared and enjoyed together.

I sat on the stairs for a few minutes, dragged myself into the kitchen, poured out a lukewarm coffee. I took it into the sitting room and delved around until I found the song I was searching for: one of Norma Winstone's albums. I curled up on the sofa with my drink, and listened carefully as she sang her plaintive lyrics which said so much about me and my life with Charlie. She describes the beauty of nature outside, 'A Timeless Place', in sad but beautiful contrast to the pain of the person looking through the window.

'*How could anybody know you [...] a mirage is all it's ever been.*'

★

Charlie had got in the habit of staying up late, watching TV or playing soft music after I'd gone to bed. He would tentatively climb in beside me when I was asleep. On one occasion I heard him talking on the phone downstairs as I went to the bathroom, the tone of his voice soft and intimate. I crept back and lay as far as I could on my side of the bed, closed my eyes and said nothing. Alone.

All that talking, our long discussions through the night, our thoughts regarding the state of the country, the world and beyond … I wondered if any of it meant anything to him. Had we ever properly communicated?

Chapter Sixty-Six

A few weeks later I received a formal letter from the solicitor informing me that Charlie had relinquished his share of joint ownership in the house and all our common property into my hands. I suppose I should have been delighted and joyful at his apologetic largesse. On the same day, I opened a letter from Charlie himself, clumsily trying to explain that what had happened between us was his fault alone and that he would always remember our time together with affection … what a joker, how jolly kind of him. For someone to whom words usually flowed easily, it was excruciating to read, coming across like a young child seeking redemption for his misdemeanours. I tore it up.

★

I was looking around at all the bags and boxes I had accumulated, after I had finally found the courage to sort out his things, grunting and sighing as I rummaged around. There were the smart clothes he hadn't worn since moving out of London, the books, the tools, and heaven knows what else. The books he'd bought as appropriate to our new start … about sailing, DIY, gardening, and even metal detectors. As far as he was concerned, making such a gigantic change in our lives was similar to taking up a new hobby.

★

There were several embarrassing moments when I dropped some of his stuff into the office. Heaven only knows how long his affair had been going on. Frank obviously knew all about it; he and Charlie had been close friends right from the start. I found it difficult to be polite, and was quite terse when I spoke to him, and threw the suitcase and a pile of bags on the floor with venom. On hearing my raised voice, the pert little secretary came rushing out of her cubbyhole. I shook off her patronising hand on my arm as she tried to say how sorry she was and all the rest of it. I suppose it wasn't their fault, as without doubt they had both been sworn to secrecy. I gave them instructions that Charlie's possessions be sent to his address, since I was sure they knew where he lived.

I swept out to my car and drove home at high speed along the quiet roads. Alone.

★

Betrayal. I recalled learning what that word meant when I was about seven or eight years old. Our neighbour Mrs Spargo baked Simnel cakes every year at Easter just as her mother and her grandmother had done before her. She always brought us a cake too. There were marzipan balls on the cake to represent Jesus' disciples. We had a slice each after tea that evening.

We ate three of the balls and I counted that there were eight left, making eleven altogether. I pointed out to Mum and Dad that Mrs V had told us in Scripture class that Jesus had twelve disciples not eleven. Mrs Spargo, her mum and her granny had obviously been getting it wrong for many years. Mum and Dad grinned at one another across the table. I even tried to work out how several hundreds of mistakes had been made over all that time as Mum smiled, saying that I always had my head in the clouds. I continued to try and explain that Jesus had twelve disciples who were his friends and they went around helping people.

I was getting quite cross and couldn't understand why neither of my parents got it wrong. Dad stroked his chin, 'You're quite right, honey. They were friends of Jesus but one of them, Judas played a nasty trick on Him.'

'What nasty trick? What did he do?'

'He kissed Jesus on the cheek as a secret sign to some bad men who came along, took Jesus away and crucified Him.'

'Is that why they show Jesus on the cross in all those paintings?'

'That's right, sweetie. Judas betrayed a good man who was his very best friend. And all of that was for money, so I guess that's why there are only eleven balls on the cake. Judas did not deserve to be remembered as a friend.'

It wasn't a word I'd ever heard before. I looked it up in my dictionary later that night as I lay in bed. Betray. Betrayed. Betrayal.

Chapter Sixty-Seven

I knew Dad was at home as soon as I drew up outside the house. Apart from his music the street was quiet until I slammed the car doors and collected my things from the back seat. I glanced up to see Mrs Spargo peering between the net curtains; she gave me a slight wave and then quickly retreated before I could respond. I thought she looked a bit cross or maybe I imagined it. She had always been our friendly neighbour and took a lot of pleasure in helping us out. Her husband Doug had passed away five years previously and her sons had both left home, got married and had children. Dad always said that Dot was trying to be helpful, his comments usually met with a snort from Mum who insisted on calling her by her married name; considering their neighbour's kindness to be embarrassing.

★

I strolled up the path with the bag of stuff I'd brought for Dad: a couple of home-made meals, some little cakes and two bottles of soft drinks. I thought it was probably time for him to take it easy on the alcohol, now that he was older. I didn't know that he kept a small bottle of rum hidden in the shed, until I caught him out drinking from a plastic cup one afternoon when I went to find some of Mum's painting things. Instead of being cross, we both fell about laughing.

I heard the music as soon as I went in through the back door. I stood and peeped into the sitting room. Dad was sitting in the big armchair, his eyes closed as he whistled along with every note of Charlie's skilful dexterity, playing 'Au Privave'. I crept in and joined in by humming along with him. It was so comforting to see him on one of his better days.

We spent the next hour catching up until he put on a record and held up his forefinger: 'Wait until you hear this one, my girl. I know we listen to a lot of instrumental stuff apart from you-know-who and a few others.' I nodded back with a smile, as he went to his collection, a pile of discs which had grown more and more over the years, filling every spare corner of the room and stuffed into any available space around the house.

He hid it behind his back, 'This, my dear, is the kind of singing known as vocalese. Pete found this at the back of his record shop and lent it to me … well kind of gave to me I guess, because he hasn't asked for it back yet.'

He grinned as he put the needle down on the chosen track. 'Such a clever interpretation of the song. Sit back, close your eyes, and listen.'

A warm rounded male voice swayed around the room: '*There I go, there I go …*'

I sat forward, 'Hey Dad surely the singer is copying that guy who plays it something like this on his sax?'

'That's right, honey: a great saxophonist, who improvised the tune: James Moody. They call it 'Moody's Mood for Love'. His use of jazz improvisation was superb. This man, King Pleasure sings the lyrics written by some guy … can't recall his name right now.'

He clicked his fingers, 'Yeh, I remember who wrote the words: Eddie Jefferson. Keep listening and hear the words at the end of the song: a worthy tribute to James Moody'

'Hang on a minute,' I held my hand up, 'This sounds like a take on "I'm in the Mood for Love".'

'That's correct, Sarah, you probably recall that old record we have of Billy Eckstine's rendition.' He came over and patted my head, 'I think it's hidden away somewhere upstairs, with some of the older stuff. I first played it to you when you were just a kid and ...'

'Yes, I remember, Dad. And I made some comment about his over-use of vibrato!'

'That's right, honey and you were only about seven years old then. You had a sensitive ear for music even at that age.'

'Well, I was properly trained, wasn't I?'

'Yep, sure thing, you've been listening to music since you were in your mother's womb.'

We both went a bit quiet then. Dad turned off the record player and we got ready to set off.

★

We were met by Matron at the door. 'Hello George, we've just finished weekly sing-song afternoon and your lovely wife's on her way back to her room.'

She put her head to one side with a smile as she addressed me, 'Lovely to see you too, Sarah. I have to say that most of the patients seemed to be enjoying themselves, but a few of them don't like taking part, I'm afraid.'

I laughed, 'Including my mum I expect.'

She gave a little giggle, 'Yes, she's such a character, your mother, always brings a breath of fresh air and her art work is absolutely stunning. I'm just on my way up to the second floor to check that everyone is comfortable, although I think that ...'

She twittered on for some time as she walked ahead. Dad and I trotted dutifully behind her, grinning at one another as we made all the appropriate responses.

'Here he is, "The Man I Love".' Mum started humming the tune. I stood and watched them as Dad went up to give her a hug. She was sitting in her armchair near the window, wearing one of her own creations, the fabric having faded and some of the hem dangling about her knees. I often wondered how the nurses were able to persuade her to wear something different.

'And there's my beautiful Sarah, come and give your old mum a cuddle.'

It looked as if she was in a positive mood; some days she wouldn't engage, hardly spoke and gazed out of the window as we tried to make small talk. At other times she was tearful or would start talking, using words which didn't seem to make much sense, making it hard to understand. Some people described her as 'eccentric', a word I have little time for. For us she was still that fiery Elsie Hodges who made an impact on others.

It's often said that childhood experiences can have a lifelong effect on the adult one becomes. Her early life had been complicated, from the anecdotes she related, often bearing a wry smile or shrugging her shoulders as if it were of little or no consequence.

I often consider how my childhood might have influenced me as an adult. The poet Philip Larkin makes no bones about the negative impact parents can make on their children in strong words in one of his poems. I cringed when I first read it. Mum and Dad were always loving, supportive and encouraging. Yet why has it taken me a lifetime to wonder where I belong?

★

Dad surreptitiously put his thumb up towards me as he lifted a cardboard box from behind the door. I asked him what it was when he loaded it into the car, but he simply tapped his nose and told me to wait and see. The next couple of hours were relaxed and happy. Dad set up the small transistor radio on Mum's bedside table and helped her find the programmes that she might enjoy. One was for the afternoon play and the other being a music channel in the evenings. The nurse dropped in to administer her medication and was highly amused. She was also taught how to use the radio, making sure that the volume was set at a suitable level so as not to create a disturbance.

Little did we know as we drove away that others on the same floor would soon become accustomed to Mum's radio choices over the next few months ... whether they liked it or not.

Chapter Sixty-Eight

D ad agreed that he was not as strong as he used to be and
decided to sell the home where I had been brought up.
There was more space in my house and the plan was to bring
Mum home as well, so that we could take care of her with some
professional help as necessary. I imagined how comforting it
would be. We would all be together again after so many long
years. I wanted them both to feel at home and to make sure that
they brought as much of their furniture and anything else they
had treasured over the years.

As always Terry had been of great help as we worked together
to move things about. Isn't it strange how some men find it
difficult to admit that they are no longer twenty-five years old,
often pushing themselves too hard to deny the reality of ageing?
Maureen and I smiled at one another when they were clearly
overdoing it. Eventually I employed a young man to help out.

I made a cup of tea and closed my eyes for a few minutes
before getting back to the job in hand. I had been playing the
same song for the nth time within the last few days: 'Morning
Star'. Some of the lyrics resonated with the sadness of recent
events, but it also gave me hope that things were about to change.
Charlie had put up discreet little speakers all around the house
when we moved in; the music coiled around, and flooded my
aching body with sad joy.

I looked to the future and imagined how lovely it would be when Mum and Dad moved in with me.

★

I was sorting out all the stuff accumulated at the top of Mum's wardrobe. Clothes which no longer fit, a pair of old slippers and at least fifty scarves. I wonder why it is that as soon as women get to a certain age, people can't think of anything to give them for Christmas or birthdays except a scarf.

Boring or what. Maybe it's because they are considered to have become boring too:

'one of the invisible of the invisible tribe.'

'Nobody can say that about my mum!' Talking to myself had become more of a habit since I lived alone.

I took one last look at the bottom of Dad's wardrobe and came across a box lodged at the back. On opening it, I found a host of small things: a pair of Christmas socks which he always wore on the occasion, a set of screwdrivers and other tools, a few postcards and other papers. Letters from his mother portrayed her trembling writing over the years. I was sorry that I never got to meet her; Dad often told us how she had risen from a painful and poor childhood into the wonderful woman that he knew.

I picked up a small, embroidered drawstring bag, my name sewn on the front in Mum's inimitable chain stitch, some of the chains bigger than others The letters strayed to one side and bits of cotton hung from the red ribbon drawstring indicating that it had probably been opened many times over. A ball of my young kinky hair fell into my hand as I loosened the ribbon. That was what Dad had been doing that day as he swept up my hair, the day that Maureen had cut it down low in preparation for my 'growing up' life at Trebean. The metal comb which he bought in the pet shop came into play shortly afterwards. I gathered up the last of the black bags and boxes from my childhood home, bumped them down the stairs and put them in a neat pile beside the door ready to take one last trip to the charity shop in the morning.

★

I paused in front of the mirror, gazing back through a long tunnel. The small brown face, the thick plaits just reaching the little girl's shoulders and the dark eyes which, for a moment, look puzzled as her head appears to move slightly to one side.

Chapter Sixty-Nine

Mark's struggle was slow and painful; all they could do was sit and hold him close as he approached his final journey. A few days before his passing, he waited until he and his son were alone before he insisted on telling him where to find three letters which he had kept locked away in his desk bureau. He held his son's arm tight as he unfolded the wrinkled paper; his voice soft yet determined as he whispered a quiet apology, making him promise not to show them to his mother because it would break her heart if she ever found out what had been kept hidden away all those years.

Kenneth read the letters that night, before putting them away. They were his wonderful loving parents; he had never wanted for anything in his life. He was a young teenager then, about the same age as Kofi is now. They had learned a lot about Cornwall's industrial history and how it influenced the wider world. That was the summer when he began to ask questions …

Coda

It's a hot sunny day in August, the quiet interspersed occasionally by the song of a solitary robin perched on a branch overlooking the field. He and his son follow a path, cross over a short wooden bridge covered on both sides by sharp brambles. They step out into the view and pause at the top of steep steps cut roughly into the cliff, overlooking the beach. The dog is straining at the leash, clearly wanting to bound off onto the shingle. The only sound they can hear is that of their shoes crunching the stones and the regular rhythm of the sea as it gently touches the shore then recedes: forward and back … forward and back.

Neither of them feels the need to talk. He gestures towards the left. They stroll across to see a natural pool surrounded on either side by slippery rocks: a perfect spot for a swim. Some distance away one can just see the sails of a small boat as it cruises along. The dog has scampered off into the water, his tail gleefully dodging about. He runs back as if to relate his excitement and shakes his wet fur all over them. His son smiles as he strokes the dog: 'Oh Jack, now look what you've done!' Jack nuzzles up against his knee before racing off again.

Looking in the opposite direction, they nod to one another as they notice figures in the near distance, seemingly the only other people enjoying the quiet beauty of this place. The people stand and hug for a few moments before they laugh together.

His son gathers a few shells nestling among the stones as they walk. The shells are small; the opening underneath is white and the top is pale pink, covered in a few brown dots.

★

Mum looks around for a while and finds a flat rock to sit on, takes a pencil and pad from her bag and begins to draw, as Dad bends towards her. She looks up and kisses his cheek before rubbing off the imprint of her bright lipstick on his cheek. I smile at them, my head to one side.

Dad and I wander about nearby looking for treasures among the stones, feeling pleased as we compare what we have found. We take some of our findings back to show Mum. We stand and pause for a couple of minutes as we watch her trembling hand as she continues her drawing; she laughs and pretends to wave us away.

Terry and Maureen come into view nearby.

'Where have you all been? We got here early and the food's all ready to go.' We all hug together, nodding our approval of Mum's drawings.

Dad squeezes his shoulder,:'OK, sounds good to me! We've brought food as well. So, let's dig in, folks.'

We are busy laying out our shared contributions and chatting away as usual. I stop to look around at this magic place, which brings such pleasure. The sun is bright and dazzling; I take up the sunglasses strung around my neck and notice two people talking as they get nearer; two men, one who may be middle-aged and the other a teenage boy, who can only be his son.

They look alike, their skin being the same colour.

The same colour as mine.

The same colour as my father's.

They both stop and pause for a moment or two. Dad turns around and approaches them, 'Hello, you must be on holiday. Welcome. We like to call this our sanctuary, our secret beach.

I'm glad you found it.' He shakes the man's hand and holds it for seconds longer than is usual as they stare at one another.

The man puts his other hand on top of Dad's before speaking. 'I read about the secret beach last year and made a promise to myself and my son Kofi that we would find it one day.' As he speaks, he takes out a crumpled piece of paper from his pocket, 'I read about it in a letter.' He hands the letter to my father with a slight bow. Dad says nothing, but steps towards the man and holds onto his shoulders as he sheds quiet tears. The man and his son give me a tentative wave. For a moment I cannot move, still clutching tightly to my little collection of cowrie shells. I stand stiff and still, my throat thick and painful as I gradually release so many years of pain and loss.

Mum places her drawing on the rock, gets up slowly up and whispers a loving welcome as she links arms with them.

Terry and Maureen step forward to join them.

I approach, places the shells in my grandson's hand and hug them both.

The full circle of my treasured family is complete.

Some References

Songs and Music

'Dewey Square' (Charlie Parker, 1947)

'Scrapple from the Apple' (Charlie Parker, 1947)

The Dream of Gerontius (Sir Edward Elgar, 1900, based on poem by John Henry Newman)

'Lady E' (Roland Kirk, 1962)

'Happy Birthday Sweet Sixteen' (Neil Sedaka. Lyrics by Howard Greenfield, 1961)

'Swingin' Shepherd Blues' (Moe Koffman, 1957)

'How Deep is the Ocean' (Irving Berlin, 1932)

'All Things Bright and Beautiful' (Henry William Monk. Lyrics by Cecil Frances Alexander, 1887)

'God Bless the Child' (Billie Holiday and Arthur Herzog Jnr, 1939)

'Moanin' ' (Bobby Timmons. Lyrics by Jon Henricks, 1959)

'You go to my Head' (J. Fred Coots. Lyrics by Haven Gillespie, 1934)

The Verdi Requiem (Giuseppe Verdi, 1874)

'The Twist' (Hank Ballard, 1958)

'Scarborough Fair' (Unknown, seventeenth century)

'The Oak and the Ash' (seventeenth-century ballad, originally a dance tune, with words added later, possibly derived from a poem by Rudyard Kipling)

'Where have all the Flowers Gone?' (Pete Seeger, 1955)

'Greensleeves' (Unknown, sixteenth century)

'Lady Be Good' (George and Ira Gershwin, 1924)

'Sometimes I'm Happy' (Vincent Youmans. Lyrics by Irving Caesar, 1923)

'Yeh, Yeh' (Rodgers Grant and Pat Patrick, 1965)

'Joyspring' (Clifford Brown, 1954)

'Cherokee' (Ray Noble, 1938)

''Round Midnight' (Thelonius Monk. Lyrics by Bernard D. Hanighen, 1949)

'Andromeda' (Chris McGregor, date unknown)

'A Timeless Place' (Jimmy Rowles. Lyrics by Norma Winstone, 1995)

'Au Privave' (Charlie Parker, 1952)

'The Man I Love' (George Gershwin, lyrics by Ira Gershwin, 1924)

'Morning Star' (Jimmy Rowles, Johnny Mercer, 1974)

'Sometimes I'm Happy' (Vincent Youmans, lyrics by Irving Caesar, 1923)

Featured musicians

Charlie Parker: American jazz saxophonist

Sarah Vaughan: American jazz singer

Al Jolson: American singer, actor and comedian

Joe Harriott: Jamaican jazz saxophonist

Billie Holiday: American jazz singer

Norma Winstone OBE: UK jazz singer

John Taylor: UK jazz pianist

Michael Bami Rose: UK jazz, tenor saxophonist and flautist

Roland Perrin: UK jazz pianist

Dave DeFries: UK jazz trumpeter

John Taylor: UK jazz pianist

Tubby Hayes: UK jazz tenor saxophonist

Stan Tracey: UK jazz pianist

Georgie Fame: UK RnB keyboard player and jazz singer

Chris McGregor: South African pianist and formed the band, Brotherhood of Breath in 1970

Featured books: Writers and poets

Chapter One: *Romeo and Juliet,* Act 2, Scene 1, Juliet: 'My bounty is as boundless as the sea.' (William Shakespeare Complete Works, Ed: Jonathan Bate and Eric Rasmussen, Random House, London, 2007)

Chapter Twenty-One: *Joe Harriott, Fire in His Soul,* p.119 (Alan Robertson, 2nd Edition, Northway Publications London, 2011)

Chapter Thirty-Two: *Paroles Sur la Dune* (Victor Hugo, nineteenth century)

Chapter Forty-Five: *The Tempest,* Act 3, Scene 2, Caliban: 'Be not afeared […] I cried to dream again.' (*William Shakespeare Complete Works,* Ed: Jonathan Bate and Eric Rasmussen, Random House, London, 2007)

Chapter Fifty: *Struwwelpeter* (Heinrich Hoffman, 1845)

TV and Radio Programmes

The Voice of America: founded in 1942, to combat Nazi propaganda, also a conduit for music and up-to-date news.

The Black and White Minstrel Show: a BBC prime-time entertainment show, featuring characters in 'blackface' from 1958-1978, finally withdrawn when recognised as racist and offensive.

Top of the Pops: weekly BBC television programme, 1964-2006

Cornish language, dialect and local expressions

Chapter Four: *Winnard:* the name of a bird particular to Cornwall, but rarely seen, a heron.

Chapter Seven: *The West Briton;* local weekly newspaper in Cornwall.

Chapter Fifty-Seven: *Emmetts:* A Cornish expression as a description of people who visit the county on holiday.

Chapter Fifty-Eight: Cornish language: *Oll an gwela,* meaning 'All the best'.

Me 'ansum: a term of endearment, literally 'my handsome' applied to any person or thing that is beloved of that moment!

Mining information: many thanks to Kingsley Rickard, who is a Cornish Bard and historian for The Trevithic Society. He is well known for his knowledge and lectures relating to the industrial history of Cornwall.

Other matters

The mention of hair, a racial feature as a recurring theme in the narrative references Emma Dabiri's book, *Don't Touch my Hair* (Allen Lane, imprint of Penguin Random House, London, 2019)

Relevant to the narrative regarding one of the methods used by Sarah as she navigates her way through life. (Chapter 19): Maya Angelou: American writer, poet and activist. This piece: 'The Mask' is available on YouTube video, a spoken word adaptation of the poem 'We Wear the Mask', written by American poet Paul Laurence Dunbar in 1896.

Chapter Twenty-Four: Notes taken from The Scottish Charity (SC021303) *Trees for Life:*
Mythology and Folklore of Hawthorn
'Across Britain there was the belief that bringing hawthorn blossoms into the house could lead to illness and death. Adults would scold hapless children for innocently decorating the home with flowers. Medieval folk also asserted that the smell of hawthorn blossom was just like the smell of the Great Plague in London.'